NEW ARCADIA

AN ALICIA YODER NOVEL

M.A. ROTHMAN

STEVE DIAMOND

Cover Art by M.S. Corley

Paperback ISBN-13: 978-1-960244-15-4
Hardcover ISBN: 978-1-960244-16-1

ALSO BY M.A. ROTHMAN & STEVE DIAMOND

Alicia Yoder Series:

- New Arcadia
- Operation Thrall
- Vatican Files

CONTENTS

CHAPTER ONE

The mist hung low in the forest, and the agent's footsteps squished through the damp ground, kicking up the aroma of peat moss—an earthy, dark, rich scent reminiscent of wet wool, with a hint of rot. In the distance, he caught sight of a barbed wire fence, the first sign of the high-security camp that wasn't supposed to be there.

Crouching low, the agent continued advancing toward the camp, but froze suddenly upon hearing a crunching and snapping sound underfoot. Dread consumed him when he recognized the sound of children's bones breaking.

The brittle remnants marked another shallow grave just outside the camp codenamed New Arcadia.

Despite the horror of the situation, the agent took another step forward.

He didn't hear the sniper round traveling at twice the speed of sound before it slammed into him.

The world turned black.

In a sound-isolated room fifty feet below Fort Meade, Doug Mason watched as two of his specialists worked on a patient lying on a hospital gurney.

One was a neuroscientist monitoring a flatscreen that had a bundle of wires attached to the patient's scalp. The other, a tiny bespectacled man who had been a practicing anesthesiologist before Mason recruited him into the Outfit.

A clandestine government agency that didn't officially exist, the Outfit and its members were an exclusive bunch, hand-picked for their special skills. These two both came from the private sector, and now served a higher calling... one that involved any number of unusual tasks, in all of which national security was at stake. Today was no exception.

Mason shifted his gaze to the head of the gurney. "Jerry, he'll be able to respond to questions, right?"

"Oh, most definitely." The neuroscientist pointed to the monitor, which displayed a variety of squiggly patterns. "We've got a classic EEG signature of unconsciousness at the moment. Mohan's going to chemically immobilize Agent

Xiang, and the sedative he's on should give up the ghost. Then he'll wake."

"It's got to be strange waking up and not even being able to blink," Mason said. He'd never witnessed a programming session before, mostly because it had only been done a handful of times, all when he wasn't on the premises.

"It's best that he can't move for a variety of reasons, but the most important have to do with the auditory and visual programming sequences." The neuroscientist adjusted a setting on what looked like a virtual reality headset the patient was wearing. "When we first began experimenting with neuro-programming, the subjects couldn't handle it. The results were miserable."

"What do you mean, couldn't handle it? Was it painful?"

The gray-haired man shrugged. "Hard to say. Before we started inducing paralysis in the subjects, they had an autonomic reaction to the process, flailed uncontrollably, and even when we strapped them to the hospital bed we couldn't get a complete lock on the programming. This is very fidgety, cutting-edge stuff. And the subjects usually don't even realize what's going on during the programming."

The anesthesiologist cut in, his Indian accent thick, yet intelligible. "Let's get things rolling." He cleaned the injection port on the IV with an alcohol swab, then injected a clear liquid into it. "This is Quelicin," he explained to Mason. "The good stuff. He'll be completely immobile. I'll attach an infusion pump to the IV so that he gets a constant four milligrams per minute throughout the procedure."

Mason watched the men work together smoothly as a team. Jerry Caldwell, was a neuroscientist, and Mohan Patel, an anesthesiologist. The two men already had a shorthand between them, and an easy, unspoken calm relationship. He didn't share their calm, feeling uneasy about this whole thing. He understood the necessity of the procedure—the news out of China looked grimmer by the day, and the Outfit needed Agent Xiang for a very special mission—but that did nothing to calm his nerves.

"I pushed a counter to the sedative," Caldwell said. "He should be awake now." He broke a capsule under the man's nose, and the smell of ammonia permeated the air. "Did he respond?"

"Yup. He's awake, Mohan," Caldwell said, eyes glued to the monitor.

Patel spoke, keeping his voice clear, and his speech measured. "Agent Xiang, this is Doctor Patel. Can you hear me?"

Mason couldn't make heads or tails of what was on the monitor, but it clearly meant something to the neuroscientist, who said: "He hears you."

"Agent Xiang, we're about to start the session. Just relax. You won't remember any of this when this is all over."

Caldwell pulled up a new screen on the monitor, this one flashing a series of patterns.

"Sending a baseline set of signals..."

A buzzing noise leaked from the agent's headset. A 3D

representation of the brain appeared on screen, rotating, with portions of it highlighted.

"Do those highlights indicate where you're setting the memories?" Mason asked.

"Yes." Caldwell tapped on one of the highlighted areas of the screen. "This will be programming run one of three."

"Why do you have to do it three times?"

"We've found that repetition helps the memories stick. And it's not just pure repetition. On the third run we induce a slow-wave sleep to consolidate the memory—"

"I thought something like that required REM sleep," Mason interjected.

"No. The slow-wave sleep that comes right after you fall asleep is when memory consolidation occurs. So I induce that state with a slow-wave frequency generator and then trigger delta waves with about ten milliamps of current through the electrodes attached to the agent's forehead and the base of his skull.

"This isn't a great analogy," Caldwell continued, "but conceptually it's similar to when your computer gets an update and you have to reboot before it can process the changes. And sometimes you have to reboot it yet again once things have been configured. The brain has a similar process."

The scientist tapped some things on the screen, and text scrolled rapidly past, along with images of places and people. All the things pertinent to an upcoming mission.

"Okay, Mohan, I've got the signals oriented. I'm about to hit go. Is he good?"

"Blood pressure is at a baseline of 115 over 78, oxygen is at 100%, and heart rate is 45. All good to go."

"Here goes."

A portion of the neuroscientist's screen blurred into streams of unrecognizable character patterns, not unlike the kind shown in the movie *The Matrix*. Mason looked over at the agent and saw Xiang's pale skin turning pink, almost as if he were having an allergic reaction or a hot flash.

The anesthesiologist adjusted the respirator, and its cyclic rate increased, giving the agent more breaths per minute. "BP is now 165 over 80, and heart rate has spiked to 115. We're still okay."

As the programming continued, the agent's skin went from pink to red, and dots of perspiration appeared everywhere his skin was exposed.

"How much longer?" Mohan said, adjusting the respirator once again, his expression tense. "BP is now 205 over 84, and heart rate is at 185."

Mason clenched his jaw as his gaze panned back and forth between the physicians and Agent Xiang.

"Almost done," Jerry said. "Five... four... three... two... one... done!"

The white noise permeating the room stopped, leaving only the sound of the respirator trying to keep up with the demands of a patient they had put through the wringer.

Letting out a breath he hadn't realized he'd been holding,

Mason felt a wave of guilt wash over him. No wonder the subject had to be immobilized for this. What kind of hell was he putting these people through? And was it worth it?

"Patient's stats are dropping back into normal range. BP is 135 over 78 and heart rate is 70. Both are drifting lower."

Mason turned to the neuroscientist. "Can he hear me?"

Jerry nodded.

"Chris? Agent Xiang, this is Director Mason. Are you okay to continue?"

The neuroscientist was watching his screen. "Can you ask your question again? I'm not sure the agent heard it. His brain is still processing the onslaught."

Mason leaned in closer. "Agent Xiang, are you okay to continue?"

The neuroscientist nodded. "EEG waves match the affirmative responses we recorded before the testing began. He's good to go."

Mason took a step back and motioned for the doctors to continue. There weren't any laws against what they were all doing, but he felt like there probably should be.

All in the name of national security.

The fires of hell didn't seem that bad compared to how Alicia's face felt as it burned from the chemicals she'd been sprayed with. She jogged in place and heard the other trainees coughing and struggling against the effects of the pepper spray. Blinking away the chemicals didn't even help; her eyelids felt like flaming hot sandpaper. She could only grit her teeth and try to ignore the pain as she bounced up and down on the balls of her feet.

"Move it, move it, move it!"

One of the instructors shoved her toward the track, and it took everything Alicia had to *not* send a back fist to the guy's temple.

She and a dozen other FBI Academy trainees were on a remote portion of Marine Base Quantico. She'd been integrated into this training class only three days ago. Yet despite the dusty surroundings, the chemicals in her face, and her complete physical agony, she knew there was one thing she *couldn't* do.

Let these bastards get the best of her.

"The more you sweat and suffer here, the less you'll bleed when on assignment. I want one and a half miles from all of you! That's six laps, for you people who aren't all that bright."

Blinking through the pain and tears, Alicia began running.

"Yoder, Sanchez, and Smith!"

Alicia and two other agents turned to the instructor.

He made a counterclockwise motion with his finger. "The other direction, numbskulls."

Alicia pressed a finger against the side of her nose, blew a seemingly impossible amount of snot in the instructor's general direction, and ran to catch up with the rest of the class.

Alicia felt much better after finishing the run—though she still felt a burning sensation in the back of her throat. She hadn't been the first to complete the six laps, but she had finished in the front third of the trainees, which would have to be good enough. Halfway through the run, she had developed a pain in her lower abdomen. It didn't feel like a normal period cramp, but what else could it be? She sure as hell wasn't going to mention it; as the only woman in this class, she wasn't about to allow that to be an excuse.

She had never run with anything more than two-pound ankle weights in college, and she'd never have imagined just how exhausting it was to run in full tactical gear. All the trainees had been completely kitted out, from military-issue combat boots to an advanced battle vest with ballistic inserts, load distribution system, and what the instructor called SAPIs and ESBIs—small-arms protective inserts and enhanced side ballistic inserts. The whole thing probably only weighed fifteen or twenty pounds, but Alicia had felt every one of them over the course of the six laps.

The last two trainees came walking back from the track looking exhausted. Their eyes were bloodshot, and partially dried snot and Lord knows what else was streaked across their faces and into their hair. They looked like hell.

Alicia now knew the feeling—quite well.

When all of the would-be agents had completed the run and settled onto the benches, an instructor stepped in front of the group and spoke.

"Okay, trainees. We've got something special today."

He hitched his thumb toward the training site behind him—a dusty ghost town that had been constructed about a quarter mile away. It had been set up in a grid pattern, with a wide main street splitting it from north to south. Yesterday, when they'd used it to go through various close-quarters combat scenarios, corpses of burnt-out vehicles had lined the street. Today Alicia saw something else out there. Something metal. But she couldn't quite make it out from this distance.

The instructor smiled. "Some researchers out of DARPA have developed a new artificial intelligence unit, and we've plugged it into one of our EOD robots."

EOD was shorthand for explosive ordnance disposal—the bomb guys. And now Alicia realized what the metal object in the main street was. A couple weeks earlier she had worked with some folks from the Army's EOD group, and she'd gotten a chance to operate one of their remote bomb disposal units. It was kind of neat, reminding her of the robot from the cartoon *WALL-E*. It even had arms that she could manipulate through a remote control.

"With this new AI enhancement, the robot is supposed

to detect and identify combatants in the field. It's been through quite a bit of testing already, but before it can be put out into the field, it's going to need a lot more work. Today is your turn to see if you can fool the robot. All you need to do is go up to it and touch the thing without it raising its red flag, meaning it saw you. Any questions?"

One of the trainees raised his hand. "Sir? How far can it see?"

"Good question. The robot will analyze anything coming within a thousand-foot radius."

A voice broadcast from what looked like a walkie-talkie on the instructor's utility belt. *"We're ready."*

The instructor spoke into a shoulder-attached mic. "Roger that." He then pointed at the man who'd asked the question. "Smith, since you're the curious type, you can go first."

The trainee launched himself from the bench and jogged north, skirting the edge of the makeshift town, then vanished between the buildings. After a moment the robot turned eastward, sensing him.

Suddenly the trainee raced into view, and the robot's arm shot upward, with something red hanging from it.

"Subject detected," the walkie-talkie squawked. *"Send the next agent."*

The instructor pointed at another trainee. "Darby, you're up next."

Scott Darby, a tall, blond, giant of a man, stood and tapped the shoulder of the guy who'd been sitting next to him. Carl something. "Hey, want to try and tag team Robo-Grunt?"

"Sure."

The two men spoke in hushed whispers, then took off at a sprint. They split up, approaching their target from opposite directions.

Was one of them going to sacrifice himself so the other could tag the thing?

As they converged onto the town, the robot seemed skittish, scanning back and forth, clearly sensing movement. But the men were ducking behind buildings before the robot could zero in on them.

Then Carl launched a rock past his target.

But instead of following the movement of the rock, the robot turned, raised its arm, then spun, kicking up a cloud of dust.

Alicia wasn't quite sure what had just happened, but the voice on the walkie-talkie said, *"Both agents identified. Send your next."*

"Cortez, you're up."

The man sitting next to Alicia jumped up and raced forward. Like the others, he ducked behind the buildings and thus delayed his inevitable defeat. His tactic was to throw up a cloud of dirt to distract the robot. But the moment he leapt from cover, the robot flagged him.

Damn, that thing is fast.

"Yoder, you're up."

Alicia stood, then tilted her head to the supply shed. "Can I use the mosquito netting?" she asked.

The instructor shrugged. "Whatever's here, you can use."

Alicia unrolled nearly fifty feet of thick mosquito netting from the spool and wrapped herself with it. The instructor and trainees watched with confusion and interest as she created a puffy ghillie suit.

When she tied it off, she checked her shadow. She could barely see anything through the layers of mesh, but she'd created the desired effect: her shadow was round—not shaped like a human at all. Alicia hoped that the AI wouldn't know what to make of her.

Keeping her hands inside the suit, she pushed out the edges of the mesh, making herself look even rounder as she trudged northward.

She didn't bother skirting around buildings. She moved straight at the robot, her heart thudding in her ears as she wobbled forward.

It turned slightly as she got in range.

Alicia kept moving.

The robot shifted back and forth like it was suffering from a nervous tic. It clearly sensed her approach. But would it identify her as a combatant?

Alicia heard the whoosh of the robot's hydraulics. She saw the red cloth clutched in its robotic grip.

It's about to raise its arm.

But it was too late. Alicia bumped directly into it and yelled, "I tagged it!" She felt a wave of triumph.

Two men stepped from the nearest building. They were dressed in street clothes and had picture badges clipped to their collars. One looked annoyed, but the other laughed.

"How did you know that your heat signature wouldn't be able to be detected through that mesh?"

Alicia shrugged. "I had no idea. I just figured if I didn't have a human outline, it might get fooled."

The other man grumbled, "Dumb luck."

"No, this was perfect," said the first man. He gave Alicia a thumbs-up. "I'd never have thought of this approach." He spoke into a handheld device. "It seems your trainee found a chink in our armor. We've got some work to do."

"Roger that. I'll dismiss the rest of the trainees for the day. Yoder, good job. We'll be back in the classroom at 0800."

As the scientists began unscrewing one of the panels on the robot, Alicia wriggled out of the layers of mosquito netting. Despite her little victory against WALL-E the Robo-Grunt, she couldn't help but feel anxiety over the training activities still to come. Unlike her classes in college, all of which provided a clear syllabus with what to expect, here she had been given absolutely no idea what the Outfit had in store for her.

She wasn't even completely sure what being an agent at the Outfit even entailed. The training seemed almost random. Last week it was working with some Marines on conditioning exercises. This week it was training at the FBI Academy. And next? Who knew?

She wished she at least had some grades to measure

herself against, unsure if she was doing well or poorly. But that might change tomorrow. She had a mid-cycle evaluation with Mason at the Outfit's HQ, and she couldn't help but wonder what Mason would have to say about her performance.

CHAPTER
TWO

It had been three months since Alicia had agreed to join the Outfit—a huge decision for her. It had not only meant moving to a new apartment in DC, it had meant leaving Princeton without having finished her master's degree in neuroscience. The unfinished degree didn't sit well with her, and now, as she drove past Lincoln Park, through the National Mall, past Foggy Bottom, and into old Georgetown, her mind was filled with doubt about her choices.

She placed a call on her phone and transferred it to the car's speakers.

"What's up, baby girl?"

The sound of her adoptive father's deep voice should have taken the edge off of her nerves, but it didn't.

"Dad, what the hell was I thinking? I feel like it was just

yesterday that I was taking classes, an ordinary student, and now I'm training to be... hell, I don't even *know* what I'm training to be. Shooting drills, CQB training, and a few days ago they put me through an entire session on vehicle engagement tactics—learning how to drive and shoot at the same time, evasive maneuvers, anti-ambush drills... Dad, this is insane."

Her father chuckled. *"Alicia, take a deep breath. Where are you?"*

She took a deep breath and let it out. It did make her feel a little better. "I'm driving to HQ for my three-month review with Mason. My nerves have me all knotted up inside. Hell, I'm trying not to throw up right now."

"There's no reason for you to be nervous. You've got this. And besides, I've been keeping tabs, and everyone so far has had nothing but good things to say about your progress."

"If you say so. It's not like they would tell *you* if I'm doing poorly. You're Levi Yoder, Super Spy. I'm just... me." Alicia's throat tightened and her heart raced. "Dad, I... I can't remember what made me say yes to this. And I mean that literally—it's like total blanks in my head. I think I might be losing it."

"I assure you, you're not losing it. And those gaps... honey, let's just say that they're there for a reason."

"What do you mean?"

"It's hard to explain. Sometimes when people go through trauma, things get blocked from your consciousness. It's totally normal."

A chill raced through her, and she began feeling light-headed. "You don't have to explain to me how the brain works—I'm the neuroscientist, remember? Or I was *going* to be. But—what trauma, Dad? Was I"—she swallowed—"was I... raped or something? What am I blocking out?"

"No, no, it was nothing like that. You just... you managed to get mixed up in something that involved the Outfit. You kicked ass, Alicia. But it was hard on you. Mason and I thought you might lose some of those memories of the incident, and honestly, I'm glad you did. You're better off, trust me. And if you're nervous about it, talk to Mason. He'll totally understand."

"Maybe."

"It's your call. But listen—I'm in DC today for a quick meeting. Maybe you could meet me upstairs for a bite to eat? How's noon sound?"

"It sounds great, Dad." Alicia wiped tears of frustration from her cheeks. She took a deep breath in, then let it out slowly in an attempt calm the roiling fear, anxiety, and nerves. "I'm sorry. I'm acting like a baby. I'm just nervous and... freaking out a bit."

"Alicia, you have nothing to worry about." She could hear the smile in his voice.

They ended the call as she pulled into an open spot on the side of the road in old Georgetown. Traffic had been unexpectedly light, and she was an hour early for her meeting, so she tuned the radio to an oldies station and tried to calm her nerves.

Even the sounds of *Earth, Wind & Fire* couldn't banish

the feelings pressing in on her. After thirty minutes, she gave up and got out of the car.

"Hey honey, you have any food I can have?"

She turned to see an old man in dirty threadbare clothing yelling at her from down the street. She grinned as she walked toward him. She recognized the "beggar" as a member of the Outfit, and the things he yelled were actually codes to notify anyone approaching headquarters if there was anything amiss. Asking for food was a sign that everything was clear. Had he asked for a drink... well, then Alicia was to leave the area immediately.

Ahead, Alicia saw a familiar sign. It featured a profile of a rooster on the left, and the head of a longhorn bull on the right. This area wasn't exactly upscale, but Alicia had gained some fondness for the dingy street front.

She walked into the Rooster and Bull, and the smells of stale beer and wood polish washed over her. The place was a dive bar... and also an entrance into one of the most secretive organizations in the world.

Dimly lit as always, the place's few tables and booths were all empty at this time of day. Behind the bar, a man toweled a glass dry. He nodded at her as she walked toward the back of the establishment.

Alicia entered the men's bathroom. A white-haired man sitting on a stool near the sink looked at her over his John Lennon-styled spectacles.

"Back again, little girl?"

She grinned. "Harold, how many pairs of tan slacks and

plaid button-down shirts do you own? That's all I ever see you wear."

"Bah!" Harold held out a white towel. "My wife always harped about the same thing."

Alicia took the towel. It looked like an ordinary towel, but she knew it had a string of RFID tags sewn into it, and acted as a key of sorts.

"Sounds like your wife was a smart woman," she said, giving the old codger a wink.

For the blink of an eye, the old grump cracked a smile, then he muttered something unintelligible as he waved her away.

Alicia chuckled as she entered the third of the bathroom's three stalls—the one with an "Out of Order" sign taped to it. She shut the door behind her, then placed the special towel on the flushing lever and flushed the toilet.

Immediately the floor dropped—taking Alicia and the toilet with it. She put her hands on the tank to steady herself as she dropped with frightening speed down an incredibly deep shaft. She'd taken this route dozens of times, yet her stomach still lurched.

After a few very long seconds, the walls fell away and the toilet-elevator slowed nearly to a stop. Alicia focused on regaining her balance as she descended into a featureless room deep underneath old Georgetown. The platform settled softly into a recess in the floor, and Alicia stepped off.

Just as quickly as it had dropped, the toilet-elevator

launched back up again, disappearing into the shaft in the ceiling.

Alicia tossed the hand towel in a nearby basket, then walked to the room's only exit: a steel door with a security panel mounted to one side. She placed her splayed hand on the panel, and a blue line passed back and forth. Then a green LED flashed, and a click echoed from inside the wall.

"Stand clear," warned a digitized voice.

Three massive locking bolts slid out of their retaining blocks on the right side of the door, and the door slowly opened outward.

Alicia remembered the first time she'd been brought here, by her father and Director Mason. The place had reminded her of a 1950s bomb shelter, except that no bomb shelters she knew of had a four-foot thick, tungsten-steel alloy door weighing eighteen tons at its entrance.

She walked through the opening, around a corner, and down a hall that ended at another door, this one with a retinal scanner. She put her eye up to the box on the wall, and with a flash of green light, the door clicked.

Alicia pushed it open and stepped into the inner sanctum of the Outfit's US headquarters.

She was in a room larger than most warehouses. Standing on a metal walkway about twenty feet above the floor, Alicia had a clear view of the cubicles arranged in a grid below her, stretching as far as she could see. No matter what time of the day or night she arrived, she always found men and women working like their lives depended on it. And very likely, somewhere out there in the world, someone's life *did* hinge on these people's work.

Four huge display screens, each fifty feet across, hung from the ceiling at the center of the space, displaying information, maps, photographs, satellite feeds, and more, and the walkway she was on continued around the edges of the giant room, leading to offices whose windows also looked down on the central work area.

She was reminded, not for the first time, of the headquarters in the movie *Men in Black*, except there were no aliens—at least, not that she knew of.

She walked down a flight of metal stairs, stepped into the cubicle bullpen, and started the long walk to the far side of the cavern-like complex. When she finally reached conference room C1, where she was scheduled to meet with Mason, the butterflies in her stomach were threatening to come flying out of her mouth.

Despite her early arrival, she found the director already waiting, studying a photograph. She looked up at the wall clock and saw to her astonishment that she wasn't fifteen minutes early, she was forty-five minutes *late*.

"Oh my God, I don't—"

"Daylight savings?" Mason said. "Did you forget the time changed early this morning?"

He stared at her with his pale, silver-hued eyes. He was in his fifties, with light brown hair and a receding hairline. Most men with his looks would have been dismissed by the general public as boring or average. Not Mason. Something in the way he held himself... his presence commanded attention. This man was the Outfit's most senior member in the US—at least, as far as she knew, and here she was showing up almost an hour late for her evaluation.

"I'm so sorry! Do we need to reschedule?"

Mason waved dismissively at her and slid the photo he'd been looking at across the conference room table. "Tell me what you see."

Alicia took a seat across from him and picked up the photo. It looked like some kind of business social. "Well, lots of Asian people, but I don't suppose you needed me to tell you that."

"Do you recognize anyone?"

She nearly shook her head when a woman caught her attention. She was only in profile, and she was a good distance from the camera, but...

"I'm not positive, but I think I do."

She felt a surge of apprehension. Her boss expected an answer—an *honest* answer—but Alicia didn't want to betray this woman's confidence. She was, after all, involved in the shady side of business.

"I... I think my father knows her."

"A very diplomatic way of putting it, young lady." Mason's stone-like expression softened, and he gave her a slight nod. "Very well, I'll talk to Levi in a bit."

He glanced at the wall clock and rose from his chair. "Unfortunately, I have another meeting at the top of the hour, so we'll have to postpone our review. I'll have my admin set something up." He walked to the door, put his hand on the knob, and looked back at Alicia. "And next time, don't be late."

She nodded.

As Mason opened the door, his phone rang, and he put it to his ear. "Hey, Levi. I'll be right up. My office." He looked back at Alicia once more. "This room is free for the next couple hours if you want to use it."

He closed the door silently behind him.

Alicia put her head in her hands. All her life she'd been an overachiever. She was always early for every engagement, meeting, class—everything. She couldn't believe she'd made such a dumb error. The training over the last weeks had been so intense, it had made her completely forget about the outside world... and ordinary things like *Daylight Saving Time.*

She'd been hoping that today's meeting would ease her anxiety. If she could just get some feedback on how she was doing—even if it was bad—she thought she'd feel more at ease. Instead, Alicia was almost an hour late to a meeting with one of the most important men in the entire Outfit. And had she not been wasting time sitting in the car, she'd likely have almost made it in time.

She remembered her father's advice, and took a deep breath.

It didn't help.

CHAPTER THREE

"*Alicia?"*

Alicia startled awake as someone tapped on her shoulder.

"Come on, baby girl." Her father motioned for her to get up. "Let's get out of here."

Alicia scrambled to her feet, blinking the sleep from her eyes. "I can't believe I fell asleep." As she followed her father out of the conference room and toward one of the headquarters' side exits, her cheeks flushed. First she'd been late to her review, and now she'd fallen asleep in the building. This day would be hard-pressed to get much worse. "Did Director Mason mention I practically missed our meeting?"

"He said you looked like your soul had left your body when you realized what had happened." Her father chuckled, draped his arm over her shoulder, and gave her a side hug. "You're a perfectionist, and you've always been super critical about your performance. I know you try to always be on top of things, but sometimes you demonstrate that you're imperfect like the rest of us."

He took the metal stairs two steps at a time, and Alicia was barely able to keep up with the man who was more than twenty years her senior.

When they were back up on street level, Alicia pointed at her car. "I'll drive."

"Is your tank full?"

"I think so, but why? I thought we were just grabbing a bite somewhere nearby." She unlocked her car and they both piled in.

"A slight change of plans. We'll grab something on the way, but we've got a good drive ahead of us."

"Where are we going?"

"To my place."

Alicia turned to her father with a furrowed brow. "Your place, as in at the Helmsley? All the way in New York? Dad, that's a four-hour drive! We could take the train instead or—"

"You have something against a road trip with your old man?"

"No, but—"

"No buts, let's go."

Alicia turned the key in the ignition, and her orange BMW roared to life. She tapped a hot-key on her car's navigation and pulled out onto the road.

"Dad, what's this about?"

"Mason's got some things cooking that might pull me out of the country for a while, and I want to make sure things are going okay with your training. So we're going home this weekend so I can put you through your paces."

Alicia frowned. "Put me through my paces? What do you mean?"

The car's navigation blurted its instructions through the car's speakers. *"Turn right on M Street Northwest and then turn left on US-29 South."*

"You've got three months of training still left to complete before you'll be going on actual missions. On the off chance I'm not around when that transition happens, I want to know for myself where you're at with your training."

"Proceed south for half a mile, then turn left on Langston Boulevard."

Alicia muted the navigation.

Her father ran his fingers along the underside of her car's roof. "You know, it's been almost seven years since I got you this. Have you had to replace the canvas yet for your car's soft top?"

"Dad, forget about my car maintenance for a second. What did you and Mason talk about with regard to me? What did he say?"

Her father blocked the sun from his eyes as she turned onto another street. "Honey, believe it or not, we had other things to talk about. Stop worrying and focus on doing your job. That's all anyone's asking of you."

"And maybe show up to meetings on time," Alicia muttered to herself.

"That too. I get particularly annoyed if someone keeps me waiting." He let out a loud yawn and put his seat back. "Wake me when we're almost there. I haven't slept in nearly thirty-six hours."

To Alicia's utter astonishment, her father was out within a minute.

Put me through my paces? What am I, a horse?

She merged onto I-395 North and wondered what her father had in store for her.

"Dad, wake up. We're almost there."

Her father lurched up in his seat and blinked away the cobwebs of sleep. He grabbed his phone, dialed a number, and put it to his ear. "Frankie, who's manning the front today?" He paused, watching the street signs as they drove past. "We're about a minute away. Tell Tony to get ready. And if you can, let Carlo know I'm coming with Alicia. Her car needs to be put away."

Driving along Park Avenue, Alicia slowed as she rolled past East 86th Street. She pulled up in front of a stately old building with two marble columns on each side of the entrance. The words "The Helmsley Arms" were emblazoned in gold leaf above the ten-foot doors.

Just as she rolled to a stop, a short man that reminded her of a young Joe Pesci ran out from the building, peered into the car, and opened the passenger-side door.

Her father stepped out, shook hands with the diminutive dark-haired man, and then motioned toward Alicia. “Carlo, this is my daughter, Alicia. She needs her car parked.”

Fascinated, Alicia watched as the man closed the passenger-side door, raced around the front of the car, and pulled open her door. He held out his hand. She stared at the offered hand for a moment before allowing Carlo to help her out of the car.

“Good to meet you, Miss. I’m Carlo Moretti.” Carlo peeked into the car and nodded. “Ah, it’s an automatic. Anything else I need to know about it?”

Alicia shook her head. “Uh, no? Just be careful with it, I guess?”

“Of course.” Carlo flashed a smile, hopped into the car, and her baby shot forward with the sound of tires squealing. He then took an aggressive right turn at the end of the street and gunned the engine.

Alicia tried not to think about Carlo’s lead-footed abuse of her car as she followed her father into the lobby of the luxury apartment building. A security guard nodded to them as they crossed the marble floor toward the elevator.

“Come on, Alicia,” her father said. “Let’s get you into a change of clothes.”

Over the years, she and a few of her sisters had accumulated quite a lot of clothes in her father's spare bedroom, both dressy and casual. Which would it be today?

"Why exactly do I need to change clothes?" Alicia asked.

"Because I don't think you want to fight in what you're wearing."

"Fight?" Alicia raised an eyebrow.

"Yeah, fight. You and I are going to spar for a bit, to get you warmed up, and then I want to see how you do in a real fight."

"I don't have any workout clothes here, Dad. And what do you mean, a 'real fight'?"

"Don't worry. I've got a spare *gi* that you can use. As to the fight, you'll see. I don't know what kind of training Mason's putting you through, and I want to make sure I get a few lessons drilled into that thick skull of yours."

Alicia rolled her eyes, knowing it was useless to argue with him. He had something in mind, and nothing was going to change it. "Okay, who am I going to fight? Because if it's you, that's not exactly fair, seeing as you're my sensei."

"Do you remember Tony Montelaro?"

Alicia recalled a big beefy man she'd met on one of her previous visits. He was head of security for the building.

"Dad! He's twice my size!"

The elevator doors opened, and her father stepped inside, turned around, and faced her, looking amused. "Unless you're hiding a few pounds on you that I can't see, I'd say he's probably *more* than twice your size. Think of it as real-world training that Mason might not put you through."

Alicia shook her head and followed her father into the elevator.

As the doors closed, her father gave her a wink. "It's for your own good, and you know it."

His phone buzzed inside his suit jacket. "One second."

As he put the phone to his ear and spoke in a hushed whisper, Alicia stared at the man who'd rescued her and her sisters from the streets, years ago. He was a man of many contrasting qualities. He lived a bachelor's life in New York City, but his adopted family, Alicia and her sisters, lived with Grandma Yoder in an Amish farming community in Lancaster, Pennsylvania. And though he presented to the world as an immaculately dressed businessman, Alicia had recently learned that in reality, he was an agent for the Outfit.

Levi Yoder, super spy.

Even before learning that secret, she knew he had a no-nonsense reputation. A few times, she'd seen her father get angry with someone… and something about his expression, and maybe the way he held himself, made those people back down. Because unlike many people who talked a big game, her father could back up that glare of his.

But she could also picture him, even now, with that warm smile he reserved for quiet moments when they were out of the public eye. He'd always been a loving father, even though there was no blood relation.

And yet sometimes these differing pieces of his personality came together. Whenever he visited the farm, he always taught the girls something about shooting a gun, martial arts, or survival skills. It was as if he'd been training them all to be ready for anything. Loving father, drill instructor, super spy. They were all the same man.

The elevator dinged, and the doors slid open. Her father stepped out and motioned for her to follow as he walked down the hallway, still on the phone, but now she could make out some of what he was saying.

"A reservation for two on Sunday... and yes, I know the place is impossible to get into. Go ahead and talk to Frankie, he'll get you in touch with our guy. Ring me back when it's done."

As he hung up, Alicia asked, "Are we going somewhere special?"

Her father paused at the door to his apartment and grinned. "One thing at a time, young lady. Let's get you into some sparring gear."

Alicia felt a bead of sweat trickle down the back of her neck as her father adjusted the straps on her padded headgear. He had cleared out the few people who'd been working out in the building's basement, leaving just the two of them to spar for the last twenty minutes.

The basement was a large open room built out as a gym, complete with state-of-the-art workout equipment ranging from stationary bikes to treadmills to a series of weightlifting stations. But the center of the gym was left open for a twenty-foot square of sparring mats.

Her father lightly smacked the padded side of her head. "All this gear is going to do is lessen the chance of you getting cuts and bruises. It's not going to keep Tony from knocking your lights out. Keep your wits about you and don't hold back on him, you hear me? I want you to give one hundred and ten percent."

Then he went over to his gym bag, pulled out his phone, and made a call. "Come on down, we're ready."

Alicia bounced up and down on the balls of her feet. She felt adrenaline coursing through her, her skin tingling with anticipation.

The elevator dinged, and a large man stepped out.

"Hey, Tony," her father said.

As the man approached, Alicia's confidence faltered. Tony wasn't just big, he was *really* big. Six foot four, probably three hundred pounds. He was a little chunky, but most of that weight looked solid. Even though he was in his fifties, the age gap wouldn't give her much of an edge against those thick arms and broad chest of his. She guessed he could probably bench over four hundred pounds.

She glanced at her father, who wore a stone-like expression with his arms crossed over his chest.

Tony wrung his large, meaty hands. "Levi, I know what you told me... but I just want to understand—"

"Tony, it's really simple. My girl's job is going to take her to some places where she might run into some unsavory types. She's a pretty good fighter, but I want her to understand what the limits are of her training. You're perfect for that. Remember when we first met?"

The large man winced. "Yeah. You nearly broke my wrist."

"Right. And I told you never to underestimate an opponent, no matter their size. Tony, here's the scenario I want you to imagine: You're a street thug and you saw some girl flashing some cash around at a bar. Now you're on the street and you're going to take her stuff. All you need to do is take that belt off of her *gi*. And since most real-world encounters are quick, you have one minute to do it. Don't underestimate her."

"You got it." Tony stepped onto the sparring mat and tilted his head to the left and right, causing his thick neck to crack. He swung his arms back and forth a bit, rounded his shoulders, and gave Alicia a slight bow, which she returned.

Then, to Alicia's surprise, Tony took on the ready stance of a martial artist.

"Hey, *stunad*!" her father snapped—the Italian slang for idiot. "When's the last time you took a ready stance when dealing with someone on the street? Get your head in this. You're on the street. She's just a mark. Get that belt."

Tony nodded, then lunged at Alicia.

She leaped to her right, catching two fingers of his outstretched hand, hyperextending them, and squeezing the finger joints together.

Tony ripped his hand back and flexed his fingers, a look of surprise on his face.

"*Yubi waza* won't work," her father barked at her from the edge of the mat. "His hands and fingers are too big for you. Fifty seconds, Tony."

The large man launched a swinging backhand at Alicia. She blocked it, but the impact sent her back several steps, and she only just managed to leap to the side as he bulled his way past her.

"Laws of physics still apply, Tony." Her father was crouched low as he shouted his comments at them. "She's got less momentum than you. She's going to—"

She snapped a devastating front kick to the gorilla's solar plexus just as he turned around to face her.

Tony grunted, but she merely bounced off of him, sending him back only a single step. Alicia realized she'd made some bad assumptions about how effective her attacks would be against someone so large.

"Thirty seconds," Dad yelled.

Tony took a step toward her. His eyes had taken on a predatory gleam.

Alicia focused on his every move, knowing if she didn't, she'd end the day face up on the mat with a concussion.

He lunged directly at her.

She again leaped to her right, only to find that this time Tony had anticipated her move. He slammed directly into her, sending her flying. She crashed onto the mat with Tony landing on top of her, and her breath whooshed from her lungs.

Before she could stop him, Tony deftly untied the knot and ripped the belt from around her waist.

Her father said something, his voice echoing across the gym, but she didn't know what. She was too busy struggling to get air back into her lungs and wondering why she saw twinkling stars everywhere she looked.

"Are you okay?" Tony asked.

The voice seemed to come from a distance, and she had to shake away the spots swimming across her vision. When she looked up, Tony hovered above her, offering his hand. Alicia grabbed it, and he gently pulled her up to her feet.

Undoing the Velcro straps of her headgear, she tossed it to the floor and took in a deep breath. "You moved faster than I thought you would."

"That's all part of the lesson," her father said. He cupped her face, looked her straight in the eyes for a few seconds, nodded, and then wrapped her in a quick hug. "As I told Tony, never underestimate your opponent, no matter their size. Don't assume a big guy like Tony isn't agile. But is there anything else you learned from this?"

"Always be armed." Alicia made a finger gun, aimed it at Tony, and shot him with it.

Tony guffawed and punched her father on the shoulder. "Sounds like something *you'd* say."

"No, seriously." Her father stared at her with an unreadable expression. "What else did you learn?"

Her father was in Drill Instructor mode. He was trying to teach her a lesson, and levity had no part in his lessons.

Alicia answered him seriously this time. "There'll always be someone who is too much for my normal methods to work against."

"That's true. But this isn't always about technique. How much do you weigh?"

"Around one forty."

He looked over at Tony. "And you?"

"About three-ten. I can't seem to get myself down into the two hundreds. It's the cannoli. They're just too good."

Dad hitched his thumb back at Tony not taking his eyes off Alicia. "Don't believe the movies where the pencil-thin karate master tosses the giant across the room. There's only so much you'll be able to do against an opponent as big as Tony. Physics is a big deal in actual fights. And it's not only Tony—sure, he's an exception. But even the average American male is five-nine and around two hundred pounds. He might be a bit blobby, but even then he'll have distinct advantages you can't—"

"Dad, I know, I know. I won't underestimate them. What about attacks to the knees, groin, neck? Sort of like chopping down a tree?"

"Groin?" Tony blanched and took a step back. "I ain't training to take shots to the nuts, Levi."

Her father smiled. "Alicia, if you have to fight an uneven battle, then I agree—chop that tree down. But you'd be wiser to avoid uneven battles if you can."

Tony held up a hand. "I'm fairly partial to my tree, thanks." He gave them both a lopsided grin. "Am I done here?"

"Go ahead," Levi said. "I'll catch up with you later. We've got some things to talk about."

"Tony," Alicia said, "thanks for the fun."

The big man let out a belly laugh and shook his head. "You Yoders are an odd bunch."

As he departed, Alicia's father draped his arm over her shoulder. "That's enough sparring for today. Tomorrow I've got something entirely different planned."

"Oh? Like what?"

"I'm going to test your vision."

"There's nothing wrong with my vision."

"Doveryay, no proveryay."

Alicia didn't speak Russian, but the rhyming phrase was something her father had taught her ages ago. Roughly translated, it meant, "Trust, but verify."

Her father kissed the side of her head. "Believe me, you'll have fun. You did well today. I'm proud of you."

Alicia stared at her father for a long moment, not believing she'd heard the words that had just come out of his mouth.

I'm proud of you.

He wasn't the type to throw out compliments, so when he said anything complimentary, it came as a shock.

Alicia's throat tightened with emotion, and suddenly a

forgotten memory pried itself loose from wherever it had been stored.

In her mind, she was holding a phone to her ear, and heard ringing on the other end of the line. Then her dad picked up. *"Yes?"*

"Dad, I need you. Something really bad happened."

CHAPTER FOUR

Growing up as a teen in a rural Amish community, Grandma Yoder taught Alicia everything she knew about the Bible and prayer, and it became her habit to pray each day before going to sleep. But when things were rough, praying to the Almighty at any spare moment felt like the right thing to do. And now, after a night's worth of nightmares, this was as good a time as any to seek guidance. Nightmares were commonplace in her life, even now, years removed from her days on the streets. Sometimes, they came as shadowy figures grasping for her, cruel fingers cutting and probing. And other times, like tonight, she awoke haunted by the ghosts of the memories lost to her. The ones her dad told her not to fret over.

Alicia kneeled at the side of her bed, her mind naturally

switching into Pennsylvania Dutch as she bowed her head to pray.

"Dear God, as I come to you in prayer, I ask for your help with the forgotten memories that haunt me. There are moments in my life that I can't seem to remember, and it troubles me deeply. Memories that I wish I could recall, but which, for some reason, remain elusive.

"I know that you understand the pain of forgetting important things. And so I ask for your grace and mercy to help me remember what I have lost.

"Lord, I pray for the strength to face these forgotten memories holding me back. I know that I can't change the past, but I trust in your power to heal and restore all things. Please give me the courage to confront these memories and find peace.

"Finally, I pray for your guidance and wisdom to help me make new memories that will last a lifetime. May I cherish every moment and create memories that I will always hold dear. Thank you, God, for hearing my prayer. Amen."

A knock sounded, and her dad spoke through the guest room door. "Alicia, anything you want from the market?"

Alicia opened her eyes. "Do you have any orange juice?"

"I'll get some extra. Be back in a bit, and I'll make breakfast."

Alicia closed her eyes again, trying to recall the memory that had startled her the previous day, but again all she could pull to mind was something about calling her father. Like a wisp of smoke, anything tangible slipped away, leaving her again feeling frustrated and empty. But all the same, praying had helped take the edge off the negative feelings.

She grabbed a change of clothes and walked into the bathroom. She had no idea what this "vision test" was that her father had planned, but she decided that now, she had her *own* plans.

Alicia was going to get some answers out of her father, even if it took tears—real or fake, and she'd had years to perfect both—and lots of begging.

She needed to close these gaps in her memory.

Alicia called out from the kitchen, "Dad, where's your box grater?"

Her father appeared in the doorway. "What in the world do you need a box grater for?"

She held up a pair of large russet potatoes she'd found in one of the cupboards. "I want to make Grandma's hash browns."

He shook his head. "I haven't had those in years. Unfortunately, I don't have a box grater."

She shot him a disappointed glance, which went unnoticed as he was busy drying his hair with a towel. "Mr. Foodie doesn't have a basic cook-prep tool? Seriously? This is no good, dad. How can you have potatoes and not—oh, never mind—I'll make a frittata instead."

Alicia diced the potatoes, a white onion, and a few other fresh vegetables she'd found in her father's refrigerator and began sautéing them in a mixture of butter and olive oil. He peered over her shoulder and nodded his approval.

"You know what would go well with that?"

"What?" she asked.

"Some *guanciale*. I picked some up this morning."

Alicia skillfully stirred the vegetables in the skillet with a few practiced flips of her wrist while her father retrieved a deli-wrapped slab of fatty meat from the fridge and began dicing it on a cutting board.

"That looks like bacon," she said.

Her father made a sputtering noise, as if she'd uttered something absurd. "Bacon? *Guanciale* is what bacon can only one day hope to be. It's a perfectly seasoned and cured pig cheek. I usually chop it up as a nice addition to my pasta carbonara, but this'll work."

Alicia used a wooden spoon to move aside some of the browning potato cubes, and her father poured the diced meat product into the pan. The *guanciale* began sizzling almost immediately, and the delicious aroma of porky goodness filled the air as he set the dining table for two. She appreciated all the time he'd spent teaching her to shoot, throw a punch, and survive in the wilderness. But teaching her how to cook had been the real gem. She joked about him being a food snob, but his taste had rubbed off on her.

Despite the rich smells of their cooking permeating the air, her mind focused on other things.

"Dad, I have to ask you something serious, and I need you to be honest with me. It's been keeping me up at night."

He reached over her shoulder, grabbed two glasses from the cabinet, and set them down before turning to face her. "Sure, kiddo. What's on your mind?"

"I want to know about what happened between when I was in school and when I joined the Outfit." She poured a half dozen beaten eggs into the pan. "That entire timeframe is almost all a blank spot in my mind."

Her father gave her a sour look and shook his head. "I wasn't trying to avoid your question the last time we talked about this. I really don't know that much about what happened, especially since I was in another part of the world during most of that time. I told you to talk to Mason—"

"I know, but I screwed up that meeting with him, and this has been eating at me," Alicia interrupted. She used a spatula to loosen the frittata from the edges of the pan and placed it in the top rack of the oven. "After he left the conference room, and I fell asleep, some fragments of memories resurfaced. I think they're from that missing chunk of time. Something about calling you."

Her throat tightened and her voice shook. "I'm sorry, but I'm having nightmares, and it's—"

"It's okay, baby girl." Her father leaned closer, kissed her on the side of the head, and gestured to the oven. "My broiler runs a lot hotter than your grandmother's, so make sure the frittata doesn't burn. I'll finish setting the table and tell you what little I know over breakfast." He grabbed a carton of orange juice and filled the glasses before walking them over to the table.

Alicia's eyes widened as her father delivered the shocking news. "I *killed* someone?" she repeated incredulously.

Her father took a sip of orange juice and continued eating his frittata, seemingly unfazed by the bombshell he had just dropped on his daughter.

As Alicia's mind raced to make sense of the situation, she asked, "Were the police called? How could something like that happen and me not be aware of it? There had to have been some kind of..." Her words ran dry and her skin prickled with a hot flash of worry. How could she have killed someone and not landed in jail, or had to face a trial, or... *something*?

Her father's response only deepened her confusion. "Nobody else knows," he said with a grin that sent a chill up Alicia's spine. "The Outfit took care of the issue. Honey, you don't have to worry about it."

Alicia leaned back in her chair. Could the Outfit really hide a person's death? As she considered the possibilities, she nodded silently in response to her own question. If what she had seen of the Outfit was any indication, they were capable of far more than she had ever imagined.

"Do you remember what I said to you in that phone call?" she asked.

"Of course. I remember everything."

"Well?" Alicia made a rolling motion with her hand and took a bite of her frittata. She chewed rapidly, the flavors lost on her as she waited anxiously for her father's response.

"You called me in the middle of the night, clearly distraught," he said. "You told me you were in your dorm room, that two men broke in and attacked you, and that one had some kind of spray that you thought was supposed to knock you out. I then asked you where they were, and you said that you'd killed one of them and knocked out the other. And you also told me that you were scared."

His face now took on a dangerous expression, as if he were reliving the moment. "I got you in touch with Brice, and the Outfit helped get you out of immediate danger."

Alicia leaned forward, her attention laser-focused on her father. "Who did I kill?"

He shrugged. "This is where Mason would come in handy, because he understands the background. All I know is that you were being targeted by some rogue characters. I never got a straight answer that made sense as to how you ended up in the crosshairs."

"And that's it?" Alicia asked. "That's all you know?"

"Pretty much." Her father made a dismissive gesture. "I'm guessing you don't remember when you and I were in a van together as part of a mission?"

"What?" Alicia's jaw dropped. "You're kidding, right? I'd *have* to remember that, wouldn't I?"

"Honey, I don't know." Her father grabbed his empty plate and glass and got up from the table. "By that time, Mason had already been working with you, so I think he'll have to be the one connect the rest of the dots. If he wants to, and sees value in it."

"Why don't I remember any of this, but you do?"

"Don't know. All I can say is you didn't know which way was up, but you were all in, regardless of not being trained yet." He glanced at the wall clock. "Finish up. We're going to be late."

Still reeling from the shocking news that she'd killed someone, Alicia shoved a large chunk of the frittata in her mouth, grabbed her dishes, and followed her father into the kitchen, muttering between chews, "Where are we going?"

"To the shooting range."

Alicia blinked with surprise. "Okay, that sounds like fun."

Her father chuckled and shook his head. "Let's see how much fun you think it is once we're done."

The car ride to the shooting range took two hours, and Alicia's father spent the entire time quizzing her on all aspects of shooting—use of a scope, windage, MOA, and all the other things she'd learned from him over the years. At least it helped to pass the time on the otherwise unremarkable trip north, and kept her from dwelling on the news about her memories her dad had dropped in her lap.

They were just west of Poughkeepsie when her father directed her to turn right onto Samsonville Road.

The trees encroached on both sides of the road, her anxiety increased along with a strong sense of claustrophobia. They were definitely in an underdeveloped part of New York.

She glanced at her father. “Are we close?”

He nodded and pointed ahead. “Look for a metal gate on the right. It should be unlocked.”

A few minutes later Alicia caught the glint of sun on exposed metal, and a sturdy-looking gate came into view.

“This is it,” he confirmed.

The gate stood unchained and open, revealing the entrance to a private road. Alicia turned onto the gravel-covered path into the woods, ignoring the sign that warned away trespassers.

“I hope this path doesn’t get too muddy, Dad. My car isn’t exactly built for off-roading.”

“I wouldn’t worry too much about that. You’re driving up a slight incline, approaching a plateau. Even when it rains around here, the water drains away quickly from the higher ground. Just keep going, Esther’s waiting.”

“Esther’s here?” Alicia’s question came out in a high-pitched squeal.

“Yup.” As Alicia drove through another gate and onto a

massive clearing at the top of the hill, her father motioned to a wood-framed shelter. "There she is."

Alicia couldn't keep the smile off her face as she drove toward the rotund figure of Esther, retrieving a metal ammunition case from the back of a silver Ford pickup. She parked next to the pickup, hopped out, and yelled, "Esther!"

The older, heavy-set woman set the ammo down, then spread her arms wide. "*Boobaleh*!"

Alicia rushed into the woman's suffocating bearhug.

Esther Rosen owned a sporting goods store in Little Italy, or as her father like to call it, "the old neighborhood." Almost every visit Alicia had made to her father's place had involved a trip to Esther's store. This gave Alicia an opportunity to talk to the older woman, girl to girl. It wasn't until she was older that she learned that Esther had a penchant for weapons and other things that might not have been totally legal to have in the city. To Alicia, Esther was like a modern Jewish mother figure, a distinct contrast from Grandma Yoder, who had never really been outside of a fifty-mile radius of the farm she'd grown up on.

Esther held Alicia at arm's length and studied her from head to toe. "You're thin as a rail!" She finger-combed Alicia's long, straight black hair away from her face, and her eyes grew misty as she whispered, "You're so pretty. It's good that you're here for training. You'll need more than just a baseball bat to keep those boys away."

She gave Alicia's father an accusatory look. "You're not feeding this girl enough! Thankfully I've got plenty of things for us to nosh on while we work on our girl's long game." She pointed at a long wooden table covered mostly with a variety of different rifles—but with a large picnic basket on the far end.

Alicia looked to her father. "My long game?"

"Esther was an Olympic shooter back in the day." He patted the side of his chest, where Alicia knew he had a gun in a shoulder holster. "I taught you how to handle a handgun, and I'm sure with what our mutual friends are putting you through, they're heavily focused on honing your short game."

He was right about that. The training that the Outfit had been running her through had involved lots of hand-to-hand combat as well as skill drills with a variety of handguns.

"Mutual friends?" Esther raised an eyebrow and looked at Alicia's father. "You haven't gotten this girl into anything that we—"

"No, Esther." He shook his head, but his expression gave away nothing. Nobody outside the Outfit was supposed to even know it existed. "Alicia's doing some work for friends in DC, and I want to make sure she's well-rounded in her education. She's good with the basics of riflery, but I want you to evaluate her and see if there's anything that needs touching up. After all, you're the expert."

"DC, eh?" Esther gave an approving nod, then turned to Alicia. "Good with the basics, are you? We'll see about that." She pointed at the rifles on the table. "How much shooting have you done with a rifle?"

Alicia shrugged. “I’ve shot a few deer with my father’s rifle, and when he’s not around, I’ve used a shotgun to get rid of pests threatening our livestock, but that’s about it. My grandmother isn’t keen on rifles.”

She scanned the table, and one of the rifles caught her attention. She touched the butt-stock and smiled.

“Pretty, isn’t it?” Esther said. “That’s one of my favorite long-range builds. I’ve got a Defiance Deviant action on it, a Hawk Hill 6.5 Creedmoor barrel, and a Foundation Centurion stock with a really sweet Vortex Razor Gen 3 scope. We’ll get to that one later today, but first—hey, don’t eat all of the Entenmann’s, you rascal!”

Dad shut the lid of the picnic basket, his mouth full of a bite he’d just taken from the chocolate-glazed doughnut in his hand. He had a sheepish expression, as if he’d been caught by Grandma Yoder taking a cookie from the cookie jar.

“Levi, did you ever teach your girl about bore or laser sighting, zeroing a rifle, or any other shooting prep work?”

He shook his head. “We’ve talked about it, but everything I’ve had her use was already zeroed for one hundred yards.”

“Pfeh!” Esther picked up a magazine-fed bolt-action rifle with a small scope attached. “Okay Alicia, let’s go over some of the basics of getting a rifle ready to shoot.”

She went to one of the shooting benches and pointed to the seat. Alicia obediently sat down, and Esther handed her the rifle.

"This is a Savage Arms bolt-action rifle." Esther's voice had switched into a professorial tone. "It shoots a .308 and can be used as a pretty decent hunting rifle, even with just the iron sights. This is a pretty common setup, and since we've got a scope on this, tell me what you know about bore sighting."

"You bore sight something so that you can get a rifle and its scope to be pointing in the same direction," Alicia said.

"And how do you go about doing it?"

Alicia studied the rifle she'd been given, peeked through the scope, and shrugged. "On this rifle, it looks like I might be able to pull out the bolt, look down the bore of the rifle so that I can see the target, and adjust the scope so that it's also on target."

"Go ahead and show me."

Alicia carefully examined the rifle, not having ever used this particular model.

"Don't worry, I'll warn you if I see you do anything goofy or dangerous. Just talk me through what you're doing."

"Okay," Alicia said. "First I need to release the magazine." She found a button near the magazine well, and pressed it. The cartridge holding the ammo popped out into her hand. She set the magazine on the desk-like tabletop and studied the lever on the bolt-action. "Looks like there's a button on the back of the bolt. I'll press that and open the bolt."

The lever moved smoothly, and Alicia pulled back as far as it would go. Then she spotted a metal button with some ridges on the back of the gun.

"I'm guessing this is the bolt release."

She pressed on the left-hand metal button, and the bolt slid out without too much fuss.

"Very good." Esther shot her a thumbs-up and then pointed downrange. "Directly ahead, there's a metal silhouette at one hundred yards. Use that as your target."

Alicia peered into the hole going through the barrel and placed the butt-stock up against her shoulder.

"Trying to get a visual..." She spotted the silhouette downrange through the barrel. "Got it."

She looked into the scope, and Esther made a critical clicking sound with her tongue.

The older woman leaned forward and patted one of several fist-sized burlap-covered bags in front of them. "Once you have your target in sight, you'll want to use something like these sandbags to steady the rifle's position. Otherwise, just moving your head from the bore to the scope is going to shift the position of your barrel."

Her father made a similar clicking sound. "I guess I should have walked you through this process instead of just talking about it."

Alicia placed several of the bags filled with sand under the front of the barrel and wedged a few near the back, forming a cradle of sorts for the rifle. "Okay, I think it's steady." She verified through the bore that she was on target, carefully shifting her gaze to the scope. "The crosshairs are on the target."

"Good. Reassemble the rifle and let's see if you're right."

As Alicia reinstalled the bolt, Esther talked about the next steps.

"As you said, the process of bore sighting is to get the scope into an approximation of the right direction. It won't do you any good if you can't even tell where the bullet's going to go. Hopefully, on your first shot, we'll get you on the target. Then we'll start making adjustments to get your scope zeroed for a center mass at one hundred yards."

Alicia slammed the magazine back into the well, and Esther handed out ear and eye protection. "Everyone put your eyes and ears on. The range is going hot."

She waited for everyone to gear up, then signaled for Alicia to commence firing.

Using the bolt action, Alicia loaded her first round, adjusted the rifle so that the stock fit comfortably against her shoulder, and switched off the safety. She peered through the scope and said, "Okay, here's goes..."

She pulled the trigger. The rifle bucked back, and almost immediately she heard the sound of metal pinging against the target.

"Hit!" Dad called out. He was peering downrange through binoculars.

Alicia turned to Esther, feeling pride at having hit the target on her first shot.

The woman made a sucking noise through her teeth as she looked through a spotting scope. "Six inches low, three inches to the left." She pointed downrange. "Do you see that orange flag hanging limply on the wooden pole?"

Alicia nodded.

"No wind, so we're in ideal conditions. We'll talk about adjusting for wind and distance later. But first, let's get you closer to a center-mass shot. Can you see the dark smudge where your bullet landed?"

Alicia looked through the scope. "Yes."

"Okay, that scope has two primary knobs to adjust windage, your left and right, and elevation, up and down. You were aiming for the center of the target. Keep the crosshairs on the center and wedge your rifle securely with the bags so it doesn't move."

Alicia readjusted the rifle and sandbags until she felt the rifle was secure. "Got it."

"Without moving anything else, adjust the knobs on your scope so that the crosshairs match up with where your bullet hit."

With intense focus on keeping the rifle locked in place, Alicia listened to the clicks of the knobs on the scope as the crosshairs slowly migrated to her desired position. "Okay. I'm dead center on where my bullet landed."

"Now aim for another center-mass shot. Let's see what happens."

Alicia adjusted her grip, aimed, and pulled the trigger.

The rifle bucked again, and Esther's voice cut through the din of the gunshot. "You jerked the trigger."

"I what?" Alicia asked as she looked through the scope. She couldn't see any new marks on the painted surface of the target. "Where did it go?"

Esther shook her head. "You rushed the trigger and ended up probably six inches above the target. You need to be slow and steady with your trigger pull, otherwise you're flinching with anticipation when pulling the trigger, and that moved your shot nearly a foot off target. And that's at only one hundred yards. Do that when your target is at a thousand yards and your shot will be in a different county. Precision shooting requires patience and trigger discipline. Your father should have taught you that. Try again. This time, slowly... and breathe."

Alicia readjusted her grip and focused on her trigger finger as she peered through the scope. Slowly she applied pressure to the trigger, and the rifle kicked back as the bullet raced downrange.

"Nope!" Esther yelled over the noise. "You didn't have the rifle under control, and I saw the barrel buck. You need to have consistent shoulder pressure to control the recoil and manage tight groupings. Do it again."

Alicia's face grew warm with embarrassment. This wasn't nearly as easy as she'd imagined it would be. She took in a deep breath and let it out slowly. Readjusting her position on the bench, she snugly pressed the rifle's butt-stock against her shoulder, peered through the scope, took aim, and focused on a smooth pull of the trigger.

The rifle rocked back against her, and she heard the ding of metal being struck.

"Hit!" Esther yelled. "Dead center. A good shot."

"Let me do it again."

Alicia had noticed how different shooting the rifle felt that time. It was almost as if it had been an extension of her arm. She adjusted, aimed, and slowly pulled the trigger.

"Hit!" Esther yelled again. "Good shot. Fifty more of those and we'll go out to two hundred yards."

Fifty? Alicia's eyes widened. This was going to be a long day.

CHAPTER FIVE

Alicia frowned at the angry oblong welt she'd picked up on her forearm. Near the end of yesterday's shooting marathon, which ended with her learning to occasionally hit targets at greater than one thousand yards, she'd managed to catch some hot brass in her shirt. The hot bullet casing had somehow worked its way down her three-quarter sleeve and wedged itself against her forearm, leaving the ugly burn mark.

She sat with her father in the rear of a luxurious sedan, and took note when they turned onto Exit 5 off FDR Drive. The signs said that this was the Houston Street/Holland Tunnel exit, which implied a trip to New Jersey.

"Dad, where exactly is this place we're going?"

"Paul's Casablanca is in SoHo," said her father beside her.

He leaned forward and tapped on the driver's shoulder. "Vincenzo, where are you going to be?"

"I-ah found *un posto*... uh, *parcheggiare,*" the man said in a mix of broken English and Italian. He held up two fingers with his right hand. "*Due* blocks *di distanza. Aspetterò* your-ah call."

"You found a place to park two blocks away and you'll wait for my call?"

"*Sì.*" The man nodded vigorously. "I'm-ah sorry, my English no so good."

Alicia's father grinned and patted the driver's shoulder. "*Non ti preoccupare,* Vincenzo. You've only been in the US for two months. It takes time."

The driver turned left onto Washington Street and then left again on Spring Street, a narrow street packed with people. Alicia saw "McGovern's Bar," spelled out in neon, glowing brightly above the crowd. Vincenzo pulled over as best he could, given the crowd.

Alicia looked over the crowd of nicely dressed people waiting outside what looked like a ramshackle building. "You sure this is the place?"

Her dad chuckled. "Don't judge a book by its cover."

The size and dress of the crowd certainly suggested that this otherwise unassuming bar was the place to be—for those in the know. But Alicia wasn't in the know. Not only had she never even heard of this place, but a visit to New York City's high-end night life didn't seem that alluring to a girl who'd spent much of her recent life knee-deep in cow manure or worse.

A man in a European-cut suit walked out of the crowd, making a beeline for their car. Dad opened his door, and the man called out with a mild Italian accent, "Mister Yoder, it's so good to see you!"

The two men exchanged kisses on the cheek, as her dad had taught her was customary in parts of Europe. "Fabrizio, I'd like you to meet my daughter, Alicia."

Alicia stepped out of the car as well, and the tall gentleman took her hand, kissing her knuckles.

"*Incantato.*" He made a sweeping motion with his arm. "Welcome to Paul's Casablanca."

He turned to her father. "Paul is currently flying back from Naples. He sends his deepest regrets that he's not here tonight."

Alicia's father draped his arm over Fabrizio's shoulder. "Alicia and I need a nice place to just watch, like always."

"Of course."

Fabrizio motioned for them to follow, and he walked with a somewhat stiff gait as a large dark-skinned man, probably a bouncer, cleared a pathway for them to the entrance. Nowhere did Alicia see the name of the club.

"How would anyone know this place was here?" she asked.

"That's part of the charm," Fabrizio said with a laugh. "This place is for those who know or would like to know. We like it this way."

We like it this way? The man spoke like the nightclub was really part of some secret society, and the three of them were card-carrying members. It was then that Alicia realized she was experiencing something she'd only heard of. As Fabrizio opened the door for her father, she glanced back at the crowd of people longing to get past the velvet rope. It didn't seem possible, but somehow this girl from the streets had become part of the "in" crowd. She felt a wave of anxiety wash over her as she worried about what kind of place her father had brought her to.

Fabrizio escorted them into the subtly lit building, and Alicia saw that the interior of Paul's Casablanca was nothing like the shabby exterior. It was well-appointed, with Moroccan-style archways, a long bar, and an open area under a disco ball with a crowd of good-looking people of all ages gyrating to the music.

Fabrizio stopped at an empty booth with a "Reserved" sign on the table. It had a clear view of the dance floor and everyone walking by. "I hope this will work for you," he said, practically having to yell to be heard over the music.

"It's good." Alicia's dad nodded. "I appreciate your hospitality."

"A seltzer for you, I presume, Mister Yoder?"

Alicia's father nodded.

"And for you, young lady? We have a full bar, and I can have Francisco make just about anything you'd like."

Alicia smiled at the idea of having a drink. It might calm her nerves. "Can I have an amaretto sour?"

"Of course. We use only Amaretto Disaronno, and do you have any preference for the sour mix? I think Francisco usually does one part simple syrup and one part freshly squeezed lemon juice."

"Whatever he recommends is fine with me."

"I'll have your drinks brought to you right away." Fabrizio turned on his heel, weaved his way through the crowd, and vanished.

Alicia gave her father a sidelong glance. He was leaning back in the booth, watching the crowd intently.

"Dad, can I ask you a question?"

"Sure."

Alicia scooted closer. "Why was that guy kissing your ass so much? Don't get me wrong, I love you to death, but why do they know you here?"

Her father shrugged and gave her a lopsided grin. "I know the owner from past business engagements. That's all. And they know I like to people-watch. That's why I brought you here. As an agent, you'll need to know how to mingle in strange places that you're not accustomed to."

A statuesque blonde approached their table, and Alicia's eyes widened. *It can't be her. Can it?*

"Levi, it's a surprise to see you here." The blonde bombshell batted her eyelashes at her father, then gave Alicia an uncertain look.

It took an effort for Alicia to keep her mouth from hanging open. This was the actress who played Veronica on a soap opera her roommate in college had gotten her hooked on.

"Buzzie," said her father, "this is Alicia, my daughter."

"Oh... oh, your daughter!" The woman's smile broadened, and she shook Alicia's hand. "It's so nice to meet you. Are you in town visiting?"

"Buzzie, let's talk later, okay?" her father said.

The woman put her hands on her hips and gave her father a pouty frown. "You said you'd call, and never did. Do you even still have my number on your phone?"

He rattled off a number from memory and said, "I'll call you."

Buzzie blew him a kiss, then smiled at Alicia. "It was nice meeting you." The starlet then turned and vanished into the crowd.

Alicia gazed at her father in astonishment. "You *know* Buzzie Henderson? Do you realize she's up for a daytime Emmy? She's... she's like... famous!"

"Is she? I hadn't realized the Emmy's were still a thing," he said matter-of-factly. "She's a nice girl, but a bit thirsty, if you know what I mean."

"Ew, Dad, I don't need to hear that from you."

A waitress brought their drinks and vanished before Alicia could even say thanks.

Her father sipped at his seltzer, then leaned closer. "I presume nobody in the Outfit has covered human intelligence gathering techniques with you?"

Alicia shook her head. "We're still on cheetahs and leopards. Humans are next week."

Her dad rolled his eyes. "You're too young for dad jokes. As an agent, you'll need to engage with a target and get information. This is a good place to practice your social skills. I come here to keep myself sharp. You and I are a lot more alike than you might think. I'm not naturally a social butterfly, but if I have to turn on the charm, I can. It's a learned behavior. The more you practice the better you'll be at it, just like anything else. You'd be surprised how much information people will volunteer. I'll demonstrate." He put down his seltzer and got up from the table.

Alicia sipped at her drink, which was excellent, and watched as her father walked onto the dance floor, scanned the room, and walked up to a girl who probably wasn't any older than Alicia.

He smiled at her, leaned in close, and said something.

The girl seemed taken aback for a second, and then returned his smile.

Alicia stared wide-eyed as the twenty-something looked her father up and down and ran her hand along the back of his arm with a growing smile that spoke volumes. Alicia knew what the girl was thinking, and it made her sick.

Her father was undeniably a good-looking guy, and he always dressed in a stylish suit when he went out. And despite his age, which was approaching fifty, he could easily pass for being in his thirties. But still. It was one thing to understand that girls—and guys—might find him attractive.

It was a totally different thing to sit here and watch some random chick blatantly lusting after her father.

He again bent down and said something in the girl's ear. She nodded vigorously, pulled out her phone, and showed him something. She then said something—Alicia only managed to lip read "your phone"—and Alicia's dad shook his head and hitched his thumb back toward their table.

The girl nodded, and her thirsty gaze followed him as he walked back and sat down next to Alicia.

"Okay, I got a girl's number even though she wanted to give me her Instagram, whatever that is. Now I want to see you try and do the same thing."

"Dad, are you crazy?" Alicia felt her chest tighten. The thought of walking up to a stranger and asking for his number was bringing on a panic attack. "It's easy for you—you look like you walked off someone's Photoshop app. I can't do that."

"I have no idea what a Photoshop app is," her father said, "but any guy would jump at a chance to give a pretty girl like you his number."

Alicia's fear was suddenly overwhelming. She shook her head and said with a shaky voice, "Dad, I can't do that."

Her father's firm expression changed to one of sympathy. He leaned in and gave her a hug, and she willed herself not to start crying. "It's okay, Alicia. I see the panic in your eyes. How about this: let's just relax and watch people. Maybe you have another drink. If you don't think you're up for it right now, that's okay. But I need you to realize you're going to have to learn to engage with a target at some point. Just maybe not tonight."

Alicia's heart was racing, and she felt a bead of sweat trickle down the middle of her back. She took a deep breath and let it out slowly.

She couldn't remember the last time she'd had a panic attack. Why were her insides turning to jelly?

Deep down, she knew why. She just hated to admit that it might still hold an effect on her. As a victim of child sex trafficking, she'd experienced every imaginable deviancy that could be inflicted on a child.

She thought she'd gotten past it.

Maybe she hadn't.

"Hey, Levi, what's up?"

Mason's voice crackled over the weak cell phone connection. Levi stood on Park Avenue, watching his baby girl's car pull away from the curb.

"Alicia is heading back to DC."

"Did you assuage your concerns over the weekend?"

"Mostly. She's a tough cookie, and I'm sure she'll do fine. I just want to make sure she gets a well-rounded education out of this. There is one thing, though..."

"Oh?"

"She's got one aspect of her training that I can't help with. The intelligence-gathering side of it."

"You mean the interpersonal stuff."

"Yeah."

Mason chuckled. *"Yup, that might be a little awkward between a father and daughter."*

"Mason, this is a real concern for me. You know her background. I don't know for sure, but I don't think she's even been out on a real date. Her life on the streets has scarred her in ways I can't begin to know. In ways *she* might not even fully realize. She needs to get past it and learn how to engage with a potential target. Otherwise she'll be in legitimate danger out in the field."

There was a long pause before Mason spoke. *"How about Annie?"*

"The Black Widow? I thought she's retired."

"It's not like I'd be asking her to do a job. I bet she'd be willing to give Alicia some training."

Levi paced the sidewalk as he remembered the last time he'd worked with that woman.

Annie looked up at the sky and shook her head. "You're nuts. But that makes you sexy as hell. Makes me wonder more and more what you're like under the sheets."

Levi chuckled. "Are you always like this?"

"Like what?"

"Such a blatant flirt. It's not exactly endearing, you know."

Annie sighed. "It's a personality flaw, but I've learned to live with it. Though you are actually someone I probably wouldn't regret fucking. Are you with someone?"

"Are you?"

"Hard to say. There's one guy I don't flirt with, because I actually care what he thinks."

"I'm thinking it's not Doc Spears. He's not exactly your biggest fan."

She waved dismissively. "He's just pissed that I used him as a one-night stand."

"Girls don't like it when guys do that, so why would a guy like it when a girl does that?"

Annie shook her head. "You really are naïve. Most guys would love no commitment, just some raunchy sex."

"Clearly Spears didn't. And regardless, it's kind of an asshole thing to do."

"An asshole thing to do? I'm not normally a backdoor kind of gal. Why, is that your thing?"

Levi shook his head. "Maybe you should flirt a little with the guy you like and not so much with the rest of the male population. Have you considered that strategy?"

"Oh, shut up. I'm thinking you're too stuffy to be that much fun."

Levi shook his head. "No, let's not get Annie involved. I have someone else in mind."

The sound of Mason's snort brought a smile to Levi's face. *"I know who you're talking about, and that might be a brilliant choice—if you can get her to cooperate."*

"We'll see. Anyway, I'm almost done with my prep work for the Russian issue we talked about. Next time we talk, I'll be in Vladivostok."

"Good. Best of luck on that. We have limited resources in that area, so don't do anything that gets yourself dead."

"Talk to you on the other side."

Levi hung up and stared in the direction Alicia had driven. He felt a growing anxiety as he recalled the spooked little girl he'd rescued from the streets.

Last night he'd seen that same expression of fear, even after all these years.

Obviously Alicia hadn't yet managed to exorcise those personal demons.

CHAPTER SIX

"What do you mean, my memories got corrupted?" Alicia said.

Director Mason sat across the conference room table from her. "I know this is going to be hard to understand, especially coming from me, a non-physicist. But about a year ago, a government project was spinning up that would have led to a bad end for the world as we know it."

He paused and scratched at his chin, and though he held a bland expression, Alicia knew better. The man's mind was always racing. In some ways, he reminded her of her father; he never let his emotions show on his face, but he was always very purposeful with what he said and did.

"Are you familiar with the term 'multiverse'?" he continued.

Alicia nodded. "Sure. It's the idea that any possible

choice you make at any moment creates an entire new universe of possibilities—which basically means that other universes exist that play out for every different choice you could have made in your life. It's like alternate history lines all existing at once."

"That's the gist of it." Mason drummed his fingers on the table and stared at Alicia with those silver-hued eyes of his. "And not only is the multiverse real, but you've interacted with it, in a way. When you were in grad school, at about the time you and I met, you received messages—memories—from one of our possible futures. These messages warned you about that government project... and as a result, that future was avoided. I know it seems fantastical, but the way it was explained to me—"

"Explained by whom?" Alicia interrupted.

Mason waved off the question. "Who is immaterial. I was told that there was a very high likelihood that some of these new memories you'd received would fade, and if they did, they would leave behind gaps. That's what you're experiencing now. Like I said, corrupted data. I didn't tell you about it because I didn't want to risk exacerbating the issue. And, to be honest, because I didn't think you'd believe what I'm telling you now."

Alicia wasn't sure whether to believe this crazy tale. Messages from the multiverse? Some clandestine government project? But all the same she was relieved to have *some* explanation, no matter how farfetched, for the gaps in her memory.

"Trust me," Mason went on, "you don't want some of those memories. Focus on developing new ones. On living your real life. Thus far, you've been doing great at that." He smiled. "I've been keeping tabs on your progress. As a matter of fact, I've got a training mission for you. You'll be paired up with a senior agent."

He slid a large envelope across the table to her, stamped with *Top Secret* classification markings. Despite the surge of excitement she felt at the idea of a training mission, she maintained her outward composure. "A senior agent?"

"Yes. It's someone you've already met. I'll send the agent here so you two can formally meet. In the meantime, I want you to stay here and go over everything in that envelope." He stood, sighing as he stretched his back. "Now, if you'll excuse me, I have yet *another* meeting to catch."

After Mason exited the conference room, Alicia dumped the contents of the envelope onto the table. It was a mix of photographs, documents written in Chinese, and CIA intelligence reports covering recent activity coming out of Southeast Asia.

Alicia had barely had a chance to briefly catalog everything when the conference room door opened and a tall, statuesque Asian woman walked into the room.

Alicia's eyes widened. "Miss Lucy? What are you doing here?"

Lucy spoke in rapid-fire Cantonese. "You're not a twelve-year-old girl anymore. You have no need to be formal with me, my little street urchin."

"But..."

Alicia blinked at the woman she'd known since her time on the streets. Lucy had an unusual background, when she spoke English it was with a slight Russian accent, was the widow of the founder of one of Hong Kong's largest triads—and a woman whom Alicia suspected was still involved in criminal activities. Alicia was suddenly all too aware of the classified data scattered across the table.

"What are you doing here?" she asked, frantically scooping everything into a pile.

Lucy smiled as she took a seat next to Alicia. "I'm going to be assisting with your training."

"You're... what?" Alicia's jaw dropped.

"I'm sure Doug mentioned you'd be working with a senior agent?" Lucy's smile widened. "That's me."

Alicia handed Lucy a satellite image of a forested area. "That's supposed to be the site of New Arcadia. It's about three miles east of the True Dragon Temple in the Shanzhi district of Taiwan."

Lucy frowned as she studied the image. She held it so close to her face that her nose was almost touching it. "I can barely detect that there's something in those woods. Whatever is at this camp has either been there for decades and has been overgrown, or someone has done a very good job of camouflaging it."

She then turned to Alicia. "What do you know of the temple complex?"

"Not a thing. I've never heard of it before now."

"It's a graveyard. More specifically, it's a columbarium, a building to hold urns filled with cremated remains. And what do you know about this area in general?"

"Again, nothing. I've never even been to Taiwan." Alicia made a sweeping motion across the table. "Director Mason just dumped all this on me right before you came in. I've only begun to go through it all."

"Summarize what you've learned so far."

Alicia noticed a slight look of amusement on Lucy's face. "You've already been briefed on this stuff, haven't you?"

Lucy shrugged. "I want to hear *your* interpretation. What's the backstory on New Arcadia?"

Alicia shook her head. In this regard, Lucy was just like Alicia's father: everything—absolutely everything—was a lesson.

Alicia retrieved one of the printouts that she'd actually had time to read. "This intelligence report gives a backgrounder. Arcadia is now best known for its pastoral beauty and rugged mountainous terrain. But in Greek mythology, Arcadia was believed to be the birthplace of the god Pan, who was the god of the wild, shepherds, and flocks. The region was also known for its association with the god Apollo, who was believed to have visited the region and had a temple dedicated to him there. The first historical mention of Arcadia comes from around the time of Alexander the Great, in association with the trade routes he established—though historians now believe that the silk and spice trade between the Western world and Eastern civilizations started in the sixth century BCE, if not earlier, long before Alexander the Great."

Alicia set the report aside and grabbed another that she'd read earlier. "Arcadia came up recently in an intercepted communication coming out of mainland China. The message included specific geolocation coordinates—the photo you're holding was taken by one of our satellites over those coordinates—and also spoke about Chiang Kai-shek's stolen property, and him being a traitor."

Lucy snorted. "Of course they call him a traitor. He's a traitor to anyone in the PRC, but he's a hero to those living in Taiwan. And the rumors of him stealing 'treasures,' around the time of the Chinese civil war back in 1949 are just the typical propaganda that always comes out of a communist-controlled society. Now, go on."

"Okay," said Alicia, grabbing another document, this one written in Chinese. "Check this out. This is an intercepted call between a general in China and one of his agents in the field. The general confirms that New Arcadia is five kilometers east of the True Dragon Temple grounds, and he says"—here Alicia read directly from the printout—"'You have clearance to go ahead and enact the Dragon's Breath Protocol.'"

Lucy nodded, but otherwise showed no reaction whatsoever. Alicia wondered if having an iron grip on one's facial expressions was a skill taught by the Outfit or just a natural thing that evolved from being an agent.

The door opened, and Mason walked in. He tossed a bunch of government-issued IDs, including a pair of black passports, onto the table. "Those are diplomatic credentials for both of you." He looked at Lucy. "Things have escalated. I'm going to need your special skills."

Lucy's expression soured. "Doug, I'm not fucking anyone for you. Go get your Black Widow or whatever other whore you've got in reserve for that kind of crap."

"I didn't—"

"I don't care what you didn't think or ask. I'm also not going to off anyone for you. I'm done with that part of my life. I'm here because Levi asked me to help with Alicia's training. That's *all* I'm doing. You got me?"

Alicia stared wide-eyed. She'd never seen Mason talked to in this manner, even by her father.

Then again, when Alicia was a kid, Lucy's nickname on the streets was *Dragon Lady*. She had no fear of anyone.

It seemed the dragon was now sharpening her nails.

"May I speak?" Mason said. To Alicia's surprise, his tone was warm, and the side of his mouth was curled up in amusement.

Lucy rolled her eyes and motioned impatiently at him.

"I hear you, Lucy. No under-the-covers work or wet operations. I still ask that you help us out by talking to some Taiwanese officials. You have a way with those folks that most do not, and it would benefit Alicia to shadow you. We need to get access to this 'New Arcadia' and figure out what's being hidden in those woods."

"Why?" Lucy asked bluntly.

Alicia saw a flicker of something in Mason's expression. Irritation?

"The State Department is keeping this hush-hush, but we're seeing Chinese troop movements that might indicate the first signs of an invasion of Taiwan. The Outfit has folks on the mainland, but there's something going on between high-level PLA officials and what we believe to be sleeper cells in Taiwan."

"PLA?" Alicia asked.

"People's Liberation Army," Mason explained. "Anyway, we don't know if the troop movements are connected to what's going on with this site, but the Taiwanese don't want anyone near New Arcadia, and we need to figure out why elements of the PLA are so interested in it. That said, this trip is purely a diplomatic effort. We've already lost an agent trying to scout the location, and I have no interest in losing another." He focused on Lucy. "I can't think of a better person to send than you—and I can't think of a better training opportunity for Alicia than simply having her watch you work. Are you on board?"

Lucy turned to Alicia and said in Cantonese, "Don't ever believe this man. This could be dangerous. You don't have to go."

Alicia felt a chill race up her spine, and her heart thudded rapidly. It took everything she had to maintain her outward composure. "I'm going."

Lucy turned back at Mason. "First-class tickets for us both. I'm not waiting in lines or getting stowed in the back of the plane this time. You got me?"

Mason grinned. "I'll do you both one better than that. In the meantime, get yourselves prepared. I figure you'll be wheels up no later than this evening."

Mason left the room, and Lucy stood and gestured to the mess on the table.

"Gather everything up; we'll check it into the confidential bin on our way out. We need to run to your apartment and get you packed. Knowing you, you probably don't have anything decent for this mission, so we might also need to do some shopping on Doug's credit card."

"I've got decent clothes," Alicia protested, trying to sound convincing.

Lucy looked Alicia up and down and shook her head. "Lesson one: baggy pants and a pullover makes you look like a tall trash bag. If that's any indication of what's in your closet, you need an entirely new wardrobe. Let's go."

"The transport to Joint Base Andrews is waiting for you both in the parking lot." The voice on Alicia's phone belonged to

Brice, one of the operations guys at the Outfit. *"Do you have any last-minute questions?"*

Alicia paced back and forth in her apartment. "How about that briefing I was promised?"

"I have two packages waiting for you and Lucy. They contain briefing details and a few other odds and ends that I managed to scrape together for you."

"Okay, I guess I'll wait to see what's in the packages then."

"Safe travels."

Lucy stepped out of the bathroom wearing a business dress and looking every bit the no-nonsense female executive. Alicia looked at herself in the mirror and wished she were half as put together. Lucy bought her six full outfits, all of them form-fitting and exposing much more leg than she was comfortable with.

They took the elevator downstairs, and as they exited the building, they were greeted by a man in an Air Force uniform, standing by a dark minivan with police lights. A logo on the vehicle's front passenger door read *Security Police* and *Department of the Air Force.*

"Ms. Chen, the jet's fueled up and ready to go," said the man. "Ms. Yoder, it's good to meet you."

He held out a silver coin to her, pinched between thumb and finger. On the face of the coin was a familiar pyramid featuring the Eye of Providence—one of the Outfit's IDs. As the airman continued to grip one half of the coin, Alicia gripped the other. A second later, the Eye lit up.

He repeated the process with Lucy, with the same results.

The airman pocketed the coin, and the two ladies got in the vehicle—Lucy in front, Alicia in the back. The airman took the driver's seat.

As they drove east, he glanced at Alicia in the rearview mirror. "Beside you on the seat are two briefcases you're supposed to take with you. They're both Outfit-secured." He then looked over at Lucy. "Do you two have your State Department-issued IDs? You'll need those to get past the main gate and onto the plane."

"Got it." Lucy pulled out her ID and clipped it to the front of her outfit. Alicia did the same.

The minivan turned right off of Dower House Road, and they passed a sign that read *Pearl Harbor Gate Hours 0500 – 2100.* Moments later they'd arrived at a well-lit security outpost.

The airman lowered his window as he pulled to a stop. They all handed their IDs to the guard, and after a quick check, he handed the IDs back and waved them through.

They entered the base, drove past the East Perimeter Road, and approached a large jet. It had a US flag on its tail, an Air Force logo on its engine, and *United States of America* painted just above the passenger windows. Alicia had never been on a jet, either military or private.

Lucy smiled. "Now *that's* a pretty bird. Don't get too used to this, Alicia. Mason's normally a cheap date. He'll send you out on a no-frills military transport, or shove you onto whatever available seat you can get on a public flight. This is new."

As they stepped out of the minivan, each with a briefcase in one hand and a duffel bag in the other, a staircase opened on the plane, revealing a man in silhouette waiting for them. Lucy started right up the stairs, and Alicia followed her lead.

The man at the top of the stairs wore an Air Force uniform. He asked for their IDs, checked them, then handed them back and welcomed them aboard. "Please buckle in quickly; we're taking off as soon as I pull up the stairs."

The interior cabin looked exactly like what Alicia expected from an executive jet: all comfort and professionalism. It even had a new-leather smell. She wondered what important government VIPs had ridden this plane before her.

A voice came over the cabin speakers. "*Welcome to the Gulfstream G650 business jet. As you get acquainted with the features of this aircraft—*"

The voice cut off unexpectedly, and a short, well-dressed Asian man hopped up from his seat in the cabin. There were over a dozen seats, but apparently he was the only other passenger.

He pointed up at the speakers. "They haven't configured everything to Military Standard just yet. Not that I'm complaining. Military Standard doesn't include soft leather headrests." He held out his hand. "I'm John Woo, deputy chief of mission at the AIT."

They shook hands, and Lucy and Woo sat down across

from each other at a small lacquered table. There wasn't another seat there, so Alicia took a seat across the aisle.

As Lucy talked to the diplomat in Mandarin, Alicia noticed a change in the way the woman held herself. Lucy seemed smaller, more reserved, and very attentive when the man was speaking. This was a role Alicia had never seen the woman play.

The man talked about himself, and Alicia, listening in, learned that he was the number two guy at what served as the unofficial "US embassy" in Taiwan. Of course, the US didn't have an *official* embassy there, because as far as China was concerned, Taiwan wasn't a separate country. They were more a rogue province of China—a key element of their "One China" worldview. The US knew they couldn't recognize Taiwan as a country, not if they wanted to maintain diplomatic relations with the PRC. So they'd created an organization called "the American Institute in Taiwan," or AIT, which served as the US embassy in everything but name.

The captain's voice came over the cabin speakers. *"This is Captain Roger Fleming, your pilot for this flight to Taipei. We are first in line for takeoff. We will be cruising at an altitude of 48,000 feet at an airspeed of approximately 500 knots to our first refueling stop at Anchorage, Alaska. Flight time is expected to be approximately six hours from wheels up to wheels down. After refueling, we will proceed direct to Taoyuan International Airport, cruising at the same altitude and speed, and expect to arrive approximately eight hours after departing Anchorage. The local time of our arrival should be approximately 0300*

Wednesday morning. This will be the only communication until we land at our destination."

Wednesday morning? It was currently Monday evening. Alicia frowned as she added up the hours, and then she realized that they'd be crossing the international date line—effectively skipping to the next day.

As the engines began revving, Lucy rose from her seat and again shook Deputy Woo's hand. "I have some things I need to talk to my colleague about during the flight. I hope later we get a chance to talk more about your summer home outside of Taipei."

Lucy gestured for Alicia to follow her toward the back of the jet, where they settled into a pair of luxurious leather seats.

"Summer home?" Alicia asked.

The dragon lady snorted as she buckled her seatbelt. "Yes. He seems very interested in inviting us for a visit whenever our tasks with the Taiwanese ambassador are completed."

Alicia felt herself being pushed against her seat as the pilot released the brakes and the jet launched itself down the runway. Within seconds they were airborne, climbing to altitude at a much steeper rate of ascent than any commercial aircraft would.

Alicia put her head back against the headrest. Woo was right. It was a very soft leather.

Alicia studied the briefcase in her lap, but saw no way to open it. She looked over at Lucy, who'd already opened hers and was rifling through its contents.

"How do you open these things?"

Lucy tapped on the top of Alicia's case. "That plaque is a biometric scanner. Put your thumb on it."

Alicia looked at the bronze plaque. The pyramid with the Eye of Providence was engraved on it. She pressed her thumb on the logo, and she felt something inside the case click. It popped open.

Inside were papers, photos, and maps. But on top of the stack was a red piece of paper with a message written in bold: *"Before departing the plane, return all contents to the case and lock it with your thumbprint. The contents will then be incinerated, and both case and contents will be safe for disposal."*

"Whoa... our cases have an auto-destruct?"

Lucy nodded without looking up from the report in her hand. "That's pretty normal."

"That's very *Mission: Impossible,* if you ask me."

Lucy grinned. "Your father is partial to 007 references. But what did you expect? We're not on this plane to hand out drinks or give blow jobs to politicians." She raised an eyebrow. "Though I'm pretty sure Mister Woo wishes otherwise. If you think self-immolating briefcases are something, just wait until you see what we end up having to deal with on location."

"What do you mean?"

Lucy shook her head. "Later. Your only concern right now is committing to memory everything in that briefcase. What you remember may be the difference between coming out of this mission alive or dead." There was absolutely nothing about her tone, her facial expression, or her words to suggest that she was kidding.

Alicia picked up the first document, and its title—"Usage of Manchurian Candidates"—reminded her of an old movie she'd watched with her father. It had been all about brainwashing some guy and turning him into an assassin. This document started off dull in comparison, mostly talking about this being a fact-finding mission leveraging diplomatic connections.

It wasn't until a passage at the bottom of the first page that things got interesting:

The Outfit captured a high-ranking Chinese officer and subjected him to memory implantation techniques. Without the Chinese official even being aware of what had been done, we successfully turned him into an asset. Unfortunately, he was killed just outside the New Arcadia grounds.

It's your task to gather information to determine what exactly is hidden east of the True Dragon Temple in Taiwan's Shanzhi district. We need to know what the Taiwanese are hiding at this site, and why the Chinese would risk destabilizing relations to acquire it.

Time is of the essence.

The intelligence you gather will be used to further the missions of several deeply embedded agents deployed in critical locations in that part of the world.

The document went on to talk about the PRC Ministry of State Security, or MSS. It was the Chinese equivalent of the KGB, and its official seal featured the ominous image of the hammer and sickle above what looked like a Chinese building.

Alicia realized this mission wasn't going to be a simple affair of glad-handing politicians. Someone had already been killed because of New Arcadia.

Alicia looked again at the first part of the document.

Manchurian Candidates.

Memory implantation techniques.

Was it possible that this was the real cause of the gaps in her memory? That she herself had been subject to this procedure, in some mission she could no longer remember, and the crazy multiverse explanation Mason had given was all bullshit?

She recalled what Lucy had said back at the Outfit's headquarters.

"Don't ever believe this man. This could be dangerous."

Alicia felt her uncertainty and fear growing.

What had she signed herself up for?

CHAPTER SEVEN

It was early morning in the village of Zhaoli, and now that Ping was eight, her mother let her go to the shore by herself to bring home whatever sea creatures she could find to cook for the midday meal. Ping had been hoping to find some shellfish, or maybe a hairy crab.

She'd never expected to encounter the sea creature now struggling on the beach before her.

It was big. Bigger than her. And covered in giant mats of seaweed.

As the monster lurched forward, Ping scampered several steps back. She was about to go get help from some of the fishermen near the docks when a giant wave slammed onto the shore, covering the creature. She thought—hoped—it would be swept back into the ocean, but it wasn't. As the wave receded, its head popped up, gasping for breath.

The monster wasn't a monster after all, it was a man.

Their eyes connected, and she saw the look of desperation on the man's face. He was stuck, half-buried in the soft sand, and the tide was coming in.

"Help..." he called out weakly, his voice barely audible over the sounds of the waves and the seagulls.

Ping wore the extra-wide shoes that her mother had weaved for her so that she wouldn't get stuck in the sand, but the man was farther out than she was comfortable going.

"Help..." he called again, just before another wave slammed onto him.

Ping's feet clomped heavily on the sand as she ran toward him.

The water receded again, and she finally got a good look at the stranger. Beneath the mats of seaweed, his shirt was shredded down to strips of white cloth that clung to his body.

"Go back," he said. "You aren't strong enough to help—"

"I'm strong enough!" Ping snapped.

She held out the plank of wood she used to set her digging tools on.

The man looked at her, then at the plank. He grabbed it, planted it in the sand, and used the leverage to pull himself partway out of the clutching sand.

"Go back so the waves don't get you!"

Ping ran back just before the next wave came crashing in. This time the man didn't disappear altogether. She could see his wriggling form, the water frothing all around him, as he used the plank to free himself.

The water pulled back, and despite his obvious exhaustion he managed to make forward progress, escaping the death grip of the wet sand and dragging himself to drier sand a bit farther on.

"Ping, what's going on?"

Ping turned and saw Elder Pu hobbling toward her, concern on his white-whiskered face.

She pointed at the man crawling out of the sea. "That man got himself stuck in the quicksand."

The old man squinted at the sight, then patted Ping on her shoulder. "Run to the pier and get some men over here."

"But—"

"Go, child! Do as I say."

Ping raced away, not willing to incur Elder Pu's wrath. She looked over her shoulder in time to see the stranger struggle from the waves onto the beach. She wished she could stay to talk to the man, but when the Elder yelled, the children of the village had learned to obey.

Elder Pu waited until Ping was out of earshot, then yelled in Korean at the stranger. "Did you escape?"

The man heaved himself up onto his feet, only to fall right back onto his knees. "What?" he said in Mandarin.

Elder Pu shook his head, puzzled. It wasn't unheard of for North Koreans to wash up on Chinese shores like this. Many were so desperate they escaped into the sea, only to eventually get caught by the tides. Few survived. But this man didn't look North Korean. His tattered shirt and his underwear—he wore no pants—weren't of the right style.

"Who are you, stranger?"

Using the wooden plank, the man levered himself up onto his feet once more. This time he didn't fall. He staggered toward the elder.

"Drop the plank!" The elder yelled, shaking his walking stick.

The stranger blinked as if confused, then dropped the plank onto the dry sand.

"Who are you?" asked Elder Pu. "Where are you from?"

The man was now almost within arm's reach. He was covered in scrapes and bruises, and one cheek was horribly swollen. He was in terrible shape, but it was the question that stopped him short.

"I... I don't know," he said.

"What do you mean you don't know? What's your name?"

The man furrowed his brow. "I... I can't remember."

It was then that Ping returned with two fishermen, all of them running.

"What's going on?" one of the fishermen asked.

"He came out of the sea," Elder Pu said. "Take him to the committee building. We will call the police."

The fishermen grabbed the man's arms, and he didn't resist. In fact he slumped, almost with exhausted gratitude, allowing them to take some weight off of his tired legs.

"Probably a Korean defector," the other fisherman said.

Elder Pu said nothing, but he shook his head. The man was beaten, half-naked, and exhausted—but he was also well-nourished. This was no North Korean defector.

But who, then, could it be?

The Nameless One. That's what the villagers began calling him. And he couldn't blame them. He genuinely couldn't remember his own name. He couldn't remember anything before that little girl found him on the beach, half-drowned, and in no condition to put up any resistance. A frustrated officer from the People's Police beat him for not revealing his identity—not that he could—and now he sat in a jail cell inside the harbor police station.

His stomach growled. He felt hunger gnawing deep in his guts—starvation, really—but he had no idea how long it had been since he'd had anything to eat or drink. When he'd asked the policeman for a drink, the man had merely thrown a cup of tea in his face.

It was a strange feeling—not knowing what he'd done, where he'd been, even who he was. And yet there were other things he knew instinctively. For instance, a single glance at the policeman's red shoulder insignia and collar told him that the man was a sergeant. And despite the sergeant's insistence on yelling at him in broken Korean, he knew that the sergeant was Chinese.

The police obviously believed he was a defector from the pariah nation of Kim Jong Un. When a woman wearing a corporal's uniform had come in earlier to take his blood, the sergeant told her, "You have my permission to take *all* of this slave's blood. Kim Jong Fatty has no soldiers, just slaves and whores."

That was this morning, and since then he'd been left to roast alone in the steaming hot building, windows and doors closed.

He leaned against the cinderblock wall and closed his eyes, and focused on his breathing. Gradually he picked up on the sensations of life outside the building. He felt the vibrations of a truck driving past, and occasionally he caught the sound of voices of people walking past.

He wasn't sure how long he'd been meditating when he heard a car door slamming shut. Suddenly the door to the police station burst open and the sergeant rushed in. His demeanor had changed entirely. He pulled out his keys, unlocked the cell, and handed the prisoner a bottle of water.

"Please, comrade, drink this. I will get you something to eat."

The nameless man eagerly guzzled the hot, clear liquid that had likely been sitting all day on the officer's suncooked dashboard. It tasted better than anything he could remember... which at the moment wasn't much.

The sergeant held out his hand. "Let me help you up."

The man took the offered assistance and stood. His legs wobbled, and for a moment the room tilted. The policeman steadied him and spoke reassuringly that everything would be okay.

Four more men entered the tiny police station, all wearing the uniform of the People's Liberation Army. The prisoner saw that one of them was a captain.

The sergeant snapped to attention as the PLA officer cast his gaze over the filthy cell and shook his head.

"Leave us, now!"

The sergeant raced out the door.

The captain held up a piece of paper and stared back and forth between it and the prisoner. His angry expression slowly shifting to one of surprise. "Sir, is it correct that you cannot remember who you are?"

The prisoner nodded. "Yes, sir. I can't remember anything from before this morning."

The captain stepped into the open jail cell and looked directly into the prisoner's eyes. "Unbelievable," he whispered.

To the prisoner's shock, the captain then took a step back, snapped to attention, and saluted. The other three men followed suit.

"Colonel Xi, you have been missing for two weeks. We are here to take you to a proper facility to help you recover."

Colonel Xi...

The name felt right. And it brought memories with it. His parents. Training to enter the MSS. Being elevated from lieutenant colonel. A secret mission.

Walking through a forest covered in a dense layer of mist...

The captain supported him as they walked out of the dingy police station into the bright and sunny day. He was helped into the front seat of a military vehicle.

But Xi was still in that suffocating forest even as he wrapped the seatbelt around his waist. And in that forest, he felt it: the sledgehammer blow of a bullet as it burned a hole through his chest.

But as the driver put the car into gear, Colonel Xi felt another memory bubbling up, this one carrying a strange name: New Arcadia.

CHAPTER EIGHT

While he read through the evening's intelligence report on the East Asian sector, Director Mason's desk phone rang. He glanced at the caller ID and snatched the receiver from its cradle. "What's up, Brice?"

"We've got news regarding our missing agent."

Mason sat up straight. The agent's burst tracker had been silent for two days, and he'd feared the worst. "What have you got?"

"Sir, this was pieced together from the comms traffic between a prefecture-level police station and its provincial military outpost, but it looks like Agent Xiang must have gotten caught by some rip currents and taken miles off course. He's now been recovered and is being spirited off to a district military hospital."

Mason let out a sigh of relief. "Do we know his condition?"

"Negative. But based on the comms traffic timestamps, the agent is likely only now arriving at the hospital."

"Keep me posted on what you learn." Mason drummed his fingers on his desk. "Has Agent Chen and her protégé arrived at their destination yet?"

The sound of typing came over the line. *"The plane landed in Taipei fifteen minutes ago."*

"Good. Let's pray that those two have less trouble than Chris Xiang did."

"You'll have to excuse my cynicism, but Lucy Chen is always trouble. Her reputation for leaving bodies for our folks to clean up is second only to Annie's."

Mason leaned back in his chair. "I just hope that aspect of the dragon lady doesn't rub off on Alicia. She's a good kid. But speaking of Annie, how's the baby doing?"

"When I left this morning, little Brice was nursing quite happily. And before you say anything, I'm just as surprised as anyone that Annie has taken so naturally to motherhood. It's fascinating to watch, the whole milk factory at work. Did you know human milk has a sort of sweet taste to it?"

Mason snorted. "That's more than I needed to hear. Keep me posted on Chen and Xiang's progress. I'll talk to you later."

Mason hung up, glanced at the wall clock, and sighed. It was almost time for him to leave, and this time he couldn't just skip the meeting—he already knew what had gotten the DC bureaucrats up in arms.

The reports coming out of China—of hundreds of Uyghurs dead from biological weapons—was enough to stir up rash reactions. The folks in the Pentagon always got their britches bunched up when the topic of biological weapons came up. And though he had intel to refute that assertion, he couldn't divulge that data. His appearance at this meeting of senior foreign intelligence representatives was under the guise of the CIA. The Outfit didn't exist...

The peace that had been maintained for over fifty years in the East Asian sector was threatening to unravel, and only a deft hand would be able to navigate these dangerous times. At the very least, he was determined to make sure nothing happened that interfered with the plans he'd painstakingly laid out.

But avoiding World War III would be nice, too.

Having parked on the south side of Constitution Avenue, between Delaware and Louisiana Avenue, Mason bristled as he fast-walked through the late evening mist toward the Capitol Building. The DC apparatchiks had changed their meeting location from the Pentagon, which had convenient parking facilities, to the one place in DC that guaranteed you'd have to walk over half a mile to get to the building's entrance.

Luckily, he had access to a car with a congressional parking permit, and after getting through security, he was allowed into the building, which despite the late hour had a few congressional staffers rushing about. The only reason anyone other than security scurried through the building was likely because the House was still in session working on some piece of useless legislature.

Mason walked into the Capitol Building Rotunda and paused as he took in the sights, sounds, and smells of what lay before him. Despite the constant cleaning and state of restoration, the building's smell reminded him of an old library. It wasn't exactly musty, but the smell for him connoted an age, which was appropriate for the nearly two-hundred-year-old building. Craning his neck at the dome's 180-foot-high ceiling, he took in the intricate details of the building's construction. The design was reminiscent of ancient Roman architecture and reminded him of the Pantheon.

The curved sandstone walls were divided by fluted Doric pilasters with wreaths of olive branches carved in the frieze above. The floor was made from concentric rings of waxed Seneca Sandstone arrayed around a central circular white marble slab. Mason glanced to his right and admired the bronze statue of George Washington standing on a stone pedestal inscribed with "Virginia" the state he represented.

Mason turned just as someone crossed from the opposite side of the Rotunda, making a beeline for him.

"Doug, sorry about the last-minute change, but somehow Senator Harkin, chairman for the senate's foreign relations committee, got word of the briefing you were going to give at the Pentagon and threw a fit."

Mason frowned at the congressional staffer, who was a member of the Outfit, and wondered for the thousandth time how anything got done in the nation's capital when nothing seemed to remain a secret. "Okay, so who exactly am I meeting with then? I'm guessing General Metcalf isn't here?"

The staffer winced. "I'm sorry, but we had to put off the general. Harkin's threatening to go to the press about an intelligence community that's gone rogue, if he doesn't get a briefing on what's going on 'right damned now' as he always puts it. He's gathered a bunch of the foreign relations committee for a briefing, so..."

"In other words, they want someone from the IC to dance for their pleasure." Clenching his jaw tightly, Mason allowed himself the momentary pleasure of imagining what he'd like to do to the arrogant senator from the state of Massachusetts. "Fine, where are we meeting?"

"It's on the Senate side, room 116 on the first floor. I'll escort you there."

The man turned and Mason followed the staffer, exiting the north end of the rotunda, and within a few minutes, found himself walking into a twenty-by-twenty-foot room.

There were about a dozen people in the red-carpeted room, some sat quietly at a long conference room table staring at their phones, others scribbled on pads of paper, while a few senators had sequestered themselves into corners of the room having private conversations.

A short, plump senator with a pencil-thin mustache glanced in his direction and immediately broke off the conversation he'd been having with a tall woman and walked over to Mason. "Deputy Director Mason?"

"That's me." Mason grinned and shook the man's hand. "It's good to finally meet you, Senator Harkin."

The man snorted and gave him an insincere smile. "I apologize for the late hour, but these matters concerning foreign intelligence don't recognize the time of day." With a loud clap of his meaty hands, Harkin grabbed everyone's attention and motioned in the direction of the conference room table. "Let's get settled, the briefing is about to start."

Harkin motioned for Mason to take the seat next to him as the other senators took their seats and staffers exited the room, closing the door behind them.

Mason panned his gaze across the room and didn't recognize many of the faces. There'd been a time when he'd made it a point to familiarize himself with the senators, since they at least held six-year stints and unbeknownst to them, they often became useful to the Outfit in various ways.

Many of the senators were a bit disheveled, as if they'd been called out of bed to attend the late-night meeting. Mason's gaze met with a ruddy-faced senator across the table from him, and Senator Martinez from the state of Texas nodded in his direction. This man he knew, having attended a few of the now-Senator's whole-hog roasts, and Martinez was certainly on Mason's rolodex of people he could reach out to, especially since the man had been a congressman for nearly twenty years before switching over to the senate. He was a canny politician who made it his business to know what was going on in DC.

The best Mason could figure was that he probably had Martinez as an ally in the group, Harkin was a snake in the grass and couldn't be trusted, and the rest were unknown quantities.

With a loud banging of a gavel, Senator Harkin spoke loudly, his voice filling the room. "Okay folks, I know you're all grumpy about the late meeting, but some of the reports out of the East Asia sector were wholly incomplete and didn't cover the latest intel coming out of China. I'll remind everyone that this is a closed session. We will be covering classified material and as always, turn off your cell phones or other electronic devices."

Several of the senators shifted in their seats, retrieved their phones and made a show of turning them off so everyone could see.

"Let's start. Earlier today some members of our committee learned of something called the Dragon's Breath Protocol being reported out of China."

Who the hell had passed this weasel of a man that particular piece of intelligence?

Mason kept his expression bland as his mind raced. This meeting was going to be awkward, but that was the least of his worries. Someone had leaked intel that only a handful of people had access to, and the last thing he needed was for the truth to actually get out.

And depending on how much had leaked and to whom, the Outfit now had people who were likely in danger.

"As far as I can tell, there is no such classified compartment nor could I find anyone who'd admit to knowing anything about such a thing. It's an odd thing when nobody in the intelligence community seems to know about something that is clearly happening, and even has a code name assigned to it. I ended up talking with someone who informed me that our guest this evening would be responsive to our queries." Harkin motioned to his left, at Mason, and said, "Deputy Director Mason, I realize that you've been called here at the last minute and you likely have no prepared remarks of any kind. I actually prefer that, to be honest. We're a rather informal bunch here, especially when the cameras are gone and the peacocks have nobody to strut for. Can you please introduce yourself to the committee, your responsibilities, and can you tell us what's *really* going on in the East Asian sector."

Mason once again panned his gaze across the long conference room table and the assembled senators all returned his gaze with expressions that ranged from those exhibiting keen interest to those who barely managed to keep their eyes open. "Senators, my name is Doug Mason and I'm a Deputy Director for the Special Activities Division of the CIA. We're primarily responsible for covert actions and other special activities."

"Covert actions?" A female senator spoke with a heavy southern drawl. "Is that covert actions only located *outside* of our country, and what exactly is it that you mean by special activities?"

"Senator, the entire intelligence community, including the CIA uses Executive order 12333 as our guiding principle behind all of our operations. It sets the guardrails on our activity.

"The CIA only operates outside the US with very few exceptions. And as stated in section 1.8a of executive order 12333, any collection of foreign intelligence or counterintelligence within the United States shall be coordinated with the FBI as required by procedures agreed upon by the Director of Central Intelligence and the Attorney General. As to special activities, those have fairly loose definitions, but are also dictated by section 1.8e of the same EO and must be directly approved by the President."

The woman, who looked to be in her sixties, maintained a puckered expression of displeasure and shook her head. No one liked having the regulations quoted to them. "That seems to me a very vague job description, if you ask me."

"Understood, Senator. We report up into the National Clandestine Service and I assure you that our activities are key to maintaining national security."

"Harriet, let the man talk." A bearded senator with a

Bostonian accent focused on the lady senator next to him. "Sounds to me like they're keeping the boogieman at bay."

Mason addressed the man from Boston. "Sir, in a way—yes, we are doing exactly that. Our operations focus primarily on counterterrorism activity."

Some of the senators began muttering to each other and before anyone had a chance to say anything else, Harkin banged the gavel repeatedly and cleared his throat. "I would remind my fellow senators that we're not here to understand or debate the merits of the CIA's mission, this is about the East Asian sector and what's going on over there. Please let the man speak before you pepper him with all sorts of questions, otherwise we'll never get this done." He turned to Mason and nodded. "Mister Mason, please go ahead."

Taking advantage of the momentary silence in the room, Mason cleared his throat and continued speaking.

"Chairman Harkin, Ranking Member Smith, distinguished members of this committee: thank you for giving me the opportunity to speak to you today.

"As to the subject at-hand: the People's Republic of China, and the so-called Dragon's Breath Protocol—as you all know, anything having to do with the PRC is a geopolitical challenge, and quite frankly, what is happening will test American diplomacy like few issues in recent memory.

"First, a bit of background: The PRC is our only competitor with the intent and means to reshape the international order: a fact borne out in the PRC's provocations in the South China Sea; its human rights abuses; its use of economic coercion; its threatening behavior against Taiwan; and, of course, some of the things we've recently witnessed hovering over our country.

"Last week, the American people saw the latest example of that reality, after the U.S. government detected, closely tracked, and shot down the PRC's high-altitude surveillance balloon that had entered our territorial airspace, in clear violation of our sovereignty and international law. And not for the first time.

"The current Administration responded swiftly to protect Americans and safeguard against the balloon's collection of sensitive information.

"We made clear to PRC officials that the presence of this series of surveillance balloons was, in a word, unacceptable. Along the way, we learned a thing or two, which I'm prepared to disclose in this classified setting, about the PRC's use of their balloons.

"We believe that the balloons are a test run for controlled delivery of some form of toxic substances. What we found inside the balloons were exploded capsules filled with the equivalent of talcum powder—"

"Excuse me," Harkin interrupted. "Did you say talcum powder? As in the same stuff we put on baby's rear ends?"

"Yes, sir, but that's my point—even though this test run was delivering a harmless substance into our territory, that doesn't mean future incursions might be as harmless."

"Understood." Harkin jabbed a sausage-like finger in Mason's direction. "Is that the allusion that the name Dragon's Breath is making? The poisoning of our citizenry? Napalm across our land? What do you expect they're planning on sending?"

"It's uncertain at this time what the exact plans are. We have people deeply embedded in that sector, hoping to learn more, and to turn the tables on them. We are not the only countries that the PRC have done this to... Taiwan has had many fly-overs with these same high-altitude balloons."

"Mister Mason," a young senator with a military-style haircut seated to Mason's left held a concerned expression. "Do you believe they're staging a multi-front campaign to sow chaos?"

"Senator, it's uncertain at this time. We have people looking into this. In the meantime, political elements are at play to give public warning to the PRC about further acts.

"Last Friday, Secretary Horowitz called Director Wang Yi to say that it would not be appropriate to visit Beijing at this time, as did the representatives from five other NATO countries.

"On Saturday, as you all know, at the President's direction, the U.S. military successfully brought down the half-dozen balloons over our territory. There are other governmental elements that are tasked with intercepting any future items as they approach our homeland."

"Son," an elderly senator at the far end of the table motioned for Mason's attention. "Is there a danger to the populace, bringing these things down? Especially on our territory."

“This lawful and deliberate action was achieved with no harm to civilians or military personnel. As to the future risks, that truly depends on what the planned payload might be from these balloons, and our ability to intercept them well before they reach out coastline.

“Realize that my people are the intelligence gathering arm for much of this effort. My team is working in cooperation with many other parts of our government, including but not limited to Homeland Security, the military, and other members of the intelligence community. Our collective response to this incident reaffirmed our core priorities: we will always act decisively to protect the American people. We will never hesitate to defend U.S. interests and the rules-based international order. We will confront the dangers posed by the PRC with resolve and keep demonstrating that violations of any country’s sovereignty are unacceptable.

“This irresponsible act put on full display what we’ve long recognized—that the PRC has become more repressive at home and more aggressive abroad.

“It reinforced the need for us to double-down on our strategy: ‘Invest, Align, Compete.’

“We are aligning with likeminded allies and partners overseas: with the G7 and the EU.”

“What about Taiwan?” Harkin asked.

“We have people in that sector, and as might be obvious, due to their proximity, maintaining a safe airspace for the island nation has its own challenges. Challenges that we are actively working on.

"We have made a concerted effort to share information that reinforces the scale of the threats posed by the PRC, and the necessity of unity in confronting them.

"We continue to oppose Beijing's unlawful acts in the South and East China Seas; hold accountable those involved in human rights violations in Tibet and Xianjiang; support the people of Hong Kong; and do everything possible to bring home unjustly detained Americans.

"Through it all, we have, and will, maintain open lines of communication so we can responsibly manage the competition between our countries.

"We do not seek conflict with the PRC. We believe in the power of diplomacy to prevent miscalculations that can lead to conflict.

"We are ready to work together on areas where our cooperation is vital—human trafficking and public health to food security, narcotics, and more—anywhere it can enhance U.S. interests and global peace and security.

"With your bipartisan support, we will stand unified in the face of this challenge. Thank you very much, Mister Chairman and the rest of the committee members.

"I'm ready to field any other questions you might have, but realize also that many things are currently in a state of flux, so I might not have all the answers yet for the questions you might ask. Nonetheless, I'll do my best to answer as fully as I can."

When he'd come in the room, Harkin told the committee that Mason didn't have any prepared remarks. *That's the difference between these people and myself,* he thought. *I'm always prepared.*

Harkin leaned back in his chair, stared solemnly at Mason for a full five seconds before allowing a smile to cross his expression. "I'll be honest with you... I wasn't expecting such candid and eloquent repartee from Spook Central. Folks in your line of work are usually as chatty as a deaf mute in a coma, so you're either really good at your job, or totally out of your depth." Harkin shifted his gaze to the others around the table. "You folks go ahead, I might have some closing questions after you guys are done."

"I'll start with a comment and a motion." It was Senator Martinez whose voice carried loudly across the room. "I've known Doug Mason for almost twenty years, and despite the reputation some in the CIA might have, I've known him to be as straight a shooter as they come. If he says the agency is doing what it can, communicating with other agencies in a need-to-know basis, and that things are in a state of flux, then that's just the way it is." He shifted his gaze to the chairman of the committee. "There's no point in squeezing for information when all we're going to get is empty air. Chairman Harkin, I motion that we table this conversation for now and bring Mister Mason back in a week to give us an update on the situation."

"I second the motion." Another senator replied.

Harkin's eyes widened for a moment and he nodded. "Very well, all in favor of Senator Martinez's motion?"

A majority of the members around the table said "aye" in unison.

"All against."

Several "nays" were uttered.

Harkin banged his gavel. "The ayes have it." He shifted his gaze toward Mason and gave him a lop-sided smile. "Deputy Director Mason, the committee would like you to return and give us an update one week hence."

Mason nodded as the chairman said a few, pointless parting words and the meeting adjourned. He couldn't have cared less about whether or not he was being asked to report back to this committee. The committee was nothing to him. He humored them so that some of the members didn't make a fuss with the media.

The thing currently racing through Mason's head was who had mentioned the Dragon's Breath Protocol to anyone on this committee.

There was a leak somewhere, and he needed to find it.

CHAPTER NINE

A bell rang and the sound of the captain's voice broadcast through the cabin. *"Customs personnel are now available and passengers have been cleared to disembark."*

Alicia closed her briefcase, and as the red paper had instructed, she pressed her thumb against the Eye of Providence and heard the lock on the briefcase engage.

Within seconds she detected the faint smell of something burning, and even though the briefcase immediately felt warm to the touch, it never got uncomfortably hot.

Grabbing her duffle bag, Alicia and her partner walked to the front of the aircraft just as one of the crew opened the passenger door.

The smells of fresh air and jet fuel blew into the cabin as

Alicia stepped off the plane and found herself at the top of red-carpeted stairs leading down to the tarmac. She panned her gaze across the expanse between her and the nearest terminal building and breathed deeply of the cool early-morning breeze. Despite having travelled in the most luxurious aircraft she'd ever been in, being stuck in a flying tube as you travel halfway across the world wasn't exactly a relaxing trip. And to make things even more entertaining, airport security made them wait nearly two hours after they landed, waiting until customs agents arrived at the terminal that serviced private aircraft for the Taoyuan International Airport.

It was now five-thirty a.m. and the airport was beginning to wake up.

Throughout the trip, Mister Woo tried several times to join Alicia and Lucy for a chat, but Lucy rebuffed any attempt at small talk, and in the end utterly banished the Deputy Chief of Mission to the front half of the plane.

The man, with his bag hitched over his shoulder, pushed past Lucy and Alicia and walked rapidly down the stairs without giving either of them a second glance.

Alicia looked over at Lucy and grinned. "I think you hurt his feelings."

"Really?" Lucy spoke with a quavering tone, and for a moment the woman held a concerned expression. She then returned the amused expression. "I'm over it." She motioned toward the building the frustrated diplomat was heading toward. "Let's get out of here."

Alicia followed Lucy down the stairs, across the tarmac and entered a building with a sign in both English and Chinese stating that it held the customs clearance area for the private terminal.

The place was practically empty due to the early hour, but it was obvious that even the private terminal's customs area was used to heavy traffic, as indicated by the two cordoned off paths, one for foreign and domestic visitors, the other had a red sign stating it was only for diplomats.

Alicia followed Lucy's lead as she led them down the snake-like path heading to the customs officer servicing the diplomat line.

Mister Woo had just gotten his passport stamped and walked away without even a backward glance as they arrived at the customs officer.

Lucy offered her black diplomatic passport and just as Alicia moved to also hand him her document, the man waved her away with an annoyed expression. "One at a time, if you please." He spoke fairly decent English. "Step back behind the yellow line."

Alicia looked behind her and took three steps back. Even though she was born in China, she'd never flown overseas before. Recalling her arrival to the US brought with it images of a nightmarish time in her life. The dark, fleeting memories of being smuggled on a ship, during the dead of night being snuck into a van, and finally being put out onto the streets to earn someone else's living. The idea of how she'd arrived on a private jet, cosplaying a diplomat was still hard for her to reconcile with how her life began.

"Please, step forward!" the man barked loudly.

Alicia blinked away the dark images as she realized that the customs officer was waving impatiently at her.

She stepped forward and handed him her passport.

"What is your business in the Republic of China?"

The Republic of China was the official name for Taiwan.

The words she'd memorized bloomed in her mind as she recalled the instructions the Outfit had left her in her briefcase. "I'm here on behalf of the U.S. Department of State on an official visit to the Taiwanese U.S. Consulate."

The customs officer ran her passport under a scanner and frowned slightly. "How long are you planning to visit?"

"Approximately one week."

The officer glanced at the duffel bag hanging on her shoulder. "Your bag?"

"It's a sealed diplomatic bag." Alicia pointed at the American eagle logo. "Department of State" and "United States of America" were printed along the circumference of the logo. Under it the words "Diplomatic Bag" were printed in English, French, Russian, and Chinese. And under that was a message only in English that said, "Property of U.S. Consulate. Only to be opened by authorized persons."

The officer didn't even give the bag a second look, instead he stamped her passport and handed it back to her. "Welcome to the Republic of Taiwan, Miss Ting."

Alicia nodded at the officer and walked over to where

Lucy was waiting with an amused expression. "You managed that well."

"I'm not stupid, you know." The briefing paperwork she'd read through on the plane had clearly stated they needed to get comfortable with the new names on their passport, but it never really talked about why. As they followed the signs that led to the transport area, Alicia asked in a hushed tone, "Hey, Miss Li."

Lucy gave her a sidelong glance. "What's up?"

"Why the new names?"

Lucy shrugged as they walked through a set of automatic doors and Taiwan's humidity hit them like a brick wall. "Believe me, this won't be the first time your name shifts around a bit when you travel. Domestic or foreign, get used to assumed names. Checking into a hotel, going through customs, all that kind of stuff leaves a trail that others can follow. The name change is for our safety." She motioned to a man standing next to a taxi stand, pursed her lips and let out an attention-getting whistle.

The man came running over and asked in rapid-fire Mandarin, "Yes, what's your destination?"

"American Institute in Taiwan." Lucy replied.

"Okay." The man blew a whistle that he kept on a chain around his neck and motioned at a line of parked cabs. One of the yellow vehicles lurched from its position at the front of the line and within seconds arrived curbside with a slight squeal of its brakes. The taxi attendant opened the rear door and then poked his head through the front passenger window, giving the driver their destination.

Alicia piled into the back seat after Lucy while the driver tapped on what looked like a navigation console.

The attendant closed the door behind Alicia as the navigation console rattled off instructions to the driver in Mandarin.

"Please take Hangqin North Road and then Hangzhan North Road to National Highway No. 2."

The cab pulled away from the curb and Alicia studied the navigation console. The computer estimated the trip to be roughly fifty kilometers, and over an hour and twenty minutes for them to get to their destination.

Lucy retrieved a buzzing phone from inside her suit jacket and put it to her ear. "Yes?"

Alicia couldn't make out anything intelligible from the crackling sound coming through the receiver, but Lucy's expression darkened.

"When will he arrive?"

More crackling from the phone.

"Okay, we'll check into the hotel. Let me know if there are any other unexpected delays." Lucy put her phone away, leaned forward and spoke to the driver. "Change of plans, we instead need to go to the Regent Taipei."

"In the Zhongshan District?" the driver asked.

"Yes."

The driver tapped at the navigation console and the device blurted out updated instructions. *"Keep left to continue on National Highway No. 2, follow signs for Luzhu. Use the right 2 lanes to take exit 8-Airport System for National Highway No. 1 toward Taipei."*

Lucy leaned to her right and whispered in English, "The ambassador got called away and won't be at AIT until this evening."

Alicia nodded. "Check into the hotel, and then what?"

Lucy patted her on the knee. "I'll show you around the city. I think you'll find it interesting."

She turned to look at the woman, but Lucy laid her head against the headrest and closed her eyes.

Alicia was fairly sure that Lucy's definition of interesting might not match hers.

After everything she'd read through in the briefcase, the brainwashing techniques, the concern over the hidden location called New Arcadia, and the instability implied by China's saber rattling, Alicia was concerned about what tonight's meeting with the ambassador was supposed to be about.

Officially the two of them were here on a diplomatic mission of sorts. An attempt to extract intelligence from the Taiwanese diplomats they'd be meeting with. Actually, that was Lucy's job. Alicia's job was to watch and learn, but she couldn't help but wonder what else was going on that she needed to know, but hadn't been told.

"Don't ever believe this man. This could be dangerous."

Lucy's warning about Mason lay heavily in her mind.

She glanced at the navigation console and sighed. The hotel was an hour away.

Lucy's steady breathing and relaxed expression showed that she'd somehow already managed to fall asleep.

With anxiety oozing from every one of her pores, Alicia shook her head and wondered if she'd ever be able to relax enough to get some sleep.

Right about now, sleep was the last thing on her mind.

What were the Taiwanese hiding in those woods that they'd be willing to kill one of the Outfit's agents over?

After checking into their rooms in the Regent Taipei, Alicia found herself walking along Guangzhou Street, with her mentor acting as a tour guide of sorts.

Lucy pointed at the elaborate old-style Chinese building on the right and said in Cantonese, "This is the Lungshan Temple. The original building was built almost three hundred years ago by people who first immigrated from Fujian province in Mainland China." She pointed past the tourist booth selling tickets. "You probably can't see it from here, but if you look at the pillars in front of the temple, you'll notice images of horseshoe crabs. They figured heavily in daily life both as a food and a fertilizer."

Their pace slowed as they waded through the gathered crowd of tourists in front of the temple. With her voice barely above a whisper, Alicia asked in English, "Are you telling me that these folks worship crabs?"

"You're such a twinkie." Lucy laughed and shook her head.

"A twinkie?"

Lucy gave her a sidelong glance as they walked past the crowd. "You know, yellow on the outside and white on the inside. You might not look it, but you're very American, just like Levi."

"Twinkie..." Alicia snorted with amusement. "That's one I've never heard, but I'll take it and wear the insult proudly."

Lucy made a clicking sound with her tongue and waved dismissively. "That was no insult, I'm simply speaking the truth. No, the people coming to the temple aren't worshipping crabs... as if. No, it's—how can I put it—a non-denominational type of temple. People come to pray for whatever they feel is needed. Whether it's to respect their ancestors, or the harvest, or even the lowly crab." She pointed at building they were approaching. "In fact, we too are going to pay our respects to the crab, but in a very different way." She glanced at Alicia. "Are you hungry?"

"Starving."

"Come on." Lucy motioned for Alicia to follow and made a beeline for a place that had a hand-drawn sign hanging over the doorway.

Alicia studied the sign and struggled to interpret the words written in fancy calligraphy. "Blue dragon?"

"Correct." Lucy nodded. "I'm glad to see you're able to

read the language you were born to." She opened the door and a bell chimed somewhere inside the building.

Alicia followed Lucy inside and studied what looked like a lobby of sorts. Dozens of pictures hung on the walls, most of them showing images of horseshoe crabs on various beaches. Each photo had an index card describing something about it.

She stepped closer to one of the images and struggled with the messily written Chinese scrawl underneath.

Keelung Harbor - 1955

Alicia glanced at Lucy and asked, "Am I reading this correctly? I think this says: *Crisp light illuminates rooster hill after the rain, gentle sun shimmers on horseshoe-crab beach in the morning.*" She stared at the words, shaking her head. "It doesn't make sense."

Lucy shifted her gaze at the photograph. "It's a poem."

"It is?" Alicia's expression noted for all to see that she wasn't impressed.

"Of course, it is." The elder woman gave a slight shake of her head. "You were likely too young to have studied classic Chinese poetry before you left the mainland, so it's not a surprise you can't recognize it for what it is."

"Miss Li?"

They both turned and a middle-aged woman dressed in a white lab coat looked at them with a quizzical expression.

"Yes?" Lucy nodded. "I called to make the arrangements."

"Of course. Everything is ready." The woman nodded vigorously and motioned for them to follow as she turned and walked through a rear exit, which had been obscured by hanging beads.

"Ready for what?" Alicia whispered in English as they walked through the beaded barrier into a back area that looked more like some kind of laboratory than a store.

Ignoring Alicia's question, Lucy followed the woman past a long laboratory bench with dozens of horseshoe crabs strapped into a tilted device that held them in place. Just below each of the crabs was a glass container with a blue liquid in it.

"Excuse me," Alicia pointed at the crabs. "What's going on here?"

The woman turned, a surprised expression on her face. "You want to know?"

"Um, yes." Alicia glanced at Lucy who was wearing her practiced emotionless expression. "If that's okay."

The woman gave Alicia a gap-toothed smile. "Of course it's okay. We at the Blue Dragon are a, how should we call it, we are a conservation and medical facility. The blue liquid you see is the blood from the wondrous horseshoe crabs we have collected from our farming enterprise. It's used by the medical industry as part of the production and testing cycle for many things, including the Covid virus and many other things."

Alicia's brow furrowed. "The crab's blood is a cure—"

"No, no, no..." the woman rapidly moved both hands back and forth as if trying to erase Alicia's words from the air. "The blood has a special protein called limulus amebocyte lysate, which is only found in the horseshoe crab. It is used by pharmaceutical companies and medical device manufacturers to help detect bacterial contamination. Special ingredients in the blood help ensure that what we put into people, whether it's a vaccine or even," the woman patted the side of her hip, "an artificial joint, is free from potentially deadly contamination. The use of what the horseshoe crab gives us all has saved countless lives."

Alicia glanced at Lucy and wondered why in the world the woman had brought them here.

With a building sense of morbid curiosity, Alicia stared at the unfortunate crabs all lined up across the long table. There was an almost invisible tube running out of each crab, and from the tube dripped the occasional drop of blue blood into a glass vial. "So, these things are sacrificed for—"

"No, they are *not killed*." The woman spoke emphatically. "They are all returned back to where they were harvested. Very much like we give blood so that others can use it, thus is it so with the honored crabs." The woman motioned for them to continue following as she walked up a narrow set of stairs.

Alicia turned her gaze to Lucy, who returned her stare with a look of amusement.

The elder motioned to the stairs. "Go ahead, this should be fun."

Going up the stairs, Alicia found herself walking down a narrow corridor lined with several doors, but the one at the end was opened and the woman waited patiently for them.

As Alicia walked into the room, the smell of something savory wafted through the air. On the far end of the room was a table that had been set up for two. On the table was a hotplate with a bubbling cauldron of some sort of liquid, as well as various plates with seemingly random raw ingredients piled on top of them.

It was then that Alicia remembered Lucy asking if she was hungry and she turned to her and asked, "This is where we're eating?"

"Please." The woman at the far end of the room called out, motioning for them to take their seats. "Miss Li, everything is to your liking, I hope."

Lucy walked over to the table, looked over the steaming hotpot and its accoutrements, nodded, and handed the woman a rolled-up wad of Taiwanese money. "Thank you. Can my friend and I now have some privacy?"

"Of course. Thank you very much for your generous donation." The woman bowed deeply to Lucy and pocketed the money. As Alicia walked up to the table, the woman gave her a slight bow as she walked toward the exit. As a parting message, the woman said loudly over her shoulder, "I'm the only one in the building for the next four hours. If you need me, I will be downstairs."

The woman closed the door behind her, leaving Lucy and Alicia alone in the rather spacious, yet spartanly appointed room.

Lucy motioned to the chair on the other side of the table. "Go ahead and have a seat. Let's get started with the cooking and you and I can talk a bit about what's to come."

Alicia sat and watched as her companion, using a long pair of chopsticks, transferred all sorts of vegetables and sliced meats into a large metal cooking vessel that had a curved divider forming a ying-yang symbol. On one side of the steaming pot was a yellow broth, and on the other side was a different broth with a distinct reddish hue.

Lucy pointed at the lava-like broth with her chopsticks, "This is Sichuan-spiced, made from a pork broth, chili oil, and a good amount of Sichuan peppercorns. It's a bit spicy and has a numbing effect. The other is more 'American' style chicken broth. Not spicy at all, but should be very flavorful." She looked over at Alicia and grinned. "Have you had hot pot before?"

She nodded. "A few times, but..." Alicia picked up a chopstick and pointed at the fist-sized bowl full of what looked like caviar, but instead of the black or maybe golden color she'd seen before, these looked strange. "What are those green and blue balls? Is that a food?"

Lucy let out a throaty laugh as she poured the contents of the bowl into the chicken broth. "Those are horseshoe crab eggs."

"They're what?" Alicia's eyes widened. "Are those even okay to eat? I mean, aren't they endangered or something?"

Lucy shook her head. "They're not endangered, but that's also why I arranged to come here. This place focuses on conserving the horseshoe crab. Those living fossils are very unusual, and very hard to breed. Let's just say that like salmon somehow manage to find where they were born and tend only to spawn there, horseshoe crabs are very similar. They need more dedicated areas to encourage their growth and spawning. I gave these conservationists a modest donation so that they can buy more beachfront area for the crab population to grow." She pointed at the plates of uncooked food and the bubbling pot of broth. "This was their way of saying thank you."

Using her own chopsticks, Alicia began unloading bite-sized pieces of bok choy, carrots, sliced lotus root, various thinly sliced meats and shrimp into the broth.

"Alicia, we're now truly alone, maybe for the first time ever. You must have questions about me that you've been holding onto for years. I'll answer anything you want to ask."

"Even personal questions?" Alicia cocked an eyebrow and studied Lucy's face, looking for any discernible reaction.

Using her chopsticks, Lucy poked at some of the items in the Sichuan side of the pot. "Anything you like."

A tingle raced up Alicia's spine and she grinned. "Why haven't you and my father gotten together? I know he likes you."

"What in the world makes you think we haven't?"

Alicia stared at Lucy for a second and then grimaced. "No, not... I don't want to know about *that*! I mean why you two haven't gotten married."

"Oh." Lucy sighed. "Ouch, you really had to ask that one, didn't you?" The woman played a bit with some of the morsels of food that had begun to float in the broth. "It's not because I'm not interested. I can't really say, because it's not my choice. He knows I'm his if he wants me."

"You're his?" Alicia was taken aback by the phrasing, and wondered if it somehow was a mistranslation. She switched to English. "What do you mean you're his if he wants you. Like a slave?"

Lucy grinned and shook her head. "You're maybe too young to understand. I would do anything for your father, and I'm fairly certain he would do anything for me. I'll be honest, this subject just makes me a bit sad. Any other questions?"

Alicia snatched a slice of the Chinese sausage from the Sichuan side of the pot, blew on it and took a bite. The savory goodness of the sausage was there, but then the odd numbing sensation from the Sichuan peppercorns hit. She didn't mind spicy food, but the numbing thing wasn't a sensation that she was used to. Grabbing a slice of lotus root from the tamer side of the pot, she bit down and appreciated the familiarity of the starchy vegetable. It was almost like a cross between a waxy yellow potato and a sweet potato. She looked across the table and noticed Lucy picking items mostly from the Sichuan side of the pot. "All of this stuff with the Outfit is new to me. How long have you been with them?"

"Almost twenty years." Lucy said matter-of-factly as she grabbed a shrimp and dipped it into a bowl filled with what looked like chili crisp. "But it's not the same as with you."

"What do you mean?"

"I've never been a full-time person with them. Let's just say I've been freelancing with them the whole time."

"Oh. What else do you do when not working for the Outfit?" Alicia asked, barely hiding the discomfort she felt at asking such a bold question. She'd known the woman for years, but talking about Lucy's occupation had always seemed like it would be off limits. All she really knew of Lucy was that she was doing well for herself financially, and she suspected the woman had ties with some unsavory sorts. What she did for a living had always been a mystery, sort of like with her father, until she'd learned about his working for the Outfit.

Lucy leaned back, stared at Alicia as she held that statue-like expression that gave no clue as to what she was thinking. "I'll tell you, but realize that this information is dangerous for you to have, especially if you say anything to anyone."

"Even my father?"

"He already knows." The woman waved the comment away. "It was almost another lifetime ago when I was purchased by my husband."

Alicia's eyes widened and it took everything she had to not gasp at what she'd just said.

"I was young, very young, and an important man purchased me from my parents since they couldn't really afford to feed us all." Lucy snatched a few items out of the pot and set them on her plate to cool. "It wasn't that unusual for such things to happen in rural China. I'm sure it still happens all the time. This man who took me on as a child bride was good to me. Gave me the best tutors, taught me everything I know, and I quickly grew to love him. There was only one complication, he was the head of one of the largest Triad gangs."

With her heart racing, Alicia hung on every one of Lucy's words. The Triad were an infamous organized crime syndicate out of China.

"We were living in Hong Kong, somewhat isolated from what was happening in other parts of the gang world, so-to-speak. However, I'd become my husband's right hand. I knew the operations. The generals that operated groups of soldiers all reported into my husband."

"Generals? Soldiers?" Alicia tilted her head. "As in part of the military?"

"No." Lucy shook her head. "The triad gangs are hierarchical and use those terms as titles. With my husband at the top, generals that report into him, and each general has his own people they call soldiers. My husband even formally enrolled me as a member of the triad."

"What did being enrolled as a member actually involve?" Alicia asked.

Lucy popped a shrimp into her mouth, chewed for a bit, and then gave her a smile. "It was actually a bit silly. He gave me wine mixed with his blood and had me drink it. Then I swore an oath to some Gods or something..." She looked up at the ceiling, her eyebrows furrowed. "I remember bits of it going something like, 'I am making a life oath to Liu, Guan, and Zhang. I dedicate to protect the country...'" her nose crinkled, "there was some other garbage about a brotherhood and various rules, but it ended with 'this is an oath I make under the witness of Holy Emperor Guan.'

"Despite the old-fashioned ritual, my husband was very progressive for the time. He felt that I was better at some things than he was, so while he focused on the drug trade, protection rackets, and other such things, he asked that I focus on the prostitution business."

Alicia's jaw dropped, not believing what she'd just heard. And how she'd said those things so matter-of-factly. What kind of person does that kind of thing?

Lucy held up her hand as if she knew what was racing through Alicia's mind. "You have to understand that if it wasn't me looking after the girls, it would have been someone else that didn't actually care about them. If I remember correctly, you experienced what some of those people are like. You might also recall that I tried to help a few of your sisters when they were on the streets."

Alicia's mind reached back over a decade. It was soon after her father had begun rescuing kids from the street, Alicia had been the first, but certainly not the last. She'd never met Lucy while living on the streets, but it turned out that some of her younger sisters had crossed paths with the other woman. Like most of the girls on the streets, they'd all been trafficked by heinous men who'd abused them. But there were always stories of someone named "Miss Lucy." That's what her sisters had called her. They talked about the lady who'd snuck sweets to them when the pimps weren't looking, or other small acts of kindness that were almost unheard of in the dangerous streets of New York's Chinatown.

"But then my husband was killed and I became a target." Lucy pursed her lips and paused; her gaze fell into her lap for a moment and for a brief second, emotions bubbled up and were reflected in her expression. "I was a threat to the generals that had worked under my husband. They wouldn't work for someone like me."

"Like you? You mean a woman?"

Lucy nodded. "And my husband's death served as an opportunity for the leaders from other triad gangs. I had to escape Hong Kong, and I did... but it took a long time for me to find safety, to assert my own control over my life." Lucy pressed her lips together into a fine line and stared at Alicia. "Your father helped me in ways I can't even begin to describe, and that's when I knew he was the one for me—even though he won't take what I've offered."

Alicia felt the sadness and yearning emanating from the

woman. Her father was the type of person who'd likely understand almost anything, but would he be able to tolerate someone who was actively still involved with organized crime? She doubted it. "Are you still involved in the gang life?"

Lucy smiled. "With the help of your father, I left much of that behind. As you know, little girls and boys will still be trafficked as long as there are deviants out there who are willing to pay for such things. But like I told your father years ago, you can't save everyone, and ultimately the only one you can truly save is yourself." She dipped her chopsticks into the broth, pulled out a clump of yellow balls, and placed it on Alicia's plate. "Try those, I think you'll find them a unique experience."

Alicia stared at Lucy for a bit, still processing all that she'd said. She wasn't sure if she'd received a true answer to the question about whether her mentor was still involved with the gangs. With her chopsticks, Alicia picked up the clump of yellow balls, sniffed at it and detected nothing other than the smell of the broth. These no longer held the pastel colors of their raw form and instead looked like a bunch of tiny egg yolks. She puffed air over the still-steaming eggs several times, popped them into her mouth, and chewed.

Her eyebrows shot up almost into her hairline. "There's really firm."

Lucy nodded with an amused expression.

Alicia chewed and shook her head. "I don't like it. It's like

I'm chewing on briny rubber balls." She nearly jumped up from her seat as her phone buzzed. She retrieved it, looked at its screen, and quickly put it to her ear. "Yes?"

"Alicia, are you with Lucy?"

It was Brice.

Lucy mouthed "Who is it?"

"I am, why? What's up, Brice?"

"I've got you on satellite and we have a team coming to your location. Lucy's phone is non-responsive."

Alicia's heart began thudding loudly in her chest as she leaned forward and whispered, "Check your phone. He says it's offline."

Lucy retrieved her phone and her brows furrowed as she stared at it. "I have no signal."

"Listen, can you hand your phone over to Lucy for a second." Brice's voice seemed calm as he spoke with an even tone, but Alicia sensed a tension behind the calm façade.

She handed the phone over to Lucy.

"Hey Brice, not sure what's up with my phone, it's not getting any signal."

Alicia leaned closer and heard snatches of the other end of the conversation.

"They know... location... compromised. Marines... AIT."

"Crap. Are you sure?" Lucy's face held a surprised expression.

Alicia heard a woman yelling somewhere outside their room and got up from her chair, she was tingling from head to toe from what was likely a dump of adrenaline flowing through her bloodstream. Something was going on downstairs.

The door flew open and as the lady with white lab coat yelled profanities at the men pouring into the room, Lucy also got up and said, "They're here. I'll talk to you when we get on location." She handed Alicia's phone back, took her own and smashed it on the ground, digging the spike of her heel into it with a loud crunching sound.

Alicia gasped at what Lucy had just done, put her own phone away and turned to the group of six Asian men, not sure how to respond. They all wore dark suits and five of them hung back as one of them approached the women. He gave them both a slight nod as the Blue Dragon lab technician smacked at his arms and shoulders, yelling for the men to get out.

Lucy glanced at Alicia and said in English, "Let's go."

Alicia opened her mouth to say something and clamped it shut, knowing that this was not the time to argue or ask questions.

Lucy put her arm around the irate woman and whispered something in her ear. Whatever it was she'd said seemed to almost instantly calm the woman down. Lucy handed the woman a few more Taiwanese bills and they all walked out of the second-story room.

One of the men spoke into his wrist and Alicia heard him say in Mandarin, "We're coming down."

She hurried to Lucy's side and whispered, "Why did you break your phone?"

“I’m likely being tracked.” Lucy said with a grim expression.

“Tracked? By whom?”

Lucy waved away the question. “We’ll be safe in the embassy.”

Alicia’s blood ran cold as she absorbed what Lucy had just said.

Safe? Safe from what?

CHAPTER TEN

Riding in the back of a panel van with no windows whatsoever, Alicia sat next to Lucy on a bench that had been welded to the bare metal floor. The security team that escorted them to the unmarked van was manned by uniformed Marines. She wasn't sure how long they'd been in the vehicle as it made its way through the midday traffic of Taipei. The only other person in the back with them was a Marine with a full kit on, including a rifle at the ready.

Alicia pointed at the Marine's weapon. "That's not an M4, what is it?"

"No ma'am, it isn't. It's an M27, the same basic gun, but it's a bit heavier, more accurate, and these all have full auto capability."

Alicia had used an M4 at the FBI training center. "The M4 I'd trained on had full auto."

"Likely the M4A1." The marine patted his rifle in an almost affectionate manner. "Prior to getting one of these, I'd been assigned a straight up M4 which only had a semi and three-round-burst selector."

"We're on Jinhu Road, approaching AIT." The driver's voice crackled from a speaker built into the roof of the panel van. *"Bypassing the southern entrance. AIT traffic control, Dragonfly is returning to the nest."*

The van made a right-hand turn and bounced slightly as it drove over two bumps on the road.

Within a minute the van had come to a stop and Alicia blinked as the rear doors opened and light from an underground garage poured into the vehicle's cargo hold.

Flanked by two marines, a man in a suit greeted them with a smile. "Miss Chen, Miss Yoder, welcome to the American Institute in Taiwan. I'm Charles Han, one of the facilitators at AIT. I've only just recently been informed of your special situation, so we are in the process of making accommodations."

The man held out his hand and Lucy took it as she climbed down from the back of the vehicle.

Alicia waved away any assistance as she hopped out of the van and took in her surroundings.

Nearly thirty parking spots filled the underground garage, with only about half of them occupied.

"Charles, do you by chance know the status of our stuff

that was at the hotel? I'd like to change out of what I'm wearing at some point."

The man turned to her, and for the briefest moment looked her up and down, before taking a step closer. "I'm sorry, but I would have taken it upon myself to make sure your belongings were brought on premises, but DC security claimed they're handling it." He motioned to the glass doors behind him. "In fact, I was asked to bring you to our SCIF the moment you arrive."

A SCIF was a Sensitive Compartmented Information Facility. It was government-speak for a secure place where classified information could be viewed and talked about.

"Is there anything else I can do for you in the meantime?" The man glanced back at Lucy who'd started walking toward the glass doors. "For either of you."

"Yes." Lucy said as she pulled open one of the glass doors. "For the moment, stop flirting with Miss Yoder and lead us to the SCIF."

Alicia's mouth dropped open and her face suddenly felt warm as the flustered man stammered an apology and rushed into the underground entrance to the unofficial Taiwanese embassy.

As Alicia approached Lucy, who still held the door open for her, the woman gave her a wink and said under her breath, "He's into you, maybe you should do something about it after tonight's meeting with the ambassador."

"Why in the world do you think I'd do anything about

it?" Alicia said in a hushed whisper as they hurried to catch up with the so-called facilitator.

Lucy put her hand on Alicia's shoulder and gave it a light squeeze. "You're very uptight. It might actually relax you."

Alicia noticed her companion raise her eyebrows twice, which she could only interpret as her being somewhat playful.

"Ladies, here it is." Charles swiped his badge on the reader next to a door. There was a chirp and the thick door began yawning open. He pressed a sequence of numbers on the touch screen above the badge reader, motioned in the direction of the door and said, "The connection to the external security team will go active as soon as the door closes."

Alicia followed Lucy into the room and the door began to close automatically on well-oiled hinges.

A conference room table dominated the space, easily capable of comfortably seating a dozen people around it. At the far end of the room were three large monitors that dominated the wall along with several video cameras that seemed to automatically follow Alicia and Lucy as they took their seats at the table.

The moment Alicia sat in the well-padded leather chair, the center screen turned on, displaying the Department of State's eagle logo.

Alicia pointed at the touch screen on the middle of the table and looked over at Lucy. "Do we need to do something?"

"Looks like we don't." Lucy pointed at the monitor as *"Secure Connection Established"* appeared on the bottom of the screen.

Suddenly the somewhat disheveled image of Director Mason appeared on the screen. His tie was slightly askew and he had the tell-tale signs of bed head that had been hastily brushed. Not a particular surprise since it was some time after midnight on the East Coast. *"I see you two have made it to the AIT compound safe and sound. That's good."*

Lucy had an angry expression as she leaned back in her chair. "Doug, what really happened?"

"Brice briefed me on the intelligence intercepts and it seems like some of your friends have connections at the Taipei airport."

Mason shifted in his chair, and it became obvious that he was in a similarly-equipped conference room, because the camera managed to keep him in the center of the screen as he reached for some printouts in front of him.

"Doug, I told Alicia about my history, so you can speak freely. Does that mean the Triad has infiltrated the Taiwanese government?"

"No. At least not that we're aware of. I'll have you know that facial recognition software isn't just a government thing nowadays. We're going to track down how the customs' security cameras were compromised, but suffice it to say that not only is Sun Yee On involved, but we've intercepted communications between soldiers of the Shui Fong as well."

Alicia recognized those names, Sun Yee On and Shui Fong, as the names given to some of the larger Triad gangs.

"Bastards!" Lucy's face turned red with anger and she took a deep breath and let it out slowly. "Both competed for common territory back when I was in Hong Kong. What the hell are they doing in Taiwan?"

Mason scratched at his chin. *"You probably already know the answer to that. Back in 2020, China had started to crack down on Hong Kong's citizens—"*

"Ah," Lucy's eyes widened and she smacked her open hand down onto the table with a loud slap. "And with the crackdown on the citizens came the crackdown on triad members as well. So they scurried away for an easier place to do business."

"Pretty much. And they clearly still remember you. This isn't a disaster, just a slight change of methods. I talked with the ambassador about an hour ago and there's going to be a somewhat informal get together that he's going to bring you to. We can arrange for security, and Brice will clear the way with the computers so your face doesn't kick off any alarms with that building's security cameras."

Alicia asked, "An informal get together of whom?"

Mason grinned. *"Believe it or not, Taiwan's Minister of Culture and several of his staff will be there. He's in charge of all of the historical and cultural elements on that island, and he should be a good starting point for information about what's going on with New Arcadia. From what I can tell, there will be a wide variety of top-ranked government officials. I see that even the commander of the ROC army has been invited. One of our people will brief the ambassador on the security issues surrounding your presence, Lucy. You know what needs to be done. And Alicia, just follow her lead. You can't have a better mentor when it comes to dealing with some of these politicians. Either of you have any questions?"*

"Um," Alicia raised her hand. "Yes. Is our stuff being brought back from the hotel?"

"It is." Mason nodded and looked down at his phone. *"In fact, I got a message just a minute ago that your duffels should be on AIT grounds as of this moment. Any other questions?"*

"Actually, yes." Lucy turned to the monitor. "What's the story with my phone? How did that happen?"

"I guess Brice didn't have time to fill you in. Evidently the triad was able to track down your cell phone's IMEI number and did something to the cell tower filters to prevent your phone's use on the island. Brice could probably explain the mumbo-jumbo around it, but you both have replacement phones waiting for you along with your suitcases. Anything else?"

Lucy shook her head. "Doug, go get some sleep, you're looking like total crap."

Mason chuckled. *"How about you, Alicia? Any questions?"*

She shook her head.

"Okay, best of luck and get us the data we need."

The monitor blinked off and Lucy hopped up from her chair and walked over to the exit.

Alicia followed Lucy and the moment she walked out of the SCIF, she noticed Charles, his gaze locked onto hers and he began to smile.

"That's enough, Chuckles." Lucy snapped at the facilitator who'd been waiting for them. "Our stuff should have arrived from the hotel, get us to our bags and whatever passes as accommodations in this place."

With a startled expression, Charles put a phone to his ear and spoke rapidly in Mandarin to someone about their bags.

Lucy walked up to Alicia and whispered, "Don't give this guy the time of day. He's weak and pathetic. You don't need someone like that, even in your bed for the night."

Alicia shook her head and laughed nervously. In her mind she nearly retorted that she'd never had anyone in her bed and wasn't about to start with some stranger—but then images of the past flooded her mind and she knew that was an outright lie.

Long-buried memories sent a shiver up her spine and she broke out in a cold sweat.

The idea of being that close to someone again made her chest tighten and it took all of her focus to not have a panic attack.

Charles put the phone back in his pocket and motioned for them to follow him. "Okay. Your things are in the guest suites. I'll take you there."

Lucy nudged Alicia out of her stupor. "Let's go."

Charles turned and walked down the marble corridor, not waiting, but expecting them to follow.

Alicia balled her hands into fists as she followed Lucy down the hallway, not so much because she was mad, but because she didn't want anyone to see her hands shaking.

After they got their stuff, it was only a matter of time before they were off to the event Mason had mentioned.

Knowing that she was mostly there to shadow Lucy and learn from her actions was soothing at first, but the idea of attending this party filled with important people still made Alicia feel like a nervous wreck.

She had no experience in parties other than the one fraternity party she'd attended. Half of the people were falling-down drunk and the other half were looking out for any signs of the campus police.

The hardest thing about tonight would be trying to look like she belonged. She was barely out of college and shouldn't even be here.

"Your guest suite is on the fourth floor." Charlie's voice announced as he pressed the up-arrow button at a bank of elevators.

She was just an Amish farm girl, and this cloak and dagger stuff was someone else's life. And yet, even though none of this felt like a life that belonged to her, Alicia told her inner voice to shut the hell up.

A bell rung somewhere and the elevator doors opened up.

Alicia took a deep breath, ordered the farmer girl to keep her thoughts to herself, and stepped onto the elevator.

Sitting on a stool in front of a bathroom mirror, Alicia watched as Lucy continued applying stuff to her face. “What’s this stuff you’re putting on me now?”

Lucy’s expression was one of concentration as she used a soft, padded applicator covered with powdered makeup all over the younger woman’s face. “This is foundation. It’s just to even out your skin tone.”

“Well, that’s better than you practically poking my eye out earlier.” Alicia tolerated the powdered makeup much better than the sharpened pencil Lucy kept nearly sticking in her eye.

“Stop being such a baby, it was only eye liner. I still can’t believe you’ve never worn makeup.”

“Are you kidding me?” Alicia frowned, trying not to move her head as the woman worked. “I’ve spent the last decade or so on an Amish farm or at school. Neither place was big on makeup.”

Suddenly an image flashed in her mind’s eye.

It was of her father applying makeup to her face, just like Lucy was doing. She couldn’t remember when that memory was from, but suddenly it bloomed so clearly that it was as if it were happening to her right now. “Would it surprise you to know that I think Dad knows about makeup as well?”

Lucy grinned as she tilted Alicia’s head and patted under her chin and neck. “Not at all, why do you ask?”

“I don’t know, but I seem to remember Dad putting makeup on me. I just don’t remember when that was...”

“Your father has many hidden talents.” Lucy leaned back

to look at her work, and dabbed a few more times at Alicia's face with the tiny pillow-like item. "Levi has shocked me in the past with some of his costume makeup skills. I'm pretty sure your father could appear in front of us and we wouldn't recognize him." The woman's look of concentration was almost comical as she dabbed at her face with a puffy stick-like applicator that had something wet on its tip.

"What's that?"

"It's concealer. Anywhere you have blemishes and such, you can apply this and it helps any of those imperfections disappear. Sometimes we cover them out of vanity. Sometimes, people in our position cover them because the wrong people might remember imperfections too clearly."

Alicia watched as the woman continued through various steps including: powder, contouring, highlighting, and blush.

Lucy dug into her makeup bag and held up what looked like a colored pencil. "Have you ever done your lips before?"

Alicia frowned. "Not with one of those I haven't. I've used ChapStick before. What is that?"

"This is lip liner. Just press your lips together and relax." Lucy did a bad job of suppressing her smile as she approached Alicia's face with the pencil. She got the distinct impression that the woman was enjoying this. "This helps give your lips a nice definition." She followed up with an application of lipstick and handed her a tissue. "Go ahead and blot."

"Blot? What's that?"

Lucy laughed. "Oh, honey. Did you learn anything besides milking cows on that farm of yours? Pretend you're giving the tissue a gentle kiss. It's just to get some of the excess lipstick off."

Alicia did as she was told and saw the evidence of her lip prints on the tissue.

Lucy held up what looked like a tiny spray bottle and said, "Close your eyes, this is a setting spray to help keep your makeup in place for the night. It'll be just like a mist on your face. Hold your breath."

Alicia heard more than felt the spray.

"Okay. All done."

Alicia got up from the stool and looked at the mirror. The person who stared back at her looked nothing like the Alicia Yoder she knew. "This is what I look like with makeup?"

Lucy touched up her own makeup and glanced at Alicia. "Damn you and your youth. You look great. I'm finding as the years go by that I need makeup more and more just to be barely passable." She turned to Alicia, who was still staring at herself in the mirror. "So, what do you think? You think you can do this yourself?"

Alicia felt a strange sense of wonder as she stared at the image of a pretty girl. All her life she'd been told she was pretty, by her family and the occasional desperate guy at Princeton, but for some reason, it was only now that she saw something in the mirror that such a label might rightfully be applied to. "I like it. I might be able to do it after some practice, but you're going to need to give me a list of all that junk you just used. I wouldn't have a clue what to buy."

"I'll get you a full shopping list, but first let me have one last look at you." Lucy took a step back and studied Alicia from head to toe. She reached out to the younger woman's neckline and fingered the necklace she was wearing. "This won't do."

"Why? I like these." Alicia reached for the charms on her necklace and suddenly felt a bit self-conscious. "I've had them for years. The Hello Kitty charm is from one of Dad's friends, and the ankh is from Dad."

Lucy frowned as she fingered the two charms. "They're pretty, but they don't go with your man-eater outfit. I mean, seriously… Hello Kitty? It feels heavy for its size, so it's probably made of platinum and gold, but that pink enameled bow, it's just not the right thing with your outfit. Take that necklace off, I'll be right back."

Alicia undid the lobster-claw clasp on her necklace and stared at the charms. She felt an irrational amount of emotion as she stared at the charms, not liking the idea of taking them off. Her father's Japanese friend had sent the Hello Kitty charm to ward off evil when she turned eighteen, and the ankh was a symbol of life that her father had given to all of his girls—they both made Alicia feel somehow more at ease. She deposited the necklace with its charms into her clutch purse, determined to keep some bit of comfort with her tonight.

Lucy walked into the bathroom and held out a string of

pearls. "Here, this is elegant and goes with your man-eater dress." As Alicia put on the necklace, her companion surveyed the results and nodded. "I think that's perfect. You're going to attract a lot of eyes."

Alicia turned to the mirror in the bathroom and stood as far back as she could to take in what Lucy saw. The person staring back was unrecognizable to the Amish girl that she'd always identified as.

The black dress was fit to follow her long, slender curves and accentuated her waistline. The pearl necklace was almost a choker, but their brilliant white color held a nice contrast to the black of her dress and hair.

Alicia ran her fingertips across the pearls and nodded.

"Looks good, don't you think?"

Reluctantly, Alicia had to admit that the platinum, pink, and gold from her necklace would likely have clashed with what she was wearing. "I guess I never thought about the idea of accessorizing for whatever outfit I'm wearing. It just... it's never been a priority."

Someone knocked on the door to the guest apartment they'd been given at the embassy.

"It's time." Lucy gathered her tiny clutch purse and said, "Let's go wow these politicians and extract whatever intel we can get."

CHAPTER ELEVEN

Having just been dropped off by a limo, Alicia's nerves tried to get the best of her as she walked into the elevator with Lucy and the Director of AIT.

"You ladies are dressed to kill." Mark Simpson smiled as he pressed the 89th floor's button in an elevator for the tallest building in Taipei.

Alicia stared dumbly at the man. He might have been the most handsome person she'd ever seen in real life. He was in his late forties, had some gray at his temples, and was dressed in a fitted suit that showed off his trim figure and broad shoulders. Even his tone of voice was like warm honey flowing through the elevator cabin.

Lucy gave the man a wink and said, "Don't worry, Mark, nobody is on our kill list today."

With her tongue seemingly tied in the man's presence, Alicia was amazed at how Lucy could respond with such seeming familiarity. Someone would have thought those two had been friends for a long time, yet tonight was the first time any of them had met.

"Have you two been in the Taipei 101 before?"

Alicia shook her head as did Lucy.

The man smiled and for Alicia, the room seemed to grow brighter with the whiteness of his teeth.

"Well, the construction of this skyscraper was completed in 2004, and it was the tallest building in the world for a few years until the Arabs took that crown with the Burj Khalifa."

The elevator rose at such a speed that Alicia's ears began popping almost immediately.

"The building has a large mall in it, lots of office space, a very nice restaurant, and at least a dozen or so floors dedicated to communications broadcasting."

A bell dinged and the elevator doors slid open.

Mark held the elevator doors open and motioned to them. "Ladies first."

Alicia walked out of the elevator and the man rushed across the hallway to another bank of elevators.

He swiped a card across some kind of reader and pressed the up-arrow. "We have one more elevator transfer after this one."

They walked onto another elevator and pressed the button for the 93rd floor.

"Some of these floors are dedicated to maintenance and not intended for public use."

They switched elevators, and as the doors closed, Simpson pressed the button marked 101F. "This place we're going to is known as Summit 101. It's a VIP club of sorts, often used to host special parties and sometimes foreign dignitaries."

"I assume you've been here before?" Lucy arched her eyebrow and gave the man a smoky look.

"Yes, on rare occasions I've been invited by some of the Taiwanese political officials." He smiled. "Though, I've never hosted anything here. That level of budget isn't something our government would support."

The doors slid open and an onslaught of sights and sounds greeted them.

Conversations, the clinking of glasses, and somewhere unseen there was the sound of someone playing the piano.

A harried-looking man wearing a tuxedo and wielding a tablet device approached as they got off the elevator. He asked in Mandarin, "Please, can I have your names."

The ambassador responded in perfect Mandarin, "Mark Simpson, U.S. representative for the American Institute in Taiwan." He motioned toward Alicia and Lucy. "These ladies are my plus-two. You don't need their names."

The man scrolled through his list of guests on the portable PC and then glanced in Alicia's and Lucy's direction. He gave Mark a head bow and made a sweeping gesture toward the rest of the floor. "I have you checked in. Please sir, I hope you and your guests enjoy. Thank you."

Alicia walked past the man, he gave her the same head bow and the elevator behind them dinged, announcing another arrival.

The man scurried toward the elevator and Alicia focused on what lay in front of her.

Just within sight there were at least two or three dozen people, mostly men, and they were almost all dressed in tailored western-style suits. One or two wore what looked like traditional Chinese suits with a short standup collar—reminiscent of pictures she'd seen of how Mao had dressed, which Alicia found odd considering they were in Taiwan.

Most had a glass of something in their hands and had broken up into small groups of two to five people.

"Ladies," the ambassador motioned for them to follow. "Let me introduce you to the person I think you're here to see."

Alicia followed behind Lucy and as they walked through the crowd, the ambassador made his way to a group of middle-aged men. He greeted one of the men with a warm smile, handshake, and then a quick hug.

The man wore a rainbow-colored sticker on his lapel and it had the equivalent of "Hello my name is" written in Chinese and the name that had been scribbled onto the sticker was unintelligible due to an ink smear.

Mark put his hand on the man's shoulder and gave it a

squeeze. "Martin, you're looking great my friend. How are you? Your husband?"

"Everything is going well, Ambassador Simpson." The ambassador's infectious smile spread to the others in the group.

"No, no, no..." Mark wagged his finger and playfully chided the man. "The U.S. has no formal ambassador in the Republic of China. You know that. I'm merely the Director of AIT." He turned to the other two men and they made quick introductions.

Martin turned to Alicia and Lucy and cleared his throat. "Mark, are these the women you'd mentioned earlier?"

"Oh my God, how rude of me." The ambassador's cheeks reddened as he nodded. "Yes, these are—"

"Tut... tut..." Martin held up his hand. "Hold that thought." He turned to the other two men and said, "Excuse us for a moment." The man motioned for them to follow him and they stopped near one of the decorative planters, away from the other people at the party. He turned to the ladies, gave a slight head bow and said, "I'm Martin Lu, Minister of Culture."

The ambassador waved at someone on the other end of the room, turned to the ladies and asked, "Are you good?"

Lucy waved him away. "Thank you, Mark. Go have fun."

Martin glanced at Mark's departing figure and then spoke barely above a whisper. "Mark said the U.S. State Department has some questions they'd like to ask in an unofficial manner?"

Lucy stepped closer to the man. They were so close that they probably could smell each other's breath. "We do. Are you familiar with the True Dragon Temple?"

"Of course, it's in the Sanzhi District just north of the city." The man's round face took on a confused expression. "Is there a problem there? You realize it holds cremated remains… I can't imagine—"

"No, not with the temple itself, but with an area just east of it."

With a furrowed brow the Minister of Culture tilted his head and asked, "What about it?"

"There was an issue about five kilometers east of the True Dragon Temple grounds."

Lucy continued to talk, but Alicia noticed the man's eyes widen the moment Lucy mentioned the area east of the temple.

Martin Lu fanned himself with his hand and shook his head. "I'm sorry, but this isn't something I know anything about."

"You must know someone who might know more." Lucy pressed the issue, speaking with a tone of certainty.

"I do, but…" The minister panned his gaze across the room and his eyes widened. "You're in luck. He rarely attends events such as this, but I see Cheng Shin-lung. I personally can't say for certain what's in those woods, but he should be able to."

"May we get an introduction?" Lucy asked.

"Come, let's see if he's in a friendly mood or not." The

minister walked toward a man who was at the bar waiting for his drink. He wore a Taiwanese Army uniform.

Martin Lu walked up to the man and patted him on the shoulder. “General, may I have a word with you?”

The man backed away from the minister with a look that spoke volumes about what he thought of that idea. He wasn’t interested.

Alicia’s eyes widened as she noticed the myriad of medals and ribbons on the man’s uniform. Whoever he was, this wasn’t some low-level flunky.

Ignoring the look of disdain that the man gave him, Martin Lu motioned toward the women and said, “May I introduce you to two lovely ladies who I think have some questions you might be able to help them with.”

Lucy approached the officer and extended her hand, which the man took and gave her a head bow. Alicia did the same as Martin Lu made the introductions.

“Ladies, this is General Cheng Shin-lung. He’s the Chief of the General Staff for my nation’s Armed Forces.” He turned to the general and said, “These ladies are from the United States State Department and have some questions that I couldn’t answer.”

“It is nice to speaking with you.” The general spoke haltingly in English as Martin Lu practically vanished from their presence.

“General, please, there’s no need for English.” Lucy stepped closer to the man, smiled and her voice took on a husky tone as she spoke to him in his native language. “We both speak Mandarin.”

A bartender placed a tall glass filled with beer on the counter next to the general.

“Excellent.” The general smiled, picked up his glass, and motioned to the bar. “Would either of you like something from the bar? The Republic of China is paying, of course.”

Lucy nodded and asked, “What are you drinking.”

“A Sunmai honey lager. It’s quite popular.”

“That sounds delicious.” Lucy nodded to the bartender. “I’ll take the same as the general.”

“Please,” the general handed Lucy his beer. “Go ahead and take mine.” He looked at Alicia. “And you? What would you like?”

Alicia stared in wonder at the sudden change of attitude. “I suppose…” she asked the bartender, “do you have Amaretto?”

The lanky bartender nodded. “Yes. Disaronno, from Italy.”

“If you can make an amaretto sour, I’d love one.”

“Right away.” The bartender responded. “And another Sunmai honey lager for you, General?”

“Yes, thank you.” The General turned his attention to the women and asked, “How long have you been in the country?”

“We only arrived this morning.”

“Oy, that’s a long flight, was it from your East Coast?”

They both nodded.

"The jet lag must be terrible for you. It must be morning where you're from. Anyway, this must be a real puzzle that you have that sent you all this way." He tilted his head toward the bartender who was pouring their drinks. "Let's wait until we have our refreshments before we get into your questions. I just hope that I can help. How long will you be in town?"

"I suppose that depends on a few things." Lucy smiled, took a sip of the beer, and made an almost indecent noise as she gushed, "this is wonderful. Like you said, very refreshing."

Alicia watched as her companion leaned against the bar, but a few inches closer to the general. To her, it was obvious that Lucy was purposefully being complimentary, being a bit hyperbolic in her reactions, and standing closer than seemed necessary. Alicia wondered whether or not it was something she could do without her skin crawling. Something about being so close to someone of the opposite sex made her very uneasy.

The bartender set their drinks on the counter, the general handed Alicia her amber-colored drink and said, "I hope it's to your satisfaction."

Moving aside the thin slice of orange attached to the rim of her glass, Alicia took a sip and the first taste was the warm almond notes coating her taste buds, followed by the sweet and sour tang vying for her attention. She nodded her approval. "It's wonderful."

"Excellent." The general motioned toward an empty

alcove with a few unoccupied leather chairs. "Let's sit and talk."

Alicia followed as the general escorted them to the far corner of the main room, and as they settled in each respective chair, Lucy made a point of shifting hers closer to where the general was sitting.

She gave him an embarrassed smile and said, "I hope you don't mind that I bring the chair closer, but we'd rather not have this discussion be overheard."

The general panned his gaze around the room and grinned. "This is a fairly public place, but I understand what you mean. Now, how can I help you?"

Alicia observed how Lucy and the general's knees were practically touching, and for a moment she wondered if Lucy was expecting her to bring her chair closer as well, but she opted to sit back and watch. That was, after all, what she was here for. Let Lucy lead, and learn from what she does.

Lucy leaned forward and asked, "We came here from Washington DC because we received some intelligence about activities in this area of the Sanzhi District, east of the True Dragon Temple."

The general's eyes widened a bit and Alicia could tell that he knew something before another word was uttered.

"What kind of activities are you talking about?" the general asked.

Lucy hesitated for a moment, likely for effect, and she leaned forward, touched the general's knee and whispered, "I shouldn't say this, but we know of the deaths in the area."

Alicia suddenly felt confused. Deaths in the area? She knew only of the agent that was killed. Did Lucy know something more than she did or was the woman ad-libbing?

"Deaths you say?" The general held a grim expression. "How can…" he clamped his mouth shut and frowned.

"We also know that your soldiers are guarding that area. There are officials in my government that are concerned about attacks coming from our neighbor to the west, and we would like to understand what their interest is in that location."

The general sat back and stared silently at both of the women in front of him for a full five seconds before saying, "You two aren't just some political envoys from your State Department. There's no way. Can I see some ID?"

Following Lucy's lead, Alicia cracked open her purse and they both showed the general their identification, which backed up their story.

"I'm sorry ladies, but this conversation has taken a turn I didn't expect." The general took a deep gulp from his glass and shook his head. "What is it you're asking of me?"

"What is your country hiding in the woods east of the True Dragon Temple that has so interested your neighbor to the west?" Lucy said it as bluntly as it could be said.

The general chuckled unexpectedly and shrugged. "I'll say this much without violating any oaths I've taken; your information is a bit stale. And without being too specific, I can say that I don't actually know what may or may not be in those woods."

Lucy shifted her chair so they were sitting side by side and it almost looked like she was leaning in to kiss the man, she was that close. "Someone must know." She put her hand on the general's thigh as she leaned ever closer.

To Alicia, what she was seeing was almost obscene in its forwardness. Her stomach roiled and she knew this was something she couldn't ever do. The idea that some guy might flirt with her made Alicia want to hide, but the idea of practically pushing herself onto someone... unthinkable.

The general's gaze was focused on Lucy as she awaited an answer. He glanced past Lucy and smiled. "My lady, you are one amazingly strong-willed and lucky woman. Were I not married, such tiger-like ferocity for your cause would attract me like no other." He glanced at Alicia. "No offense young lady. You're a beautiful flower as well." He gently removed Lucy's hand from his thigh, stood and motioned in the direction of the bar. "You see that man in the dark suit?"

They both turned and nodded.

There was nothing unusual or particularly identifiable about the man. A middle-aged Asian man, wearing a business-appropriate suit, and would have blended in with any crowd in the business district.

"You asked some very specific questions." The general motioned toward the generic-looking man at the bar. "Ladies, if there's anyone who likely knows about the motivations of our friends to the west and the area you're talking about, it would be that man, Tsai Shih-ming. He's the head of the National Security Bureau."

Alicia had read a briefing about the NSB. It was Taiwan's equivalent to the CIA.

"Can you introduce us?" Lucy asked.

The general shook his head. "I'm sorry, but that man and I do not get along. And besides, it wouldn't be appropriate. You'll have to excuse me. I have to go."

The uniformed man gently nudged his way past Lucy, walked through the crowd of people, and vanished from sight.

Alicia looked at Lucy and the woman was checking herself in the mirror. "Did that go as expected?"

"We at least have confirmation that something's going on." Lucy shrugged. "We have another lead, so let's keep pulling the thread and see what we find."

Alicia followed Lucy as the woman pulled out her ID and walked over to the bar.

"Mister Tsai?" Lucy approached the man with a large smile.

The man turned and eyed Lucy with a look of suspicion. "Yes?"

Lucy held up her ID and extended her hand. "I'm Ruth Li, from the U.S. State Department. I was wondering if we could talk for a bit."

Alicia had always been a student of body language, and she'd spent a lot of time with her father just watching people. It was a game that they'd played when she was younger, and from those early years of practice the man's reactions told her a lot. The furrowed brow, the tension in his shoulders, and the way he practically bristled at Lucy's offer to shake hands told her this guy wasn't in the mood for chit-chat.

The man breathed heavily, ignoring the offered hand, and shook his head. "Why is someone from the U.S. government approaching me at this public event? There are proper channels for such things, and you should know that, *Miss Li*." He said her name with a derisive tone, almost as if he knew that wasn't her real name.

Lucy's smile broadened and she stepped closer.

Alicia winced. Lucy was either oblivious to the signals this man was sending or she didn't care and knew she could break through the man's resistance.

"Mister Tsai, my partner and I just arrived this morning and we haven't yet arranged for the proper communique to the NSB." Lucy stepped even closer, and her voice took on a husky tone. "But when I noticed you were here, I had to take advantage of this chance meeting." She glanced at his empty glass and motioned to the bar. "Can I get you a drink?"

The man glanced in Alicia's direction and she felt a shiver as his frown deepened.

He gave Lucy a cold smile and said in perfect English, "I saw you whoring it up with General Cheng. The old man might sully his honor for some cheap tits and ass, but I will not. Get away from me." He turned to the bartender and tapped on his glass. "Another seltzer."

Lucy walked stiffly away from the man, anger oozing from every pore. What the head of Taiwan's intelligence agency had said had clearly made her mad. She whispered, "I'll need to reach out to Mason to open the front door."

"That's not unexpected, right?"

She shrugged. "These things take time, and I'm not sure how much we have, given the intel we have."

Alicia stepped closer to Lucy and whispered, "What was that you told the general about multiple deaths in the forest? Were you adlibbing or was that the truth?"

"It's real." Lucy frowned as she pulled out her cell phone and began texting someone. "Mason gave me some reports about the Taiwanese government suppressing and even disappearing entire families from a nearby village. Evidently there are a lot of very upset villagers who claim that the government had killed and cremated entire families that had gone into those woods. We don't know how much of that is truth or just hearsay, but it seems oddly specific."

"You sure spooked the general when you brought it up." Alicia turned back to the bar, and the man was still there, nursing his sparkling water. With a growing sense of frustration building up within her, her mind raced through scenarios as Lucy continued tapping a message onto her phone, presumedly texting to Mason or someone at the Outfit. "Let me try."

"Try what—?"

Alicia walked away from Lucy and made a beeline for the man at the bar.

He turned to face her just as she was within arm's reach and shook his head. "Young lady, you're not listening—"

"Mister Tsai, I'm not here to try and deceive you." Alicia began speaking rapidly in English, not letting the man get a word in edgewise. "I've been sent by my government to try and get some intel that could save countless lives, but the problem is that time is of the essence. My friend tried an approach that I personally find appalling, it probably works better than it should with most men, but I'd honestly rather speak candidly. Can you at least talk to me? Maybe we can trade information?"

Alicia noticed Lucy approaching from the corner of her eye and motioned her away. Surprisingly enough, she listened, walked to the other side of the room, and visited one of the stations set up with finger foods.

The man looked at her with the same expressionless stare her father had always used. "You're very young, aren't you?"

"I am young. Only twenty-three. But—"

"Word of advice, young lady. People in our vocation never speak candidly. You always keep something back, because you never know when you'll need it."

"Can we start over?" Alicia extended her hand. "I'm Alicia Yo...der." She stammered, realizing her mouth had run ahead of her brain and accidentally voiced her real name.

Amazingly enough, the man shook her hand and looked at her with a puzzled expression. "That's an unusual family name for an Asian girl." Other than a slight foreign accent, the man's English was excellent. "You don't by chance know a Levi Yoder, do you?"

Alicia took an involuntary step back and shuddered as a sense of dread washed over her. How could this man have so quickly come up with her father's name? It was at that moment that she realized several things: if this man knew her father, that could either be a very bad thing or possibly one that's positive. Also, of all the billions of people on this Earth, how in the world could she have met someone who was literally on the other side of the planet that knew of her father. Was Dad somehow famous in intelligence circles? She knew almost nothing of such things.

"I see that you do." Without her even needing to respond, the man read it from her reaction. "Who is he to you?"

"He's my father." The man's eyebrows raised just a bit. "I was adopted as a child."

"Interesting." The man held up a finger and said, "Wait right here." He pulled out his phone and put it to his ear.

After a few seconds he nodded his head and began having a conversation with someone in Japanese.

Alicia knew enough to recognize the language, but had no clue what the man was saying.

He turned to her and asked, "Levi Yoder, from New York?"

She nodded. At this point there wasn't much use in trying to deceive the man. Alicia had already screwed up, but what did her father have to do with this man, and why was he suddenly talking to someone in Japanese?

Mister Tsai nodded curtly and said, "Hai" to whoever

was on the phone. He turned to Alicia again and asked, "Did you receive a gift on your 18th birthday from someone in Japan?"

Alicia puzzled over the question and her eyes widened. "Yes. How could you possibly know that? It was a necklace with a charm." She opened her purse, dug out her necklace with the Hello Kitty charm on it, and showed it to the man. "It was this. I almost always wear it. It's supposed to keep evil away."

The man pulled the phone away from his ear, aimed the phone at the charm Alicia was holding and took a picture. There was silence for a few seconds and suddenly the head of the Taiwanese intelligence agency nodded curtly to whoever was on the phone, said something in Japanese as he turned on the video conferencing feature, and then handed Alicia his phone. "Tanaka-san wants to see you."

She held the phone and saw a wrinkled older man on the tiny screen. "Hello." Alicia spoke in English. "I'm sorry, I don't speak Japanese."

"So... you are the eldest girl your father talked about." The man spoke in heavily-accented English. *"I recall him using the name Alicia. It is good to see you as a young woman. I hope my small gift has brought you some peace and safety. Give my greetings to your father and tell him that Tanaka-san remains forever in his debt for what he did for my granddaughter."* The man smiled and bowed his head. *"It is my privilege to meet you my little lotus blossom, but please return the phone to the man who gave it you."*

Alicia handed the phone back and her heart raced as she wondered who that man was, and what in the world had her father done... saved his granddaughter from some criminals? Maybe helped pay for some medical procedure? She had no idea. Dad didn't say much about the man who'd sent the Hello Kitty charm for her birthday, other than he was Japanese. That in and of itself wasn't so strange, since Dad had spent years in that country long before he'd adopted her.

Mister Tsai was speaking to the man on the other end of the line in rapid-fire Japanese. All Alicia could make out was the occasional "oh!" or "hai!" neither of which meant anything to her, but each time, the head of the intelligence agency gave a curt bow to nobody in particular, which seemed a bit dramatic since he'd switched off the video.

The man pocketed the phone, turned to Alicia and pressed his hands together in front of his face, as if in prayer, and gave her a quick bow. "I apologize for my rudeness."

The man's tone seemed sincere, and for some reason his entire demeanor had changed after hanging up with the mysterious old man.

"Miss Yoder, you wanted to talk about something?"

"Yes, please. I'd love to." Alicia pointed at the phone, which the man had put back into his suit pocket. "Who is Tanaka-san?"

Mister Tsai smiled and shook his head. "That is not important to know. I have promised to Tanaka-san that I will help *you* with your cause as much as I can."

Alicia felt tingles up and down her body as a sense of

elation flooded through her. She took in a deep breath and let it out slowly, trying to calm her excitement at not having made a disaster of this engagement. “Okay, where do you want to talk?”

The man motioned to the floor-to-ceiling sliding glass doors. “There, on the balcony.” He glanced over at Lucy, who was watching from afar. “My promise to help extends only to you, I don’t want your companion within earshot. What I share is for you, and if you choose to share that information, it is on your conscience, not mine.”

“Okay, I’ll tell her and meet you on the balcony.”

Mister Tsai nodded and walked toward the sliding glass doors.

Alicia hurried over to Lucy, explained the situation and when she mentioned her conversation with someone named Tanaka-san, her eyes widened. “You know who that is?”

Lucy motioned toward the balcony. “Trust me, it’s not important for you to know who that man is. Go, get the data we need, and for God’s sake, don’t let that man edge you too close to the balcony.” She gave Alicia a playful grin. “The last thing I need is to explain how you ‘jumped’ off the top of the Taipei 101. Oh, and by the way... awesome job. But seriously, go get our data.”

CHAPTER
TWELVE

It was surprisingly cool up on the balcony, but that made some bit of sense since she was standing around one thousand feet above the city streets. Alicia looked over at Mister Tsai as he shooed away the last of the guests who'd occupied the balcony and slid the glass door closed, giving them some modicum of privacy.

He kept himself just outside of arm's reach, leaned close to the balcony edge and said, "Five kilometers east of the True Dragon Temple, you say?"

Alicia nodded. "I'm going to be quite plainspoken about my purpose here, what I know, and what I hope you can fill in with more details. I'm here to help my partner gather intelligence on what has caused concern in some circles. We know about the Mainland Chinese infiltration of spies onto your island. That's probably not a closely guarded secret, it stands to reason that you'd spy on each other. But something happened east of the True Dragon Temple that has caused deaths. There's evidence that elements of Chinese intelligence are very interested in what's at that location. I also know that the army is guarding an outpost in that vicinity. Couple that with the recent domestic threats we've had from the PRC sending high-altitude test flights of balloons over U.S. territory. You can understand why our intelligence community would be concerned about the possibility that those tests will be deployed with something other than talcum powder in the future. What can you tell me about the current situation in those woods?"

Mister Tsai harrumphed and raked his fingers through his hair. "You have a right to be concerned, as do we, for that matter. Yours isn't the only country that those balloons have traveled across." He gave her a sidelong glance, and a hint of amusement shone on his face. "I suppose I shouldn't be surprised that the U.S. has a fairly strong spy network in my country. I'll try to ignore the ramifications of such a thing. Where can I begin...

"Let me first ask of you that this information be kept away from the public. If some of this would be known by others, it would certainly be embarrassing to those in power, but more importantly, it could lead to social unrest that might lead to unimaginable consequences."

Alicia nodded. "I can assure you that almost everything I deal with is of a classified nature. I'm sure my government will treat anything related to this topic as a national security item that only a limited set of people will ever know about."

"I suppose that will have to suffice. That location has had several code names over the years, none of which are particularly important—"

"New Arcadia?" Alicia asked.

"Yes, that is one of them. It was a hidden facility that conducted medical research. It doesn't matter the specifics of the research other than to say a terrible mistake was made during the time that the facility was last active.

"It turns out that there was some kind of breach in protocol that resulted in the release of a toxic strain of organism."

"Organism?" Alicia frowned. "You mean like an animal?"

"No, more like a virus, but I'm unclear on the details of such a thing, to be honest. My background isn't in medical research. I suppose you could look at it as the same level of breach as what had happened in Wuhan with the Covid virus. Regardless of how it escaped, the fact is that it did, and whatever it was, it was virulent and deadly.

"The chaos that ensued ended up with the deaths of hundreds of people who were previously infected. Unfortunately, even when the person was killed, they were still contagious. The only sure way to contain the spread of this horror was the burning of the host's body." The man pressed his lips together into a thin line, wielding a grim expression. "Many of the people who were incinerated to prevent the spread were children. An entire scouting group that happened to be in the woods at the time of the breach had been quarantined, confirmed to have been infected, and then ultimately cremated. Their remains were buried in shallow graves in the woods."

"That's horrible." Alicia winced, imagining how bad this must have been to actually have to kill children. She felt the chill of the night air seep into her bones. Shallow graves and ashes. These were the things nightmares were made of. The way he described the situation, they'd barely avoided yet another pandemic, possibly one that could have been much worse than Covid had been.

"It was only after the cleanup had begun that we realized that someone had infiltrated the facility and stolen several vials of the pathogen."

The man's voice was thick with emotion. Alicia's breaths came too quickly and for a moment she felt lightheaded. Using a technique her father had taught her, she focused on her chest's rising and falling, willing it to slow the rapid pace of her heart and thus her breathing. All the while, she felt a growing sense of discomfort in her lower abdomen, almost like period cramps, but it wasn't the right time for that. "Do you know who took them?"

"We of course suspected the PRC. Nonetheless, from that moment on signs were placed throughout the woods, enforcing a ban on entry for anyone. There was a strict shoot-to-kill order put into place for any unexpected people who came within range of the facility. We expected that between the signs warning people away and the cordoned off area, nobody would come within range, but one day a man arrived in the dead of night. He tried to infiltrate the boundaries of the facility. He was taken out by a sniper's bullet."

"Were you able to identify him?" Alicia asked.

Mister Tsai nodded. "The man was a member of the Chinese secret police. A person in a very similar position to my own."

Alicia clenched her jaw tightly, knowing how much chaos this would sow with the people at the Outfit. What would their reaction be? "Are there still samples of the pathogen in that facility?"

The man snorted. "Not as of two days ago. We've razed the entire site, burnt it all to the ground. It was the only way we knew we could be sure that the pathogen was neutralized." He pulled out his phone, made a few swiping motions, pulled up aerial images of a forest fire, and showed it to her.

Alicia stared at the evidence of the inferno, likely taken from a helicopter or maybe even a drone hovering a few hundred feet above the woods. In the distance she saw hints of what had to be the True Dragon Temple.

He swiped his thumb across the screen and showed a screenshot of a local newspaper with the headlines describing a freak firestorm north of the city. It had images of the burnt devastation as firefighting crews battled to keep the conflagration at bay. "The evidence you might be looking for has been destroyed. Out of an abundance of caution, we simply had no choice. I'll be honest, we can't be sure that the missing vials weren't simply a clerical error or that they truly were stolen. And if they were stolen, we can't be one-hundred-percent sure who took them.

"However, before we part ways for this evening, I can leave you with one interesting piece of intelligence that your analysts might find thought provoking. Recall that I mentioned there was a spy from Mainland China that got shot and killed. In his possessions were some very unusual items, including a type 74 flamethrower, and nearly a dozen incendiary grenades."

Alicia tilted her head and puzzled at what the man had just said. "That doesn't sound like someone who was trying to steal something, it sounds like someone who was trying to destroy something."

"Odd isn't it?"

"If China had stolen it already..." She gasped as the puzzle pieces fell together. "They'd want to destroy any remaining samples so that nobody else had access to it."

"That is a plausible scenario." The man sighed. "Whoever has taken the samples, these people may not realize just how dangerous this thing that they have is. Just like with what happened in Wuhan, one little mistake is all it takes." He pushed away from the railing, and held out his hand to shake Alicia's. "As much as I would love to continue a conversation with you, I have to leave. I hope this conversation has helped you, and I pray something good comes of it."

The man opened the nearby sliding glass door, and

closed it behind him, leaving Alicia to her thoughts on the cold, breezy balcony.

Alicia's mind raced in a thousand different directions at once.

There no longer was a New Arcadia. It was gone.

Yet the danger hadn't diminished, in fact it had likely grown exponentially.

The sliding glass door opened and Lucy walked onto the balcony. "Did you get something from him?"

Alicia stared wide-eyed at Lucy and said, "We need to get out of here and talk with Mason."

It had been only a few days since Colonel Xi Bo managed to extricate himself from the muddy tide flats outside a coastal fishing village. At first, his memories were like phantoms in the night, whispers that promised to tell a tale, but never quite divulging their secrets.

The day-long stay at the Jinzhou community hospital had helped him address the dehydration and the scrapes and bruises he'd received recently, but nothing new came popping back into his head.

Outside of random fragments spanning the last few years, he still couldn't remember much of his past. He spent much of that stay wracking his brain, trying to dig further back into his past, but he couldn't remember a thing. There were certainly things that he knew had to have happened, but those gaps in his memory were impenetrable: he couldn't remember attending school, entering the military, he could only recall a vague image of his parents. The only thing he'd held onto was the few fleeting memories of his most recent mission, being promoted to colonel, and a few other key things that at the moment seemed somewhat random and pointless.

Since then, he'd talked to several people at various levels of the People's Liberation Army both in person and on the phone. From his interactions with them, they were able to piece together a timeline and set of events that had occurred. A doctor that he talked to on the phone made the determination that the best potential remedy for his acute retrograde amnesia was to go back to where he'd been assigned and see if familiar places and people would help reawaken his lost memories. They'd arranged for his travel back to his home base, which was nearly eight hours northeast on a plane, and now he was north of Harbin as the vehicle he was in bounded over rough terrain. He looked down at a map and studied his surroundings.

They'd left Harbin nearly three hours ago and were now driving through a remote region east of Yuchin. They were less than one hundred miles from the Russian border, traveling on what seemed to be a maze of ancient paths and riverbeds that cut through the dense forest. The boulder-strewn terrain made for a challenging ride, and even though it was certainly easier than walking, the vehicle he was in had clearly not been designed with comfort in mind.

He glanced at his driver, a sergeant, and wondered what the man had been told about him. The man had remained tight-lipped throughout the journey, only speaking when spoken to. “How much further?”

The man pointed north. “The base is only another fifteen minutes. Is the ride too bumpy for you, Colonel? I can slow down if you like.”

“Go ahead as you normally would.” His stomach flip-flopped as the vehicle flew down an embankment. “Do many people use this... road?”

The sergeant shook his head and he held a white-knuckled grip on the steering wheel. “Not so much. The base is a bit isolated, but that’s kind of the point now, isn’t it? We can’t have people knowing too much about what we’re up to.”

“No, I suppose not.” The colonel had no idea what he was talking about, which frustrated him to no end.

The sergeant looked over at him and said, “Better hang on, sir, this next one is a stomach-lurcher.”

The colonel barely had time to react before the vehicle went right over the edge of a steep-walled ravine. For a moment he thought the car would flip end-over-end, but the sergeant deftly threaded them through the boulders and trees, and when they reached the bottom, he turned the wheel sharply left.

He smacked his head sharply on the side of vehicle, and for a moment saw flashes of light in front of his eyes.

Shrugging his shoulders, the sergeant muttered, “I hate that path.”

The colonel loosened his death grip on his seatbelt and yelled, “Then why the hell use it?”

The sergeant glanced at him with a surprised expression. “Sir, because the only other way in and out of the base is to follow this ravine for another hour and a half in the opposite direction. But if we go this way…” He pointed up ahead. “You see? We’re already here.”

Sure enough, the ravine opened into a valley surrounded by mountains on all sides. A few armed soldiers stood watch as they drove past them, entering the naturally secluded military camp.

As the sergeant pulled up to a manned entrance, PLA soldiers approached on both sides of the vehicle. They yelled out, “Identification!”

Bo pulled out the sheaf of papers he’d been given at the hospital, which served as the only identification he had at the moment, and offered it to the soldier approaching the passenger’s side.

The soldier reached for the papers, paused, and the young man snapped to attention and saluted. “Colonel, welcome back. We had feared the worst.”

The worst? He remembered only bits and pieces of his prior mission. Images of the woods as they appeared through night-vision goggles loomed large in his mind’s eye.

A distant image of a barbed wire security fence, and the smell of peat perfumed the air.

The colonel winced as the phantom pain bloomed in his chest. The doctors at the hospital had checked, and there was nothing there. No reason for the pains, yet when he recalled the last moments of his mission, the memory of the burning pain deep in his chest felt almost like he'd been stabbed.

Bo returned the salute and one of the guards peered into the driver's side window to address the driver. "Sergeant, please take Colonel Xi to the research and tactics building, the general wants to meet with him."

The driver put the car in gear as the metal barrier sunk into the ground, allowing them to drive onto the clandestine military base.

The colonel took in the sights of his surroundings and only a couple buildings struck familiar chords in his shattered memory. All of the concrete buildings were unmarked, yet he knew the one with the green entranceway was the mess hall. He could even remember its interior, with the long benches and the food being served was almost always reconstituted field rations. One of the side-effects of being in such a remote location was that the supplies they received was almost never of the kind that included anything that was perishable. That much he remembered.

As the sergeant drove past an open area with soldiers practicing their field maneuvers, Bo spotted the building at the west end of the valley. The building with the yellow door was one he was very familiar with.

He could picture himself walking past the entrance into an open area with hallways receding north and west. On the south wall was a large picture of Mao. Bo remembered walking into the north hallway and knew there was a lab there, but couldn't remember anything about it.

This place was definitely where he belonged, but there was so much data missing from within his head, he could only pray that somehow it came back to him.

The sergeant parked in front of the building and motioned at the yellow door. "Sir, it was a pleasure driving you."

"Thank you for getting us here safely." Bo hopped out of the car, gave the sergeant a crisp salute, and walked into the building.

It was exactly as he remembered it. The picture of Chairman Mao was where it was supposed to be, and everything else was in its place. Bo hesitated as it dawned on him that he had no idea where the general's office might be, or if there even were offices in this building. That information was eluding him for the moment.

Somewhere in the distance, he heard the sound of footsteps and seconds later, Bo spotted a man approaching from the western hallway.

He immediately recognized that the man wore a type-seven camouflage training uniform.

Bo looked at himself, and winced. He was wearing

threadbare civilian clothes borrowed from the leftovers at the community hospital that had taken care of him.

As the man approached, he noticed the two stars and sheafs of wheat on the collar, and immediately snapped to attention and saluted the general.

The general returned the salute and smiled broadly, clapping his hand on his shoulder. “Bo, it’s so good to see you returned, albeit not undamaged.” His brows furrowed and he had a look of concern. “I was told about your memory loss. How much can you remember?”

Bo shrugged. “I’m afraid not as much as I’d like, General Hong.” He only knew the man’s name because it was clearly spelled out on his uniform. “But things come back in waves. Sometimes I just see or hear something and it unlocks yet another memory.”

“Do you remember me?”

Bo winced and shook his head. “I’m afraid not, sir. I apologize.”

“No need for apologies.” The general motioned for him to follow. “Let’s go back into my office and we can talk.”

They began walking through the western corridor as the general peppered him with a series of questions, most of which he couldn’t answer. But when asked what was the last thing he remembered before finding himself on the beach, Bo felt as if he were reliving the last moments of his mission.

“It was the dead of night, when even the insects have gone to sleep. The moon was behind the clouds and the world looked green through my night-vision lens. The mist hung low in the forest, and as I approached my target, I remember my footsteps squishing through the damp ground, kicking up the aroma of peat moss—an earthy, dark, rich scent that was reminiscent of wet wool, with a hint of rot. In the distance, I saw the barbed wire fence.

"Crouching low, I continued my advance toward the camp. The ground was softer than it should have been, as if it had been freshly dug up. I froze, hearing the sound of a crunching and snapping sound underfoot. I'd feared I had triggered a land mine, but it was the ash-covered bones of a recently buried body.

"The last thing I remember is walking through a veritable graveyard of bodies, and then..." Bo rubbed at his chest as he took a seat in front of the desk in the general's office. "Something happened. Even though I have no scar nor indication that I'd received any injury, I remember my chest burning, almost as if I'd been stabbed or shot. The next thing I remember is being aware of myself once again on a remote beach near a place named Jinzhou."

"Amazing..." the general shook his head. "I'm sorry that you suffered in your mission, and I intend to help in whatever way I can to get you back those missing memories."

Hong's tone and expression seemed sincere and Bo felt a bit more at ease.

"We just received the latest satellite image of Chinese Taipei." The man leaned over, extracted a photograph from a stack of papers, and placed it in front of Bo. "What is it that you see on that satellite image?"

Bo picked up the glossy photograph and looked over it. It was an image of the area surrounding the city of Taipei, and his eyes panned toward the north, noticing the landmark of a temple whose name eluded him at that moment.

For whatever reason, he remembered that to the east of the temple was his objective. He looked closer and frowned. There was an obvious scorched area where he believed his target should have been. Even though the image was black and white, it was clear that there was an oblong section of land that had been burnt recently. In fact there was a bit of a hazy streak across the land that originated at the site of his objective. A clear indication that smoke was still rising from the site when this photograph was taken. No signs were evident of the fence or the building he'd spied beyond them. "It looks like the area was burnt to the ground."

"Exactly right." The general let out a hearty chuckle. "I'm very sorry that you didn't come out unscathed from the mission, but it's obvious that you managed to complete the Dragon's Breath Protocol, as requested. I will make sure that your successful effort is known by those above me."

Bo stared at the image, and felt nothing. The name Dragon's Breath Protocol rang no bells for him, and he couldn't remember what it was that he'd been asked to do.

Evidently he was the one responsible for burning that section of forest. But for what reason? A growing sense of frustration welled up within him. He looked up at the general and admitted, "I can't remember doing it."

Hong nodded. "Maybe that is the burning sensation you

mentioned feeling in your chest. A fragment of memory left over from the fire you started at the site of your mission."

"Maybe..." Bo wondered if that could be it. But the suggestion felt... wrong.

The general stood and walked over to the colonel who hopped up from his chair as well. Hong put his arm over Bo's shoulder and patted his chest. "Let's get you briefed on what we've done with the results of your efforts, and I believe as you get back into a normal work environment, your memories will return."

"Yes, sir." Bo wasn't sure if it would work, but it was the only thing that seemed reasonable. Without his memories, he was nothing, and Colonel Xi Bo found that outcome to be unacceptable.

It was time to reclaim who he was.

CHAPTER THIRTEEN

Alicia and Lucy sat in the SCIF at the Taiwanese embassy, watching the secure video feed of a conference room broadcasting from the underground headquarters of the Outfit. Alicia leaned over and hit the mute button, shutting down the microphones hanging from the ceiling. "Do you recognize everyone?"

Lucy shook her head. "Not everyone. You obviously recognize Mason and Brice on the far end of the table. The black gentleman to Mason's right is Sekou Cooper, he's the Director of Intelligence for all operations in Africa. Next to Sekou is Richard Wong, Director of Intelligence for Asia and the Pacific Rim. The woman opposite him I don't know, but if I had to guess, she's probably the replacement for Adam McCallister, the DI for the Americas who was really old and ready to either keel over or retire."

"Out of curiosity, what's Mason's official title? Does he head up the whole thing?"

"No, but listening to him you'd sometimes think he does." Lucy gave a sour look at the video screen. "Doug Mason is officially the head of OCID, the Organized Crime and Intelligence Division. His jurisdiction is a bit odd, because he handles issues that happen in pretty much every part of the world, but he mostly deals with assets the Outfit has coming out of organized crime. He's also the senior person Stateside, but there are others he reports to. I have no idea what the hierarchy of the Outfit looks like above Mason, I just know there are people above him. Everyone has to report to someone, Alicia. That's the number one constant in this business."

"Interesting." Alicia pondered what Lucy had just said and it made sense. Especially with Lucy's past dealing with organized crime, that's likely how she got sucked into the Outfit, even if only on a freelance basis.

Another person walked into the conference room on the video screen and Lucy said, "That's Gregor Manheim. DI for Europe and Eurasia. I think he has parts of the Eastern bloc, including the former Soviet breakaway republics, and Russia itself, while Richard handles all the rest of Asia and the Indian subcontinent."

Alicia felt the butterflies in her stomach dancing a jig as she realized that everyone in that room had probably read the report she'd put together about what the Taiwanese spymaster had told her. What if it hadn't been good enough? Clear enough. What if—

"Okay folks, we're all situated in DC." Mason spoke with a calm, yet authoritative voice. *"Taipei, I see you folks are ready. Alicia, I believe Lucy has already filled you in on who everyone is except for Bridget Litchford. She's the new DI for the Americas."*

Alicia stared at the control console which showed the microphones as still being muted. "How did he know?"

Lucy sighed. "The man reads lips."

"Yes, I can read lips fairly well, but the rest of the team here can't, so you can come off of mute. I'm locking us down."

Alicia reached across the conference room table, toggled the mute button, and heard the sound of metal sliding against metal. She turned to look at the SCIF's door and noticed a tiny red light blinking above it, and the touch screen next to the door displayed "Locked" in red letters. All done through some remote command. *Neat trick.*

"Okay, everyone has read the report coming from the team in Taipei. I'll summarize the situation briefly:

"We have intelligence saying that the PRC has gone out of their way to steal what seems to be some kind of biological agent that the Taiwanese had been working on. And our so-called allies to the west were so damned afraid of what it could do, they ended up slaughtering men, women, and children to prevent a possible worldwide pandemic." He turned to Brice. *"Do we have any intel on what it was these idiots were developing in those woods?"*

Brice cleared his throat and spoke with a nasally tone. *"I did manage to get into the Taiwanese government systems, the equivalent of our JWICS."*

The Joint Worldwide Intelligence Communications System was colloquially known to members of the intelligence community as "jaywicks" which was the system the U.S. government used for transmission of top secret and sensitive compartmented information.

"Given how little time has elapsed since learning about this issue, I'm not done searching, but so far, the computers have come up with only a few pieces of information. Evidently that site formerly known as New Arcadia was doing medical research on things that I can only describe as being ominous. At least one of the things they were investigating was the use of prions. For those not familiar with what a prion is, it's what we've heard of before as the cause for mad cow disease, but in a medical sense it causes the proteins in an animal's brain to assemble and fold abnormally." Brice picked up his notepad and began reading from it. *"Some of the symptoms from prion infection are rapidly developing dementia, difficulty in walking, hallucinations, muscle stiffness, confusion, fatigue, and difficulty in speaking. A few key points, prion infections have no treatment and are always fatal."*

Always fatal. The words seemed to cause the congregation of officials to collectively flinch. Alicia's blood ran cold as she imagined what being infected might be like.

"Unfortunately, that's all I've been able to dig up so far. I've got folks continuing the search and have enlisted some DoD computer resources to help scan through the Taiwanese databases.

"One thing that I should note is that in my research, I found

that it's almost impossible to destroy prions. Boiling them, using radiation, alcohol, even dunking them in acid won't do anything. The only real way to destroy prions is with intense heat. We're talking heat well above 1,000 degrees Fahrenheit."

"Good God, that's hot enough to melt rock!" Sekou exclaimed with a pleasant Nigerian accent.

"Likely why they burnt the place to the ground." Alicia said as she recalled the images of the conflagration the spymaster had shown her.

"Exactly right." Mason nodded and turned to Brice. *"Were you able to look into whether that weapon could be aerosolized?"*

"I talked to one of our bioweapons experts and he confirmed that it should be possible to create an inhalable version of these prions. That being said, it wouldn't take more than a few inhalations of contaminated particles in the air to get a potentially fatal dose. He actually had a lot to say on the subject, and the highlights are basically, the more you take in, the faster the onset of the symptoms. But his biggest caution was that it would be utterly insane for anyone to use prions as a weapon, largely because it would be almost impossible to detect and the decontamination process, if spread over a wide area, would be practically impossible."

A nuke was what came to Alicia's mind as being the only way to clear out an entire area with enough heat to remove such a threat. Clearly an impractical option.

Mason shifted his attention to Bridget. *"We need to get someone who isn't a total political hack to help us work on this Taiwan issue. First: what the hell were the Taiwanese even thinking with this line of research, and secondly, figure out a way to get our government more engaged with the Taiwan-China thing. We don't need a massive escalation, and this sure looks like it has the makings of one."*

"Understood." The woman nodded. *"Senator Martinez is helpful due to his seniority, and I have a few contacts with the representatives out of Utah that can be trusted to be adults and do what's needed."*

"Well," Mason drummed his fingers on the table and held a sour expression. *"Now that we know this damned thing could conceivably be put into a powdered form and spread over a wide area, what do we know about the PRC's actions with those damned balloons of theirs? I don't need to ask Bridget, we know the Americas are under threat, but Sekou, Gregor, Richard, have your areas been affected by those balloons?"*

Sekou shook his head but Gregor spoke with a slight German accent and said, *"Eastern Europe and Russia have had their airspace crossed multiple times by these high-altitude balloons. We've monitored communications between the EU governments and China and there was always an excuse coming that the flyover was purely accidental. In none of the cases did members of the EU pursue it any further, and the balloons ultimately flew over the Atlantic Ocean. What happened to them afterwards is unknown."*

"Both Taiwan and Japan have also been affected by these Chinese tools of terror." Richard said as he scribbled something on a notepad. *"In fact, a balloon crossed over Hokkaido only yesterday. The PRC claimed that it was a weather balloon which*

had picked up a stray wind current, nonetheless it was shot down by one of Japan's Self-Defense Forces jets and fell into the Pacific Ocean."

"Brice, what's the situation with our Manchurian asset?" Mason asked.

The mention of the Manchurian asset immediately caught Alicia's attention. It was one of the most ominous aspects of the briefing she'd received on the flight to Taiwan.

"I have bad news on that." Brice flipped forward several pages on his notepad. *"We lost his transmission signal somewhere east of a town called Yuchin, it's in the northern part of China, very close to the Russian border."*

"Do you think our asset has been discovered?" Mason asked.

"I doubt it, mostly because it happened just ten minutes from a remote military base that we know is hidden in a valley nestled between two mountain ranges. He'd been traveling for three hours or so at a somewhat constant speed, so if he'd have been discovered, I'd expect it wouldn't have been while traveling. Also, that part of the world is wilderness. It's got to be insane to get assets into and out of that area, especially using the route they were taking. It wouldn't be shocking to me if during that trip, they ran into a rather bumpy ride and our asset accidentally smacked his head on something in the vehicle, thus potentially rendering the transmitter nonoperational. And from what I could tell from the terrain maps we have of that area, they were going pretty fast for that terrain. Not exactly sure how they managed it."

Mason frowned. *"So, we think we know where our asset was going?"*

"Yes." Brice nodded. *"And given what we know, it's almost a certainty that's also where the stolen bioweapons content was taken."*

"Wait a minute," Lucy interjected. "How do we know where those vials of stuff were taken?"

Brice looked to Mason, and the director shook his head. *"Sorry, that I can't divulge in this meeting. Suffice it to say that we have good intel on this information."*

"That brings us to next steps." Mason declared. *"I presume we cannot remotely activate the asset?"*

"I'm sorry." Brice shook his head. *"I tried several different ways to get a read on him. We can't."*

"Which means we need to get someone into that base to interact with the asset." Mason turned to Richard. *"I know we have nobody in that particular military base, but do we have any female assets that might be local?"*

Richard frowned. *"If you mean pillow-talk candidates, no. The women I have in operations are mostly all grandmotherly types. The few younger ones that I have that speak Mandarin aren't in operations, they're administrative."*

"Oh crap..." Lucy grumbled and shook her head.

"Don't even think about it, Lucy." Mason remarked.

"You didn't hear me volunteer yet; don't tell me I can't go if I choose to."

"Actually, this time I'm saying absolutely you can't." Mason spoke with a tone of finality. *"You don't realize it, but there's a hornet's nest of activity from your old Triad friends looking for you. The last thing I'm going to allow is you going from the frying*

pan into the fire. There are cameras on practically every rural street corner in China much less in the cities. Your friends will inevitably find you, and even if they can't get directly to you, they'd figure out a way to get every member of the Chinese police and army looking for you within their borders. No. This time you can't do it."

"What does pillow-talk candidate mean?" Alicia asked.

"No." Lucy shook her head and sent Alicia a look of warning. "I forbid it. Your father would certainly forbid it. Absolutely not."

Alicia felt her cheeks getting warm as she glared at Lucy. "All I'm asking is what does it mean?"

"All it really means is someone who is young enough and pretty enough to pass for a sleeping partner." Mason said. *"It might seem primitive and crude, but it's not uncommon in some parts of the world for women to get past security and even extract intel from someone by getting very close to them. Even top-secret military bases."*

"You're not doing it, Alicia." Lucy again shook her head. "I told you about Doug, he's going to put you in danger. I can't let you do this."

With a sense of righteous indignation flooding through her, Alicia felt the hairs on the back of her neck stand on end as she confronted the woman who'd been nothing but kind to her. "Is there any other choice? Are you seriously thinking that a viable choice is to wait and see what the Chinese want to do with their stolen bio-weapon? I for one don't want to see my family or other innocents get hurt."

Lucy returned Alicia's angry gaze. "Not everything is your responsibility. You're still in training."

She turned back to the monitor, feeling a sense of embarrassment at having the confrontation witnessed by a bunch of strangers. "Director Mason, if there's nobody else, I'm willing to do this, but I need a lot more information on what exactly it is that I have to do."

Mason nodded and turned to the others. *"Anyone else with a young, passably attractive Asian female operations agent with Mandarin skills?"* When everyone else shook their head, he sighed. *"Lucy, I'm going to send two security details to the embassy and collect both of you. We'll talk again after I finish getting a few things straightened out on my end. Anyone else have anything else they need to say?"*

"Doug, Alicia's not ready to go." Lucy said with a growl.

"Okay, that'll wrap it up for now. Thanks for attending on such a short notice."

The video feed ended and the door to the SCIF unlocked.

Alicia got up and as she saw Lucy get up from her chair it dawned on her that they were both still wearing the same clothes from the Taipei 101 party. She tried desperately not to think about how embarrassing it was to wear a slinky and somewhat revealing dress on a video call with people at work. "If Mason is sending folks over, I'm not going dressed like this."

Lucy turned to her and spoke with a tone that broached no argument, "You're not going on this mission."

CHAPTER FOURTEEN

Night was falling as Alicia entered a part of town that looked a bit rough around the edges. The streets were so tightly packed it was impossible for two cars to drive side-by-side without one of the vehicles pulling onto a walkway. Alicia asked the driver, who was a member of the Outfit, "How in the world can you remember where anything is around here. There's no signs."

The man patted the side of his navigation system. "The overhead maps are very useful for learning the streets, but this place I know very well." He pointed at a building and said, "You see there, there's a sign hidden between the awning of the Hot Pot and Pho restaurants. We're heading south on Lane 123 off East Nanjing Road."

He turned left and somehow the street got even narrower. "We are now on Alley 4. Very simple."

Alicia shook her head and thanked all that was holy that she didn't have to drive in this place.

Homeless people, prostitutes, and the occasional roaming gang of street toughs occupied the passing side-walks. Oddly enough, this was exactly the kind of place Alicia would have expected to find an entrance to one of the Outfit's properties. After all, the U.S. headquarters was in a very dingy part of DC, literally underneath a seedy old bar.

It began to rain, sending many but not all of the side-walk-dwellers running for shelter.

"We're getting close to the night club," her driver said.

"A night club?"

The driver cracked a smile, the first sign of any emotion from the guy, but said nothing.

They stopped in front of a plain-looking building where two men stood on either side of a set of double doors, protected from the elements by a red awning. Techno music hummed from somewhere inside.

Her driver didn't say a word, so Alicia grabbed her duffel and stepped out of the car. The minute she closed the door behind her, the driver revved the engine and vanished into the night.

"You're not going on this mission."

Lucy's command repeated in her head and Alicia found herself smiling. Brice had briefed her on the half-hour long drive to this place, and even though the mission was ridiculously dangerous, she felt oddly comfortable with what was being asked of her. Understanding the stakes—the millions if not billions of lives in danger—caused a subtle shift in her mindset and perspective. To succeed at this would require something that in the depths of her soul, she knew she had to overcome, and overcome it she would.

At this point, she'd given herself no other choice, burning the metaphorical bridge behind her.

Alicia stepped up to the two men who were the size of sumo wrestlers. "I'm supposed to meet someone here."

"I'll need to see some ID, Miss Yoder," said one. His voice was so gravelly it sounded like rocks rubbing against each other.

Alicia wondered how the man knew her name, but she pulled out her passport and hesitated, realizing that it had a different name on it.

The man shook his head. "Not that kind of ID, ma'am."

It took only a second before it clicked in Alicia's head. She dug the coin out of her pocket and held it out. The bouncer grabbed the other side of the coin, and the LED lit up.

The two men stepped aside and motioned for Alicia to enter.

As Alicia opened the door, she braced himself for an auditory onslaught. But despite the sound of techno music coming through the door, the inside of the building was utterly silent. And when she shut the door behind her, she heard only the muted sound of the music—coming from *outside*.

Or, apparently, from the door itself.

The whole thing was a ruse.

Alicia panned her gaze across the entrance and had a severe case of déjà vu. She was positive that she'd never been here. After all, it was the first time she'd ever been to Taiwan, but had she been in a place that looked similar… maybe? She couldn't remember. The gaps in her memory hinted at something, but it was just out of reach.

She stood inside a wood-paneled lobby, fresh with the scent of wood polish and pipe tobacco. A reception desk stood across the room, manned by a short, matronly Asian woman with her hair bundled up with an elaborate set of clips.

"Miss Yoder, I was told to expect you tonight." The woman spoke English with a light British accent. "ID, please."

This time Alicia knew what to do. She held out the coin, and when the attendant grabbed the other side, the coin began glowing.

"Very well, ma'am. It's very good to meet you. I'm Mrs. Yang, the proprietor of this establishment."

Alicia looked around. "I'm sorry, Mrs. Yang, but what is this place?"

"That's a simple question with a complicated answer. This establishment meets the needs of those who seek its assistance. And I believe you are here with such a need."

"Actually, I'm here to get ready for a mission."

Mrs. Yang motioned toward a hall on Alicia's left. "Ah, yes. Director Mason left me with some instructions to exercise on his behalf. Please, follow me."

The hallway was lit by old-fashioned sconces with lightbulbs that flickered as if they were aflame. At the end of the hall a door stood slightly ajar.

"Ma'am, this is our quartermaster's section," Mrs. Yang said. "When you arrived, it was this wing that was unlocked." She stopped before the door, stepped to one side, and motioned grandly. "After you."

Alicia pushed the door open, and was surprised by how slowly it moved. It was six inches thick and must have weighed many hundreds of pounds, but its hinges were well-oiled, as it moved soundlessly. She stepped through, and lights flickered on, revealing a room filled with largely unmarked lockers. But she didn't see any way of opening them.

Mrs. Yang motioned to a pole in the center of the room. At about eye level was a visor, like one might see on a submarine's periscope. "If you will, Miss Yoder, please peer into the biometric scanner."

Alicia put her eyes against the visor. A green light flickered, and a series of clicks followed. She stepped back and looked around. Several of the lockers had popped open.

"Let's start with this side of the room, shall we, ma'am?" said Mrs. Yang, gesturing.

She paused, looked at the well-dressed woman and then panned her gaze across the rest of the room. This all felt like she was in some secret lair in a John Wick film. Between the headquarters and this place, the Outfit certainly had a flair for the dramatic.

Alicia's curiosity pulled her to the first open locker. Inside she found a change of clothes, including black leather boots, socks, bra, and underwear, along with a military uniform that she immediately recognized as being from the PLA, the Chinese army. The insignia on the collar indicated that the uniform belonged to a staff sergeant. Beneath the uniform was a red-colored passport for Mainland China. She opened the passport and saw her face staring back. "Interesting."

There was another ID in a red booklet, this time her military ID, again with her picture, along with a Chinese driver's license.

"It's a necessary element for any agent working behind enemy lines." said Mrs. Yang. "You can leave behind your old passport. It isn't needed. Also, please change into your uniform. It should fit you properly."

Alicia turned to face the woman. With her gray-streaked hair and wrinkled face, she had to be in her late sixties at least—but her voice was strong, she had perfect posture, and she gave off a youthful energy.

"How long have you been doing this?" Alicia asked.

"This, ma'am? What do you mean?"

"Walking people through whatever it is I'm doing."

"You mean prepping for a mission?"

"Is that what this is?"

"Of course. And as to how long I've been doing this..." Mrs. Yang pressed her lips tightly together and hummed. "I suppose this would be my fourth decade. Yes, just about forty years."

Alicia's eyes widened. "I guess I'm in good hands."

"Most certainly, ma'am."

"You can call me Alicia."

"That's very kind of you, ma'am, but I think after forty years, I'd be more likely to spontaneously combust than to fall out of protocol."

Alicia laughed. She liked this woman. "Should I change right now?"

"I think that would be for the best." Mrs. Yang motioned toward a table next to the biometric scanner. "Please keep your Outfit-assigned ID, since it is keyed to your biometric signature. The rest you leave with me, and I will happily take care of it."

When she was done, Mrs. Yang motioned toward the next locker. "Shall we continue, ma'am?"

Inside this locker was a thinly padded vest. Alicia removed her military jacket and shrugged into the vest. "Kevlar?"

"It serves the same purpose as what people wear in the military, I am sure. However," said Mrs. Yang, smiling, "I think you'll find the vest to be very effective and concealable."

Alicia adjusted the straps and put her jacket back on. "I don't know how effective it would be in comparison to what the U.S. military wears. In my training at the FBI Academy, I wore a battle vest with SAPIs and ESBIs—small-arms protective inserts and enhanced side ballistic inserts—and I certainly wouldn't think about wearing anything over them."

"Yes, well... the Outfit provides its agents with the best of what's available. Military grade doesn't always mean the best—frequently the opposite in fact, regardless of country. The best is what you're wearing. Then again, the military has different priorities on some things."

The third open locker held a sturdy knife with a six-inch blade and holster. The locker also contained a wallet, already stocked with some Chinese money and a Bank of China Visa card.

"Miss Yoder, I should inform you that weapons laws are different in China than in the U.S. You'll notice that you've not been given a firearm, and that is on purpose. It would draw undue attention to you and your mission, since almost no members of the Chinese army or police force carry them, unless there's a very specific reason. Nonetheless, I'd recommend that you keep the weapon you do have concealed."

"Okay, don't wave the knife around," Alicia said. "Got it."

Mrs. Yang led her to the fourth and last locker. It held a cell phone and a contact lens case. "Please activate the cell phone by swiping your finger on the fingerprint reader."

Alicia did as she was told, the phone lit up and began buzzing with an incoming call. "Hello?"

"Hi Alicia, it's Brice. This is the second part of our little talk that I promised would happen. Are you familiar with how to put in a contact lens?"

"More or less. I learned how to put them at my dad's place when we dressed for Halloween one time."

"Okay, unscrew that cap and put the contact in. It has no corrective vision attributes since you don't need it; you'll see what it does."

What it does? Alicia unscrewed the cap and examined the lens submerged in the contact solution. The otherwise clear lens had a bunch of silver threads running through it. "What are those silver strings in there for?"

"They're fiber-optic channels interlaced with bundled arrays of carbon nanotubes. Trust me, you won't see them when you put it on. Put it in your right eye, since that's the one I had measurements for."

"O-okay." She stammered, both excited and hesitant at the same time.

She scooped the contact onto the top of her index finger and stared at the quivering lens. This was the part she hated. As she moved her finger closer to her eyeball, she wondered why anyone would willingly opt to wear contacts. The idea of putting something directly on your eye seemed nuts, yet here she was doing exactly that.

"You know the drill, just press it on gently and it'll just suction cup right onto your eye. It should automatically orient itself once you blink a few times."

Alicia did as she was told, and the world turned blurry as she blinked the excess contact solution away. She dabbed away the wetness, then looked around, not seeing anything out of the ordinary. "Okay, now what?"

"Look at your phone and go to the home page. You should see an app with an eyeball icon."

"Clever."

"I thought so." Brice quipped. *"Anyway, tap on the eyeball icon to activate it, and you shouldn't have to do anything else afterwards. As long as you have a signal or a Wi-Fi connection, you'll be good to go."*

Alicia looked at her phone and the moment she tapped on the app she saw a "linking" message flicker into view in front of her right eye. It was just like a heads-up display. It was a strange sensation, because the text looked like it was just within arm's reach, but as she panned her gaze around the room, she could tell that the image must be somehow projecting into her eye. "Okay, it says it's linking."

She glanced at Mrs. Yang and the proprietor's face suddenly had a red square surrounding it with "unknown" flashing underneath it.

"Woah, when I look at Mrs. Yang, it's highlighting her face and saying 'unknown.'"

"Excellent!" Brice exclaimed. Alicia heard a few keystrokes across their connection and felt the phone buzz. *"Go look at the text image I just sent you."*

Alicia looked at the text and saw the face of someone she didn't know. Even though she didn't recognize the face, her contact highlighted the balding man in a green square and the text underneath it spelled out *"Larry Correia, author"* in glowing text. As she stared at the image, more biographical data began scrolling upward.

"That's pretty cool." She turned away and then focused back in on the image. It started over with the name and occupation. "So, it identifies who I'm looking at and gives me some bio data if I keep looking."

"Yes, and I color-coded things for you based on a three-point assessment of where the identification came from, criminal associations, and active warrants or other similar types of alert flags." With an enthused tone of voice, Brice began speaking in a rapid-fire manner as he explained the invention. *"I actually collaborated with one of your father's friends, a guy named Denny, who you might know."*

Alicia smiled and pictured the tall, thin, black man as he poured her a drink at the bar he owned. She'd know Denny since she was a little girl, but never realized he was a tech guy.

"Denny happened to be a classmate of mine ages ago. Anyway, back to the contact lens. We can do this now because of the latest silicon advances that allow me to quickly calculate the hashes that I use almost like a fingerprint for the image you're looking at, transmit the hash to the phone, and then I can do quick lookups..."

Alicia grinned and let Brice drone on as he explained stuff that was beyond her interest or comprehension. She pulled up a browser and flipped through random images, each of the people were quickly identified, with varying levels of bio data associated with them. As soon as Brice exhausted his stream of explanations, Alicia asked, "So, most of the pictures I'm seeing here on my phone your lens is picking up and able to identify them, but it didn't identify Mrs. Yang. Is there—"

"For the lookup, I'm using the backend APIs for accessing NGI, the FBI's next generation identification system, NCIC, INTERPOL, the passport image database through our State Department and about one hundred other country's passport services. Hell, I'll even fall back to Google's reverse image lookup if I have to. However, I've pretty much scrubbed all of the members of the Outfit from just about any of those repositories, so the lookup doesn't work well on us. With one exception."

Her phone buzzed again.

"Take a look at the picture I just sent."

She looked and it was a picture of an Asian man. Her contact lens immediately wrapped the man's image in a green square. "So that's what he looks like. Colonel Xi Bo of the PLA is our Manchurian candidate?"

"That's the target I told you about." Brice said. *"As I said earlier, I'm tracking your progress through this phone. Keep it on you at all times. You'll need to reactivate the phone hourly, otherwise your contact lens will lose sync with the phone, and only you can activate the phone. Given that, when you arrive at Harbin, I'll make sure to have your transportation ready. Check your phone upon arrival, it'll tell you what vehicle to look for. Any questions?"*

"No. I'm good for now."

"Best of luck, and be careful."

The phone line went dead and she pocketed the phone.

She turned to Mrs. Yang and asked, "What's next?"

"Follow me, ma'am."

Mrs. Yang led her back down the same hall through which they'd entered, but instead of leading to the lobby, it took them to a set of stairs going down. Alicia was certain that the lobby had been here. It was a straight hall—no way could she have gotten turned around.

"Hold up. Where's the lobby?" Alicia asked.

Mrs. Yang simply motioned toward the stairs. "Ma'am, the train is waiting for you."

"Train?"

As Alicia spoke, she heard a click behind her and turned back—only to find herself facing a blank wall.

"Wait a minute," she said. "Where the hell's the hallway? Where's the locker room?" She spun around and realized she was standing in the room by herself. "Where's Mrs. Yang?"

The matronly old woman was gone.

"What the hell is going on?"

Alicia's mind raced as she pushed against a seemingly solid wood panel. Were the hallways on some kind of casters and moved silently while her back was turned? This entire building had suddenly taken on a haunted house vibe.

"I hate funhouses! Is anyone listening?" She spun again in a quick circle, but saw no movement, and heard no response to her yelled question.

Whatever was going on, at this point Alicia had nowhere to go but down.

She descended the stairs. They led to a tiny train platform, no more than ten feet wide, where a sleek railway car was already waiting, its doors open. Once again, Alicia had no choice but to board.

The doors slid closed behind her, and a disembodied voice announced, *"The train will be departing in ten seconds. Please hold on to a rail or you will likely be thrown backward. This is your only warning."*

"Lovely." Alicia took a seat and gripped one of the poles.

"Five seconds. Four. Three. Two. One."

Alicia slid backward as the train accelerated at a rate rivaling that of a race car. Within seconds, wind keened loudly outside as the train flew through the darkness.

Given the train's obvious speed, Alicia had no idea how long it would take to arrive at her destination. And yet the minutes passed, and all she saw was darkness. She checked her phone repeatedly. Thirty minutes. Forty. An hour.

How long is this tunnel?

Alicia startled awake and for a second thought she'd gone blind.

It was still nearly pitch black in the train compartment as she traveled at unimaginable speeds along the underground track. Reaching for her phone, she noticed that she hadn't just taken a little nap, she'd been asleep for nearly five hours.

Through her right eye, she saw scrolling messages as her contact lens reactivated.

Alicia stretched and felt like a new person after that long nap. Six hours in total had passed before she felt a shudder in the cabin. The howling sounds of the wind changed their pitch as the train decelerated. The disembodied voice returned. *"We will be arriving at the Harbin Safe House in approximately five minutes. Please disembark only after the train has come to a complete stop."*

Harbin?

Wow! That was much faster than she could have ever imagined. Alicia had figured the train might have taken her across the Taiwan Straits to Hangzhou or maybe even Shanghai, but Harbin? That was something like 1,400 miles away.

She did the math in her head and supposed it could be possible—*if* the Outfit had an underground train that ran under the East China Sea, under the Koreas, and all the way up to Harbin. Was it even possible? And all of this dedicated to the Outfit's own personal use, a train that rivaled the speed of Japan's bullet train?

Evidently, the Outfit had exactly that kind of train.

When the doors opened, Alicia stepped out. An elderly man waited on the platform, and greeted her with a salute.

"Miss Yoder," he said with a thick Chinese accent, "can I please see your ID?"

After Alicia went through the process of mutual identification using the coin, the old man gestured to the stairs behind him.

"Welcome to Harbin, Miss Yoder. Your transportation will be waiting outside."

CHAPTER FIFTEEN

Sitting in the back of a taxi, Alicia took in the sights, such as they were, as they drove through Yichun. The city's main claim to fame, evidently, was their lumber and mining industry. It was a modest rural city, nothing like Taipei or New York, yet it was odd how densely packed it was for a relatively small population. Maybe it wasn't in the Chinese DNA to create anything that resembled a suburb in the U.S. It was either ultra-dense packed in housing, or rural expanses where the next-door neighbor was practically in another time zone.

The driver motioned to the right, "That's the Shunhe Department Store. Very famous. Very very famous."

Alicia studied the crowded open-air market, packed with hundreds of tiny stalls strewn throughout a large plaza, all of them occupying every nook and cranny between the established brick-and-mortar locations. Even though Alicia might have come from the farming areas of Pennsylvania, she was pretty sure the Amish had set up more extensive shopping venues than this place.

"Very very very famous." The driver pointed at another location, seemingly at random.

She nodded as her only response, while seriously questioning this guy's opinion on what ranked as a famous place.

The navigation device spoke through a crackling and obviously damaged speaker, *"Head west on Daxue Road toward Hongqi Street."*

"We are going to the motorcycle store, right?"

"Yes, yes, yes. A very famous location. I'll show you."

The navigation device began blurting out a series of confusing directions as they approached a roundabout.

"At the roundabout, take the 2nd exit and stay on Hongqi Street heading to Xuefu Street, Keji Blvd, Technology Avenue, Guang fu Road, Bin jiang Road, Wan xin Street, He da Hwy."

It was almost as if the thing was having a seizure trying to describe all the tiny roads the roundabout connected.

"Turn right onto Guang fu West Road."

The taxi took the first right.

"Turn left onto Jian ye Lane."

Alicia spotted a familiar logo to the right and breathed a sigh of relief.

"Turn right onto West Chang'an Road."

The taxi pulled up to the small Yamaha motorcycle store sandwiched between a noodle shop and a book store. Just as the driver was going to speak, Alicia pointed at the store and said, "The very very very very famous Yamaha store. I can see that."

The driver gave her a look that she couldn't quite translate, but he didn't seem amused. He tapped impatiently on the computer screen, which was displaying the price for the fare.

Alicia paid the man, hopped out of the car and the taxi sped away.

Shivering from the chill in the air, she was thankful it was near summer time in this part of the world. If she recalled her geography correctly, they weren't too far from Siberia, and if this area was chilly now, she could only imagine what it would be like in the winter. Alicia suddenly felt grateful for the insulation provided by the vest she wore under her military uniform's jacket.

She walked into the store's equivalent of a parking lot, which was really nothing more than a sort of concrete patio of sorts. It had about twenty different motorcycles displayed around its storefront and she couldn't help but smile at the memories that replayed in her mind.

Her father had long ago taught each of the kids how to drive a manual transmission car as well as the basics on how to operate a motorcycle, though he refused let them drive anything with only two wheels unless he was there to supervise.

Her father's words rang loudly in her mind. *"At least with a car, you have some metal between you and the idiot next to you. It's not that I don't trust your ability to make good choices, it's that I don't trust everyone else on the road."*

Little did he know that when she was at Princeton, one of her roommates had a Honda Rebel 500 that Alicia would occasionally play around with. She'd relished the fun of riding the motorcycle around school with the wind in her face.

As she examined the bikes on display, she was relieved to see all the familiar parts and pieces where she expected them to be. Front brake lever on the right-hand side of the handlebar, clutch was on the left. The familiar gear shift and rear brake were next to the left and right foot pegs respectively, and she trailed her hand over the center console and smiled.

Alicia was surprised at how excited she felt at the idea of riding a bike again.

A middle-aged man walked out of the tiny glass-enclosed office and said, "Can I help you?"

A green square framed the salesman's face and in front of her hovered the man's name and occupation: *Kenly Xing, salesman for Yamaha Motor China Co., Ltd.* It was going to take a while for her to get used to that contact lens projecting people's names and occupations into her eye.

Alicia nodded. "Which of these bikes is powerful enough to go off-road."

"What do you mean?" The man looked puzzled.

"Well, if I were to ride the motorcycle off of the normal highway—"

"That's not recommended."

Alicia's brow furrowed and she continued, "Nonetheless, if that's what I needed to do, which of these has the strongest engine?"

The man walked over to one of the motorcycles and patted its seat. "This one has a 250-cc engine. It's the most powerful one we carry."

Alicia looked over the bike and tapped one of the tires with her boot. "These are very smooth tires; will they have traction off the road?"

"That's not recommended, you know."

"I *know* it's not recommended." Alicia was getting annoyed at the man. This wasn't how a person gets a sale... she pulled in a deep breath and let it out slowly, realizing she was in China. The communists didn't necessarily have the same motivations that she was used to in a capitalistic society. This guy was getting paid regardless, and probably didn't give a crap about whether he sold anything or not. "How much gas can it hold?"

"The tank's capacity is 11.5 liters. More than enough."

How the hell does this guy know what enough is? *Breathe, Alicia, just breathe.*

Alicia did the mental math on how far she needed to go and realized this would probably be fine. "Okay, how much?"

"Do you have cash?" The man asked.

She had some, but certainly not enough to buy a motorcycle. "I have a credit card."

The man shook his head. "We don't take that."

Alicia glanced at the office where he'd just walked out of and saw several credit card logos displayed prominently on the window. She pointed at the office and said, "The Yamaha office you just walked out of seems to say differently. See that Visa logo, it says you accept Visa."

"It's wrong." The man didn't even glance backwards. "I accept cash. If you don't have cash, then you have a good day." He turned and walked back into the tiny glass-enclosed store, sat on a stool and began fiddling with whatever was on his cell phone.

Alicia's jaw dropped and felt a surge of irrational anger wash over her. She took several steps back and then marched away from the store to breathe and collect her thoughts.

Her stomach growled as she spied a street hawker with a steaming kettle and a portable wok tossing food together for a waiting customer.

She watched as the elderly man tossed the food in a searing-hot wok, and Alicia knew without question that this man had been cooking like this for much longer than she'd been alive.

As he served up the customer, he looked over at her and said, "Today I'm cooking Cantonese style. You want beef chow fun?"

With her mouth watering, she nodded.

"That will be ten RMB."

She paid the man the equivalent of one dollar and forty cents and watched as the man, who had to be in his seventies, retrieved wide rice noodles from the steaming water, and quickly made short work of the other ingredients as he began tossing marinated beef slices in the sizzling wok, a squirt of dark liquid from one plastic bottle, a dollop of a sauce from a separate container, and it was almost like an orchestral arrangement as the man tossed everything together unerringly and within minutes poured a steaming-hot noodle dish into a wooden bowl, quickly sliced up some tomatoes, cucumbers, and red peppers, and handed it to her with a set of chopsticks.

As she tasted her food, which was delicious, the man was already preparing another customer's order. It was at that moment that Alicia realized that she'd love to travel some day and explore places like this. Tiny out of the way places like this remote area had so much to show people, only if they looked. There was always good in the world. And there were always talented people, true stars that were only known to those who lived in the area.

She wolfed down her meal and even though her belly was full, Alicia scooped the last of the noodles into her mouth and handed her dish and chopsticks to an elderly woman who wiped the plate clean, sprayed it with some liquid from a squirt bottle and put it back on the cart for the cook to hand out once again.

Alicia's stomach gurgled as she realized how unsanitary

this process was and forcibly turned, trying to ignore what she'd just witnessed.

Just as she was about to pull out her phone and see if there was any other place she could go that would sell her the transportation that she needed, she heard a commotion nearby.

"Look out for shorty!"

"Chase her, look at how she runs!"

"She's just an overgrown duck, look at her waddling!"

Alicia looked across the street and caught sight of four teenage boys teasing a fleeing child who had no chance of outrunning them.

With a surge of anger she yelled, "Pick on someone your own size, you cowards!"

"Oh, shut up and do something about it!"

Alicia bolted from her position and ran across the street, just barely dodging a passing motor scooter.

The boys' eyes widened as they realized she'd called their bluff and scattered in all directions. They hadn't been close enough for the HUD of her contact lens to display any information, and the young girl came up as "Subject Unknown." She must have been too young and not in any database yet.

She approached the still-crying girl who'd been teased by them and realized that she was older than Alicia had initially thought. Probably thirteen or so. The girl was a dwarf and had likely suffered this type of teasing for most of her life. Alicia crouched down and said, "It's okay. You don't need to let them upset you like that."

The girl was struggling to breathe from having been chased, and Alicia wiped away the girl's tears and shook her head. "The boys are gone. They're just stupid and don't know any better."

The girl sobbed and looked miserable. "They're right. I'm short and useless."

"Nonsense!"

The girl was startled by the ferocity of Alicia's forceful response.

Alicia cupped the girl's chin in her hand and said, "I want you to remember this: God only lets things grow until they're perfect. For some it takes longer than others... for you it clearly didn't take as long."

The girl's mouth dropped open as she stared wide-eyed at Alicia, not knowing how to respond.

"Lin, have the neighborhood boys been terrible to you again?"

Alicia turned and noticed the motorcycle shopkeeper standing behind her as the girl held up her arms and cried out to her father.

The man picked her up and rubbed her back as she cried on his shoulder. He looked at Alicia and sighed. "Are you still interested in the motorcycle?"

Alicia stood and felt a surge of hope. "I am."

He tilted his head in the direction of the store and said, "Let's go find you a proper bike."

It took all the self-control she had to not smile or have any outward reaction other than to follow the man as he carried his daughter across the street and back to the shop.

He handed the girl his phone and said, "You can play in the office until I'm done with this nice lady."

The man turned to Alicia and with a sheepish expression said, "I checked and it seems like Visa may be okay. It just requires a bit of paperwork."

Alicia nodded, and at this point she didn't really care why he'd changed his mind. She pointed at the motorcycle they'd previously looked at and said, "How about that one?"

The man pressed his lips together and said, "You mean to take it off the road?"

She let out a sound that could only be described as a honk as Alicia choked on the laugh that had nearly burst out of her. "Yes. I need to use it off the road."

The salesman motioned for her to follow and he led Alicia to the back of the lot. "This might be suitable."

Alicia smiled as she noticed the knobby wheels for added traction in the dirt. "250-cc motor?"

"Yes, and an 11.5-liter gas tank, which I will be happy to fill for you."

Alicia dug out her, or rather the Outfit's credit card and handed it to the salesman. "Sold."

At this stage, the price really didn't matter. She needed what she needed.

"Do you have a helmet? It is required by law, but most police don't seem to enforce it."

"I'll take one. I think I need a size medium."

"Just to be sure," the man pulled out a measuring tape and said, "please measure the circumference of your head and tell me what it is."

She wrapped the measuring tape around the top of her head and then looked at the measurement. "Fifty-six centimeters."

"I would suggest a small. It is better for safety if the helmet is a little tight rather than too lose."

Alicia nodded. "Okay, I'll try the small."

The salesman patted the black bike and said, "I think I have one that is the correct size that matches the bike's colors very well. I'll be right back."

Alicia patted the seat of the motorcycle and couldn't help but smile at the idea of riding it around, but at the same time she kept reminding herself that there was a lot of potentially unpleasant business ahead. Those sobering thoughts helped keep her exuberance in check.

The man came out with some paperwork and a large box, which he handed to her. "First, try on the helmet."

She opened the box, removed the full face-mask helmet and smiled. It was so shiny and new. Not even a hint of a blemish on it.

Alicia removed the care instructions from inside the helmet, pulled it over her head and even though it was snug, it was a comfortable fit. She flipped up the visor and smiled, "This will work."

The salesman nodded and handed Alicia her credit card and some papers to sign.

Even though she wasn't paying for it, the Outfit was, Alicia noticed the price and was surprised at how relatively inexpensive it was. It made her think of the possibility of maybe getting one when she was back in the states, but she doubted it would be this cheap over there. This price was likely due to the motorcycle being manufactured in China, regardless of the brand it was associated with. As soon she finished signing, the man handed her a set of keys and patted the gas tank. "It's already full."

Alicia shook hands with the salesman, who looked tired and much less enthused about the sale than she was.

The man returned to his office, and Alicia waved to his daughter who was looking in her direction.

The girl smiled, and then hid her face behind her father's leg.

With Alicia's heart thumping loudly, she pulled out her phone, and tapped on the eyeball icon. This time it pulled up several options and she selected option number two.

Alicia straddled the motorcycle, flipped up the kickstand, inserted the key, held in the clutch and started the motorcycle.

It started right away and the feeling of the engine rumbling underneath her was an awesome experience.

She flipped down her visor, put the bike into first gear and slowly let out the clutch.

The bike inched forward and Alicia panned her gaze across the street, and for the first time she understood the term some gamers around her had used: Augmented Reality had been sort of an abstract thing in her mind, but now with her contact lens in place and the magic of the programming that Brice had put together, she saw the street as it really was, but it now had an arrow pointing to the right.

It was the direction she needed to go.

With a sense of fear and excitement, Alicia let out the clutch and advanced onto the street. It was now time for the truly dangerous part of the mission.

CHAPTER
SIXTEEN

Alicia made her way to within a mile of her destination and was surprised at how well the motorcycle had taken to the uneven terrain. It was her thighs that were having trouble with the trip. She'd learned fairly quickly that going over rough terrain while resting on her backside like she normally would when riding was a wholly uncomfortable and jarring experience. Instead, she had to put more of her weight on the foot pegs, effectively raising her butt up off the seat so that when she hit the heavy bumps and ruts in the road, she could use her legs to more easily absorb the pounding the motorcycle took from the rough path she traveled.

The green arrow still showed that her path continued straight ahead, but in the overhead map it showed that she'd be taking a right into a hidden valley.

Slowing down, she shifted into neutral and rested for a moment, removing her helmet and breathed a sigh of relief as a cool breeze blew across the forest trail. She wiped away her sweat-dampened hair and put her phone to her ear as she checked in with Brice.

The phone rang once and it was immediately picked up. "I'm approaching the site."

"I can tell. Good progress, and I can confirm that General Hong is currently enroute to Beijing to attend a meeting of the military heads, as we thought would happen."

Alicia nodded. "Good. That'll make things easier on me. Do you know how much time I have before he might come back and blow my cover?"

"Don't depend on that as your limiting factor." Brice warned. *"You need to go in, complete your objective as quickly as possible, and get across the border as we talked about. Remember, he doesn't need to be there to blow your cover, all it takes is a phone call and him talking to the wrong person. Don't be over-confident in any plan, because that's how things go to hell."*

"Understood." Alicia took the admonishment in stride. For a moment she'd allowed herself to think this was going to be easy. But Brice was right, she needed to always act as if any and all parts of this plan could go awry. "I'm going in. I probably won't be in communication again until I'm running out of here like the hounds of hell are chasing me."

"Don't think that they won't be." Brice said. *"Obviously, you're the best judge of conditions on the ground, but realize that*

however you plan on getting out, almost certainly you're going to have a tough time of it until you make it out of the country. Best of luck, and just so you know, I'll do what I can to tie up the base's phone lines for the next twelve hours or so."

"Thanks, anything you do is appreciated. I'll talk to you on the flip-side."

Alicia pocketed her phone and decided to strap her helmet down onto the back of her seat. She put on her soft PLA camo cap, shifted into first and slowly let out the clutch.

She rode the motorcycle along an even and well-trodden dirt road, giving her thighs a bit of rest. It only took about two minutes for her to come upon the turn off to the right.

With the cool wind blowing in her hair, she felt invigorated even as she spied the first of the soldiers, whose only reaction was to look in her direction as she rode past them.

It was another quarter mile or so before she slowed and approached the manned entrance to the base.

Several soldiers approached, their weapons hung limply at their sides, more curious than concerned.

Alicia switched off her bike, then got off and pocketed the keys as one of the men called out, "Have you taken a wrong turn somewhere, comrade?"

She shook her head and gave the man a toothy grin. "I'm here on General Hong Zuocheng's orders."

"Oh?"

Another soldier approached and asked, "Do you have a copy of these orders that we can inspect?"

"No. They're not those kind of orders." There were five soldiers at the entrance, and three of them had approached, one within arm's reach. Their identities flickered onto her HUD, cataloging them for a later report she suspected she'd have to write. She spoke loud enough for the three of them to hear her. "I've been sent to help Colonel Xi... relax a bit."

The nearest soldier burst out with a laugh, and the other two smiled. They knew what "relax" was a euphemism for, or at least they certainly believed they did.

The nearest soldier stared at her, his head tilted, and a wolfish grin on his face. He approached, dragging his gaze up and down her body, when suddenly he reached out and grabbed a handful of Alicia's ass, giving it a firm squeeze, his smile growing larger, exposing his misaligned and chipped teeth. "Maybe after you help the Colonel 'relax' you can experience what it's like to be with a real experienced soldier."

In her mind, Alicia felt another subtle click as a piece of a mental puzzle fell into place. Purpose. Purpose to accomplish her mission and a growing desire to not be held hostage by the fears she'd been running from since being rescued from the streets.

A sense of calm determination fell over Alicia as she turned to the soldier and glanced at his collar. She smiled, reached up to his face and dragged her fingertips along his jawline.

In a blur of motion Alicia slapped him hard across the face, dropped low, sweeping his legs out from under him.

The corporal crashed onto ground and she yelled, "I'm a proud Staff Sergeant of the People's Liberation Army, and I honor my senior enlisted and officers alike! You need to remember who you are, corporal. Remember who you are, and what your role is in our army. If you fail to remember this, I will ensure that this incident is reported directly to General Hong. Do you hear me? Do you?"

"I do!" The corporal scrambled to his feet and saluted Alicia. "I'm sorry, Sergeant. I apologize for my behavior. It will *not* happen again! I swear to you."

The other soldiers motioned to the ones manning the guard gate and the metal barrier began lowering into the ground.

She looked over at the two other soldiers, and realized that she outranked both of them. "Where can I find Colonel Xi?"

One of the men stepped forward and said, "I just recently left the research and tactics building, and he was there. I can escort you if you like."

Alicia hopped onto her motorcycle and hitched her thumb to the seat. "Hop aboard, it'll be quicker that way."

The soldier hesitated and held a worried expression.

"Come on, you're not afraid of riding on a bike with a woman, are you?" Alicia felt a sense of amusement as she watched the soldier screw up his courage and finally hopped onto the back half of the seat.

Alicia started the bike and said, "Unless you want to fall off, you probably want to hold on."

The soldier's voice quavered. "Where?"

She rolled her eyes and said, "Just hold onto my waist."

The moment he did, she sped forward and the soldier grunted with fear as he held on for dear life.

"Far end of the valley. Building with the yellow doors."

Alicia nodded and then accelerated across the level ground, going faster than she'd yet been able to on this motorcycle.

Feeling the stinging cold of the wind at speed normally brought a smile to Alicia's face, but the reason she smiled this time was from the image burnt into her mind of the soldier after she'd dumped him on his ass. More than that, she smiled because of what him being on his ass *meant*.

For one of the first times in her life, she'd pushed back against someone wronging her.

She had a hard time imagining how this mission would progress, but if nothing else, she had that moment to remember for as long as she lived.

The so-called research and tactics building was about half of a mile from the entrance of the base, and as Alicia opened the kickstand and shut off the motorcycle, the soldier who'd accompanied her nearly fell to the ground as he scrambled to get off the bike.

Alicia did her best to hide any of her reactions to the

soldier's behavior, who was clearly freaked out about having been on the motorcycle. She was both amused and somewhat put off by how afraid the soldier had been. His bearhug across her waist left a dull throbbing pain across her lower abdomen, something that seemed to be coming up more and more. Either she was going to be getting her period early or there was something going on down there. A problem worth checking out... but not here, and not now.

As the panic-stricken sergeant worked to calm himself down and get things together, Alicia finger-combed her hair and with a bit of creative hair manipulation, she managed to bundle it all up under her cap.

"Are you good now?" Alicia asked.

The soldier nodded and gave her a queasy smile. "I've never been on a motorcycle before."

"You don't say?" Alicia shook her head and gave the man a knowing grin. She motioned to the yellow doors. "Lead me to the Colonel."

They walked into the building and the first thing Alicia noticed was the far off sound of a phone ringing.

No, not just a phone, multiple phones were ringing and seemingly going unanswered.

"I'll do what I can to tie up the base's phone lines for the next twelve hours or so."

Alicia pressed her lips tightly together and clenched her jaw so as not to burst out laughing. Brice was doing exactly what he had promised.

Knowing him, he probably infected a bunch of

computers with a virus that autodialed all of the phones on the base.

The building smelled of mildew. Not the kind of scent she'd have expected in a place that conducted research on deadly things.

They walked along a cinder-block hallway, and Alicia paid careful attention to the number of intersecting passages they'd crossed and soon enough they were at an unmarked door that was partially ajar.

"Hello? Hello?" A man's frustrated voice leaked from within the office, following by the sound of a receiver being slammed down onto a handset.

Alicia motioned to the sergeant. "You can leave me now."

The soldier nodded and walked back the way they'd come.

Alicia watched as the receding soldier pulled his phone from one of his pockets, and put it to his hear. "Hello? Who is this?"

His voice echoed down the hall as he pocketed his phone and Alicia heard the phone in the Colonel's office start ringing again. *"Who the hell is calling?"*

Alicia knocked on the door and walked in. Sitting behind a desk was a familiar face. One she'd only seen in electronic form.

Colonel Xi slammed the phone down and picked up his buzzing cell phone. "What is it?" The man's face contorted with frustration. "Hello?" He hung up the cell phone and his office phone began ringing yet again. He looked up at her. "Do you know what's going on with the phones?"

She smiled and motioned for him to follow her. "Colonel Xi, I'm here on behalf of General Hong. Let's go for a walk, and believe me, you'll want to leave your phone behind. Someone in Beijing was running some kind of comms test and it has messed up all of the phone lines in this area."

The Colonel stood and shook his head. "I can't get anything done with all of this noise." He walked around his desk and they shook hands. "You have me at a disadvantage, you know my name, but I don't have yours."

Alicia smiled. "Staff Sergeant Ye Ting." She had to almost yell it as all the phones in the building seemed to be ringing at once. "You can just call me Ting. Let's get out of here, the noise is getting on my nerves as well."

Alicia led them back the way she'd come and as they stepped out of the building, the Colonel's gaze was distracted by the motorcycle. "Is that yours?"

She nodded. "It is."

The colonel walked over to the motorcycle and pause, breathed in the late afternoon breeze and smiled. "Do you hear that?"

"Hear what?" Alicia asked.

"Exactly. None of those damned phones ringing." He held a shaking hand up to his head for a brief moment. Then looked over at Alicia and said, "So, General Hong sent you?"

"He did." Alicia nodded, feeling a bit nervous about the

lie. “Colonel, I was told about your memory problems and I’m here to try and help.”

“Oh, thank goodness! Finally.” The man’s eyes widened and he smiled. “Please, call me Bo, and I’m afraid the memory issues are very real. I need… I just need my memories back. I get flashes, but they only make the gaps in my memory seem more pronounced.”

Alicia knew the feeling.

“And the constant ringing of those damned phones isn’t helping. It makes it feel like knives are stabbing into my eyes. I’m sorry… Ting, was it? Do we know each other and I’m just not remembering?”

Alicia noticed soldiers coming out of some of the nearby buildings, and she pointed at the motorcycle. “Bo, do you want to take a quick ride with me?”

“Where? I mean, yes, but where to?”

Alicia straddled the motorcycle and started it. She pointed at the north end of the valley where there were no buildings and just an open meadow up to the edge of what looked more like an unclimbable cliff than a sloped mountain. “Over there, that’ll give us an opportunity to talk undisturbed.”

Bo hopped onto the motorcycle with practiced ease and gently held onto Alicia’s waist as she accelerated away from the rest of the base’s inhabitants.

Alicia and Bo walked side by side as the Colonel explained the problems he'd been having.

"Ting, I'll be honest, it's been driving me crazy the idea that people know me as someone who I barely recognize. They speak about things that we've done together and it just draws a complete blank in my mind. It's frustrating beyond words."

Alicia listened and again felt the strange kinship with the struggles this man was enduring. She had her own blank spaces within her memories, and the more he talked, the more she began wondering whether or not she herself had undergone some kind of brainwashing technique. She knew nothing of how the Outfit had managed to blank out his entire history. And even though she had nowhere near the issues he was going through, she still had those annoying gaps and worried about their origin.

Mason's explanation about some sort of multiverse, and the effects of it on her memories, still felt dubious at best. That seemed much less believable than whatever was done to this poor man.

But she was here on a mission, and part of that mission was to give this man back what was missing. The way it was explained to her was that his memories were locked behind multi-level verbal cues that were not unlike solutions to a puzzle. They were all words or phrases that he was highly unlikely to ever hear in his day-to-day life, and she was about to employ the first of those words.

"Bo, do you understand English?"

He shook his head. "Not more than a few words here and there. I've never had the need to learn. Why?"

"There's a word in English called *'providence'* – it's a word that means the protective care of God or of nature as a spiritual power. It's a concept that I sometimes think about. Like that there's a higher power watching over us. Things that happen—whether it's the loss of memory, or a tragic event —I truly believe they happen for a reason, and in the end, it happens for the better. What do you think?"

Bo stopped walking and stared at the ground. He blinked repeatedly and wasn't speaking.

She touched the back of his arm. "Are you okay?"

He shuddered for a moment and nodded. "I am. I just had a strange sensation almost like I was here in this place before. Talking with you... or maybe it wasn't you. Something about this," he pointed with both hands at their surroundings, "all of this seems foreign yet familiar. I'm not sure." His brows furrowed and he continued walking.

The effect of the keyword was both dramatic and lackluster. Alicia wasn't sure what to expect, but maybe a sense of déjà vu was the appropriate or expected results. She readied the second word and asked, "Have you always envisioned yourself as a military officer? Did you have any other ambitions growing up?"

"I don't remember my childhood at all." Bo grimaced and the furrow between his eyebrows deepened. "As I'm trying to remember, it almost seems like I can picture something. No, wait... I remember fishing. I just... I'm not sure. I'm sorry."

Alicia felt a wave of guilt as she saw the man plainly struggling with thoughts that were almost within reach. It was something she related to all too well. "You know, as a child I always wanted to be like my father. He was a *mason*, and built our childhood home."

Bo grunted as he put his hands to the sides of his head and clenched his jaw.

"What's wrong?" She asked, as the man stumbled to one knee, obviously in some kind of pain.

"My head. It's something... wrong." His voice strained with whatever his mind was going through.

Wracked with guilt over the man's agony, Alicia rushed to his side and whispered the third and final phrase, "*Chris Xiang.*"

He gasped and would have fallen face forward if Alicia hadn't grabbed his shoulders and held him upright.

The man's eyes were closed, his breathing was ragged, and he was sweating profusely.

"Bo, are you okay? Can you hear me."

He remained unresponsive for a full thirty seconds.

Alicia put her hand against his chest, and his heart was racing faster than she could count. Whatever it was that the Outfit had done to this man, it seemed inhumane, even if he supposedly volunteered for this mission.

"Bo, can you hear me?"

His eyes fluttered and he shook his head.

"Are you there?"

Bo's eyes opened, they were bloodshot, and he looked

directly at her, his chin quivered. "Bo was my brother; my name is Chris."

The man collapsed into her arms and began weeping.

Wracking sobs of anguish as Bo—no, Chris—muttered words about his brother being dead.

"I felt his death in my chest. I've been feeling it since becoming aware on that remote beach."

Alicia had no idea what to do as the man cried. She rubbed his back and made soothing noises as if comforting a child. "It'll be okay."

"He was my twin. It'll never be okay." And the man's entire body shook as he experienced a level of grief that seemed unimaginable.

A twin. Likely identical. All the pieces connected and locked into place in Alicia's mind. All the intelligence reports. The passing comments from Mason and Brice. Now it made sense. Somehow the Outfit had managed to sneak a twin into a position of consequence for national security. The full scope of the plan likely wouldn't ever be explained to her. At least, not to her satisfaction. But a little piece of the puzzle bothering her had snapped into place. It made sense.

Wiping the man's face with her sleeve, Alicia found herself in the odd position of mothering someone who was older than her by more than a couple of years.

It took several minutes before Chris managed to gain any semblance of control over his grief and in the end, he gave Alicia a hug and whispered, "Thank you."

She patted him awkwardly on the arm and smiled. “Are you okay? Can you remember everything?”

“I remember everything, even the implanted, phantom memories left over from my brother.” The man stood and shook his head. “But I am far, *far* from okay.” He looked at their surroundings and held a grim expression. “We need to burn this place to the ground.”

CHAPTER
SEVENTEEN

It was late at night and Alicia and Chris were in his private sleeping quarters. The building had grown silent as everyone had eventually decided to disconnect the phone lines and turn off their cell phones. Brice's trick had effectively annoyed the entire base into isolating itself, which was brilliant. But now what?

Alicia sat in front of the tiny desk in Chris's room as the faux Colonel sat on the edge of his bed and grinned at her. "What are you smiling about?"

He shrugged. "I guess it's just lucky that the second-ranked officer on the base gets his own room. Were it anyone else other than the general, we'd be dealing with bunk beds and at least a half dozen or more roommates. What time is it?"

She looked at her phone, likely the only one on the base that hadn't been powered off, and said, "Not quite midnight."

They'd already talked tactics before coming back into the building, knowing that they couldn't dismiss the possibility of his room having a listening device. Theirs was a common goal: destroy the content from the vials that were stolen from New Arcadia and somehow get the hell out without being captured or killed. None of these things were a sure thing, but the first thing they needed to do was wait for midnight.

That was when the night watch was on duty, and there were less people patrolling the area.

Chris lifted his mattress and retrieved a large hunting knife that looked very reminiscent of the kind that Rambo had made famous. He offered the hilt to her, but she shook her head, lifted the side of her jacket, and displayed her own sheathed weapon. "You know how to use it?"

She gave him a venomous glare.

He held up his hands and grinned. "Hey, I had to ask." Chris attached the Rambo knife's sheath to his belt, drew out the knife and then reseated it. "I'm ready."

Alicia hopped up onto her feet and nodded. "You lead."

With the sound of a diesel generator humming nearby, Alicia puzzled over the writing on one of the twenty-five-kilo bags of fertilizer and motioned for Chris. He was standing outside the supply shed, watching as a vehicle patrolled the base's perimeter. "Hey, come here for a minute. I stopped learning Chinese when I was ten, and none of what I learned covered these words. I don't recognize some of these words; can you tell me what the ingredients are in this fertilizer?

Chris leaned down as Alicia put the light coming from her phone up against the bag. "It says it's a nitrogen fertilizer made from ground limestone, cow manure, calcium sulphate, dolomite granules, ammonium nitrate, and urea." He turned to her and asked, "Are you sure this will work? Didn't you say the virus needs to be burned at over 1,000 degrees to even have a chance of breaking down?"

"Assuming we know what was taken, it's not a virus, but actually a protein of sorts." Alicia shrugged. "I might have dropped out of grad school, but I spent nearly six years at one of the best schools in the world, pretty much acing my undergraduate studies, and I remember my organic chemistry pretty well. If we can get the ammonium nitrate in this fertilizer to melt and start an exothermic chain reaction, the explosion should raise temperatures to over 3,000 degrees within the reach of the fireball."

"How much of this do we need?"

She looked across the empty field at the shadowy outline of a large building and then down at the pallet. "I figure there's about 60 bags on this pallet, which is roughly about 1.5 tons of this stuff." She counted up the pallets and said, "Ten pallets, so roughly fifteen tons of nitrogen-rich fertilizer. I'd say we need all of it, just to be sure."

Chris's eyes widened. "All of it?"

"Well, yeah. I'd rather not take any chances with something that has a hundred percent fatality rate. Now, I'm not a physics person, the math involved for those equations always were a problem for me, but I figure the shock wave it'll produce is going to result in that entire building acting like a giant grenade. We won't want to be anywhere in the area when it goes off." She frowned. "The question is, how are we going to get all of this," she pointed to the building about one-hundred yards away, "over there?"

Chris stared in the direction of a patrol vehicle as it approached on its normal sweep of the area and chuckled. "Let's see if we can get some help." He made large sweeping motions with his arms, trying to get the soldier's attention just as he was about to pass them by.

The vehicle's brakes squeaked as the car skidded to a halt.

Chris motioned for the driver and yelled, "Come here, comrade."

The soldier hopped out of the still-running vehicle and walked over with a puzzled expression.

Alicia recognized the corporal. It was the same snaggle-toothed soldier who'd grabbed her ass when she first arrived at the base.

The man's eyes widened as he spotted her standing next to the Colonel. "Sir, how can I help?"

Chris motioned in the direction of the open supply shed. “We need this shed emptied for a shipment that will be arriving first thing in the morning. Do you know anyone on duty who can operate the forklift?”

“Sir, I know how, and I’d love to help, but I’m on patrol right now. I can do it after my shift, if that’s okay?”

“I suppose you didn’t catch that I need this shed empty by *first thing in the morning*.” Chris hitched his thumb toward the nearby barracks. “Wake someone to cover your patrol while you do this.” He pointed at the far end of the meadow. “I need the contents of this shed deposited in the receiving area of the research and tactics building, understood?”

“Understood. Anything else, sir?”

Chris nodded. “Make sure that both fuel tanks for the generators in that building have been filled. We can’t take any chances with losing power, especially in that building.”

“Consider it done, sir.”

“Dismissed, corporal.” Chris returned the soldier’s parting salute, and the corporal bolted for the barracks.

Alicia nodded and whispered in English, “That’ll help with the heavy stuff. And smart move on the generator refill, I presume it’s diesel?”

He nodded.

“I don’t suppose you have any timers for any explosive actuators handy do you, and know anyone who can rig them?”

Chris shrugged. “My brother might have known, but none of those memories are with me. I know where the weapons are stored, we can take a look and see what choices we have available."

"Can we?" Alicia felt a bit surprised, but then realized what role Chris played at this base. "I guess as the number two out here, you probably can do whatever you like."

Their attention was drawn to a nearby building as two soldiers raced out of the barracks. One of them was the corporal who piled into the passenger's side of the vehicle while another soldier took the wheel and sped off into the darkness.

"I wouldn't say I can do anything," Chris said, "but I think this much I can do. Let's head over to the supply depot and see if we can find us some explosives."

As the lights flickered inside the small concrete storage facility, Alicia was surprised at how sparse the supplies were inside the building, especially since it served as the supply depot for an entire base.

Several items caught her attention: night vision headgear, several boxes of uniforms, boots, and other non-perishable goods. On the far end of the room, she saw the first sign of any weapons, and it was a dozen or so pistols. Not exactly what she'd have expected to find.

She grabbed the night vision gear, which seemed to be attached to a helmet, and clipped it onto her belt for the moment. Alicia had plans for that. "Is this the supply room for the *entire* base? It seems like fairly meager pickings."

"I'm surprised they have as much as they do, to be honest." Chris locked the door behind them and panned his gaze across the shelves. "You have to realize how out of the way this place is. There's no electricity or other utilities running into this camp, and everything is run off of solar panels, batteries, and generators. And if I recall, this place has one or two communication hardwires coming in from the nearest city. If it weren't for a fairly regular delivery of diesel and the equivalent of MREs, this place would probably cease to operate within a month. I was trying to read through the files that the general left for me, but from what I can tell, this place is a pet project for the general and his senior commander in Beijing. It's running on a shoe string budget. He told me that's part of why he's in Beijing, to stir up some more funding without making anyone suspicious."

"Fair enough." Alicia walked deeper into the building, scanning the shelves for anything that looked like it could be useful. She found more pistols, all of them looked fairly generic and certainly unrecognizable to her eyes, since they likely were all Chinese-made. She spotted two short bullpup style rifles, but when she looked at the barrel, it was obvious they were low caliber, and probably wouldn't work for what she needed. She began to feel a growing sense of anxiety at the lack of choices when she stopped and stared at one beast of a rifle. It had a bipod clamped onto its barrel, a huge muzzle brake, and put a smile to her face. She picked it up. "Woah, this sucker weighs a ton."

Chris walked over and ran his fingers over the sticker on the shelf. "It says it's a 'Type 10 sniper rifle with a 5-round magazine, shooting 12.7mm x 108mm multi-function rounds.'"

Alicia readjusted how she held the rifle, which had to weigh about thirty pounds, and studied the unfamiliar layout of the gun. She pressed on what looked like the magazine release button and the heavy cartridge fell into her hand. The magazine was full of red-tipped ammunition. "What's a multi-function round?"

"It could be anything, but luckily there's also a Russian description which clarifies things a bit." Chris ran his finger along the Russian text, which he was clearly able to read. "It says the rounds are made for armor piercing and lateral expansion, which I take it to mean that they expand or explode after penetrating armor, which makes sense since something like this is typically used against hard targets."

"Good enough." Alicia slammed the cartridge back into the magazine well and peered through the attached scope. "All we need is the armor piercing part, but this is going to be dicey."

"Why?" Chris asked.

"I have utterly no idea if this scope is zeroed, and if it is, what distance is it zeroed to." Alicia set the heavy gun down for a moment. "There's only one way to find out."

"Great..." the embedded agent gave her a sour look.

"We've got the rifle and some ammo." He pointed to a wooden box on a bottom shelf. "That box with Russian letters stenciled on it says, 'Grenades'."

Alicia walked over to the box, peered inside, and saw what looked like a bunch of plastic grenades. "During training I threw exactly two grenades, and those were the only grenades I've ever thrown in my life."

"How'd it go?"

She snorted. "I didn't get anyone killed, which I guess means I did okay."

"That's all you can hope for, I suppose." Chris picked up one of the fist-sized grenades and nodded. "Pretty standard. Type 86 high explosive anti-personnel grenade."

Alicia stared at the object in his hand. "But they look like they're made of plastic."

"They are, for the most part. The Chinese have a slightly different design than the American-made variety. This has a core of high explosive in its center, and embedded throughout the hard plastic are over one thousand 2.5mm metal balls. Those balls are about half the size of BBs. They're taking the place of the metal fragments we're used to coming off of the American design, and frankly it's nasty business." He tapped at the side of the grenade and said, "These tiny little pieces of shrapnel travel faster and further than what you'll see with most other fragmentation grenades. Anyone within twenty feet of this thing going off is probably going to have a very bad day as they get turned into Swiss cheese."

Alicia scanned the rest of the shelves in the area and found no other explosives or other rifle options that made sense.

“Hey, put this on.” Chris handed Alicia a holster, which he’d grabbed off one of the shelves.

As she adjusted her belt for the over-the-waistband holster, Chris did the same and handed her one of the pistols from a nearby shelf. She gave the pistol a quick once-over, popped out the magazine, and seated it again.

“It’s a QSZ-92. Basically a 9mm Chinese-built semi-auto with a fifteen-round magazine.” Chris pulled back the slide, chambering a round. He looked over at her as he holstered his weapon. “You should probably carry with one in the chamber. When you need to shoot someone, the last thing you’re going to want is to fumble around with the gun trying to chamber a round.”

Alicia felt a bit uneasy as she chambered one of the rounds and flipped on the safety.

Chris gave her a look.

“What?”

“Did nobody ever tell you that when you carry, you carry with a round chambered? You want as little as possible between you pulling out the gun and firing it. That’s why we train so much in the Outfit. If the gun has a safety—which this one does—you practice thumbing it off when you draw. Especially when you carry concealed. But fumbling to rack the slide of your pistol when drawing in a tense situation?

When fractions of a second matter? Suicide. Believe me, it'll save your life. It's saved mine."

Alicia shook her head and holstered her weapon. When she got back, she'd put herself through every intense pistol class she could. The FBI program wasn't nearly good enough. "To be honest, I'm the one who'll be driving the motorcycle, so if I'm needing my gun while driving us out of here, we're both in a very different situation than either of us had planned."

"Point taken." He grinned as he picked up the sniper rifle. "I'll carry this, you carry the box of grenades. If anyone stops us, it will look a little less odd if I'm the one with the rifle."

Alicia grunted as she picked up the box of what had looked like toy grenades. It was much heavier than it looked.

"You okay?" He asked.

"I'm good."

He unlocked the door and turned off the lights.

Alicia stood in the pitch black, waiting for their eyes to adjust, and also so that when they opened the door, a bunch of light didn't pour out into the nighttime, making it obvious that they were walking out of the building with a bunch of questionable items.

Slowly, some of the shadows within the building began to have varying shades of darkness, a sign her eyes were adjusting pretty quickly. Five feet in front of her, Alicia saw what looked like the Chris's shadowy outline. "You know, I should probably call you a name or be offended or something that I'm the one standing here holding the heavier of the items."

"Haven't you heard?" The shadowy outline chuckled in the darkness. "It's a new world with women always proving how they're better than men."

Alicia smiled and shook her head. "Oh, shut up and let's get a move on."

Chris opened the door into the late-night darkness and somewhere in the distance, they heard the sound of a vehicle approaching.

Alicia wiped strands of sweat-soaked hair from her face as she dumped the last of the large bags of fertilizer into the large open space in the center of the research wing of the building. This research wing was designed so that several experiments could be conducted at the same time while each of them was isolated from the other.

Each of the labs were connected to a shared central office space, making this wing of the building look very much like a hub and spoke type of design, with the central office space being the hub.

Panning her gaze across the so-called hub, it was now filled with a giant pile of nitrogen-rich fertilizer.

Chris pressed another grenade arm-deep into the pile of fertilizer, and then grunted as he grabbed another five-gallon can of diesel, pouring its contents over the large pile of fertilizer.

Alicia smiled. "It looks like you're planting grenades and watering them."

"I'm looking at what I hope to be a bountiful crop." He looked over at her and said, "You realize this is way more fertilizer than that McVeigh guy used in the Oklahoma City bombing, right?"

"I know, I studied that bombing in organic chemistry, if you can believe it. But he also had some high explosives to kick start things and big barrels of fuel oil." Alicia's eyes burned from the fumes coming off of the fertilizer, which smelled strongly of ammonia. She looked over at the receiving area where the soldier had deposited everything. It was only twenty feet away, but it had taken a full two hours of back-breaking work on both of their parts to carry the bags of fertilizer to the center of the room, empty the bags, and repeat the process nearly six hundred times. She looked over at Chris as he nearly slipped walking around the pile of diesel-soaked fertilizer. "Do we have the target ready?"

"I was going to ask you about that." Chris held up a flat panel of duct-taped grenades and motioned to the window above the receiving area's roll-up doors. "That's the window you'll be facing, is this big enough of a target?"

Alicia studied the large panel of explosives and shrugged. "I don't think we have any choice. It's going to have to do."

He looked up at the window and panned his gaze across

the room. "What temperature did you say the diesel needs to be at before it'll ignite?"

"It depends on the type of diesel, but if you get diesel to anywhere from 130 degrees to close to 200 degrees Fahrenheit it'll start to create a vapor that can catch a spark. Below that, diesel won't typically catch fire." Alicia pointed at all of the wood from the pallets and said, "I figured we'll build a fire over on that side of the room that slowly heats this room up. However, this building is made of concrete and the active flame will only last so long, making it an unreliable source of ignition. We need to balance between getting our asses out of this place and setting up the conditions to getting the diesel warmed up enough so that it *can* ignite." She pointed at the window where the grenades were going to be placed and said, "We need an ignition source, which the grenades will certainly take care of, assuming I can hit one them."

Chris looked back and forth between the service door and the pallets. "Okay, I get it. But what if you don't manage to hit the grenades, will this stuff auto-combust at a certain temperature?"

"It will." Alicia frowned as she tried to recall details from her undergraduate years. "And if I'm remembering correctly, it's something like 400 degrees. But I doubt that the fire will get this room anywhere close to hot enough for that."

The agent walked over to the service door, opened it and pointed at the large shadow of a generator, which was currently off. "I don't know crap about chemistry, but I know enough about servicing those things to know that the uncooled exhaust from this type of generator is something close to 700 degrees."

"But how do you know when it's going to turn on?"

"That's easy." Chris waved dismissively. "Generators don't run 24/7, and in this case, they run long enough to charge the bank of batteries this building runs off of, and then shuts down for a cool-down cycle. I can just flip a switch and turn it on manually. But if I disconnect a couple of the cooling pipes, I can route the heated exhaust from this thing into this place—"

"Oh, and it potentially ends up getting this giant pile of crap hot enough to not only set off the diesel, but melt the ammonium nitrate into a volatile form and then—*Boom*!"

"Exactly." Chris nodded. "So, let me see if I have this right. We light the fire over there," he pointed at where the pallets were stacked up near the giant roll-up doors. "I flip the switch on the generator with the routed exhaust, and we get the hell out." He frowned. "Then you either hit the target and the place explodes, or... this is where I think I don't get it—"

"I hit the target and the place doesn't explode right away, or at least I sure hope it doesn't. It'll catch the diesel on fire because some of it is already at its flash point. With the diesel on fire, it'll cause the heat to rise in this building really quickly, which should at some point trigger an exothermic chain reaction and then—"

"Then *boom*?"

"Yes, then the boom." Alicia smiled. "As long as everything works. I think it will, but your exhaust thing is a good safety measure. However, I don't think we can depend on it being the key factor on triggering the explosion. It'll take a lot longer than we need it to. We really need an ignition source or the timing on this is going to be all sorts of awkward." She glanced at her phone, which was smeared with all sorts of unspeakable filth. "How long will it take for you to do your exhaust trick?"

"Give me five minutes. It'll be quick." He pointed at a large set of metal drawers. "There's tools right there. I'll go get the ladder, stick the grenades up there with more duct tape, and you start working the fire angle."

Alicia pulled out the lighter they'd found in one of the office drawers and stepped away from the fuming pile of crap. She looked over at Chris, then at herself, and shook her head. They were covered from head to toe with foul-smelling fertilizer. Amish farmers get pretty dirty when mucking stalls and other chores, but she may never in her life have been as filthy as she was at this moment.

With adrenaline coursing through her, Alicia's skin tingled, and it seemed like all of her senses were heightened. She felt a sense of exhilaration as they put the last bits of their plan into motion. Like getting a runner's high without having to do the actual running part she hated.

If Alicia had any sense whatsoever, she'd be pissing her pants with fear, but for some reason, the real danger she was in calmed her like no drug ever could.

Alicia knew that in less than fifteen minutes, she'd either be dead, incarcerated, or running for her life.

There weren't any other options... and yet the lack of choices somehow *freed* her. A weight lifted from her shoulders. Her fears didn't leave—maybe they never would. But understanding the fear was just another emotion, which meant she could control it.

Control. Control over herself. Over her future.

Or at least the next fifteen minutes of it.

She assembled the pallets into a large pile and smiled as she flicked the lighter.

CHAPTER EIGHTEEN

Alicia lay prone in the darkness as Chris moved into position. She was wearing the hard helmet with the night vision gear attached. Her motorcycle was ten feet away, a sleek shadow in the night. She flipped up the night vision gear and peered through rifle's scope. She saw the tiny square of light in the top right portion of the window and adjusted her aim.

She'd already chambered one of the large .50 caliber rounds and the safety was off.

The barrel was held up out of the dirt by the bipod, and Alicia adjusted her grip on the large rifle. She'd never fired anything of this caliber that wasn't mounted on the back of a vehicle, but prayed the lessons Esther had taught her would hold true for this sized rifle.

What if she missed? What if the scope wasn't zeroed?

She was about five-hundred feet from the building, and knew that the bullet would sail across the dark meadow and arrive on target in less than two-tenths of a second.

It was almost no time... but this was a semi-automatic. Anything was possible.

"You ready?"

Chris's whispered voice came from somewhere out of the darkness behind her.

She stuffed the wads of torn cloth into her ears, the best she could do for ear protection, and as planned, she patted the ground twice with the toe of her boot, all the while keeping her focus on the target.

She heard as much as felt the scuff of Chris's boots and she pictured him winding back to throw the first of two grenades at the base's entrance.

The discarded spoon from the first grenade fell to the ground with a metallic *ting*, and the world seemed to slow to a crawl.

Her thoughts remained laser-focused on both her target and the time that had elapsed. *Five seconds for the first of the grenades to explode.*

Peering through the scope, she adjusted her aim once again. Holding the butt stock firmly against her shoulder, she knew this thing was going buck backward, and with much more force than the .308 she'd fired with Esther.

Four seconds before the first explosion behind me.

She couldn't worry about anyone behind her, that was Chris's job. But this rifle was going to make a lot of noise.

She'd done all the calculations in her head a dozen times. Two tenths of a second for the bullet to cross the five hundred or so feet to the target.

The nearest building that wasn't currently filling with exhaust fumes from a generator was about 1200 feet away. It was one of the barracks that housed at least one hundred soldiers.

Three seconds.

It would take about a second for the sound of her shot to reach that building.

If she hit one of the grenades, the sound from that explosion would get to the barracks just ahead of the sound of her shot.

Two seconds.

She'd have time for one more shot without any more worry about the noise.

She felt her heartbeat in the tip of her trigger finger.

One second.

And just as she counted to zero, she was between heartbeats, the crosshairs were exactly dead-center on the window, she pulled the trigger.

The rifle exploded with near-deafening sound, and the muzzle flashed brightly as the gun bucked hard against Alicia's shoulder.

A sharp-sounding explosion erupted behind her, but everything was still moving in slow motion.

It was almost as if she could see the bullet streaking across the air through the scope, and in a fraction of a second

Alicia saw a large burst of light flash just as the bullet struck nearly a foot above the window.

With only the slightest adjustment she launched another round, knowing this was the last one she could afford to send.

And almost instantly, a burst of light and sparks exploded from just inches under the window.

Instinctively, Alicia sent a third round, absorbed the shock and jumped up from her prone position as explosions erupted from multiple directions.

At this point her ears were ringing and she couldn't be sure of anything as she flipped down her night vision gear, hopped onto her motorcycle, turned the key, and gunned the engine.

Chris jumped on the seat behind her, screaming in her ringing ears, "Go, go, go!"

The world had a greenish hue as the bike launched forward. She skirted around the vehicle barrier, which was still up, as Chris shot one of the guards who was still moving.

Turning the throttle, they blasted past the base's entrance and Chris yelled, "You did it! There's flames shooting out of the research building's window."

"Ahead!" Alicia yelled as a pair of patrolling soldiers raced toward them, guns drawn, and bullets flew in both directions.

Suddenly the night turned into day and Alicia yelled as she was momentarily blinded.

Chris grunted and Alicia felt the motorcycle almost get flung sideways by the tremendous shockwave that hit them.

Pain in her chest bloomed as she accelerated along the dirt path, only barely able to make out her surroundings.

The world grew dark once again and Alicia blinked the tears from her eyes. Her contact lens showed the route that Brice had programmed in. "Hold on, this is going to get uglier."

He tightened his grip on her as the bike plummeted down a ravine. It took everything she had to not lose control as they nearly smashed into a giant boulder.

The ghost-like arrow pointed her north and she barely kept the bike upright as she followed a craggy path through the woods. "Do we have anyone behind us that you can see?"

"No, and to be honest... I doubt they'll have a clue we're even gone for days. I told you that was a lot of fertilizer."

Chris sounded like he was in pain.

"Fine, you're right." She yelled over the sound of the motorcycle's revving engine, all the while her ears were ringing loudly. "It was a lot of fertilizer, maybe even too much. Does that make you happy?"

"Getting home would make me happy." Chris leaned against her back and his right arm quivered.

"Are you okay?" Alicia felt a sudden pang of fear as she recalled the grunt he'd uttered as they were hit by the shock wave.

"I'm fine, just tired. Focus on getting us there in one piece and I'll buy dinner."

Alicia clenched her jaw as she gunned the engine and launched up the side of a shallow ravine, sighing with relief as they exited the forest and entered a large open grassland.

Alicia hopped off her motorcycle and held the phone to her ear. "Brice, we're at the river, Chris says the water is freezing, too cold to swim. It's still pitch-black outside, but from what I can tell from the reflection of the moon on the water, this river is *very* wide. Is there a bridge we can get to?"

"That's the Amur river, and it's about a half a mile across where you're at. There's no bridge you're going to be able to cross without the Chinese stopping you. Don't worry, keep your eyes open, there should be someone coming. I've given them your coordinates."

Chris hobbled up from the bank of the river and her eyed widened as she spotted a large patch of darkness on his military uniform.

"You're bleeding!" Alicia raced to him and put his arm over her shoulder, helping him walk up the slope. "Brice, Chris is hurt. And it looks pretty bad."

Someone nearby yelled in Russian.

Chris yelled back and he turned to her. "Someone's coming from the river. Let's go."

"Brice, is our contact coming out of the river?"

"Yes, one of our people, Yuri, he's going to get you across.

Make sure Yuri know about Chris's condition, he'll know what to do."

Alicia helped Chris as they walked back down the slope toward the dark waters of the Amur River.

Her night vision gear had started to flicker midway through their hour-long ride to this spot, and at this point it had completely gone out. All she could see was the moon's light scattered on the ripples of water, and as Alicia strained to make anything out of what might be coming, she heard the sound of water lapping against wood, and it was getting louder.

Suddenly, she spotted the raft approaching.

Chris was getting weaker. She felt it as he leaned more and more of his weight on her.

A man leaped across the water and offered his arm to Chris, who was barely able to stand up.

Two other people hopped off the raft and in less than a minute, Alicia and Chris were both lying on the floating platform. Chris lay flat on his stomach while she stared up at the brilliant stars above, her ears still ringing from firing the sniper rifle and the other explosions.

The last thing she remembered was the sound of a quiet electric motor purring as it sent them floating across the river, and to freedom.

Alicia had woken up about thirty minutes earlier and learned that they'd been brought to a lonely building outside a town called Obluchye. A doctor had spent the entire time she'd been awake working on Chris's injury. He was unconscious, and had an IV attached to his arm. He didn't look good.

But now that whatever adrenaline had been in her system had flushed away, she felt every bruise and scrape that she'd somehow previously managed to ignore. Even where she'd nestled the butt of the rifle, she felt the throbbing bruise from those three quick shots that she'd launched. But that was the least of her issues.

The doctor turned to her and spoke in broken English, "Please removing shirt."

"No." Alicia shook her head and pointed at Chris. "How is he doing?"

The doctor glanced at Chris and shook his head.

Alicia's heart dropped to the pit of her stomach.

"He's no good." The doctor said with a thick accent. "Needs surgery. Needs drugs." He pointed at Alicia's chest. "You crying out when checked you asleep. Let me see problem."

Alicia winced as she shifted her arms to remove her jacket. The doctor undid the straps to her vest and carefully removed it along with her undershirt. With the amount of pain she feeling at the moment, the idea of her sitting upright topless in front of this guy didn't even phase her. She had no mental space for modesty at this point.

"This hurting you. Take breath."

Alicia clenched her jaw as the doctor pressed gently on her ribs, using just the pads of his fingertips he slowly moving from rib to rib, his expression not changing as he pressed higher and higher and finally nodded. "Good news. No broken rib. Very lucky." He picked up the vest and pressed his finger into a hole.

"I got shot?" Alicia's eyes widened and her mind replayed that moment that they bolted from the shattered remains of the base's entrance and encountered two soldiers.

Chris was firing.

The soldiers were firing.

That was when the world switched from night to day, and the chaos got switched to an eleven as the world literally exploded all around them.

That's when it happened.

"I think you'll find the vest to be very effective and concealable."

No truer words could have been uttered by Mrs. Yang.

Alicia looked down at her chest and the fist-sized purple bruise for the first time. Had she not been wearing that, she'd likely not have survived long enough to even get to the river, much less escape into Russia.

The doctor was talking, but for some reason, his voice was coming out as if he was speaking in static.

The world tilted and she found herself being caught by the elderly physician and slowly lowered to the makeshift examination table.

He continued to speak and the world grew dark.

CHAPTER NINETEEN

Three Days Later

The driver that Mason had arranged to pick her up at the airport dropped her off on the side of the road in old Georgetown. Ahead of her was the familiar sign with the profiles of a rooster and a longhorn bull. The sign was just above the entrance to the seedy bar known as the Rooster and Bull.

The familiar place brought a smile to her face as she entered the bar, the smells of stale beer and wood polish washed over her like they always did. Alicia remembered a time when the smells had bothered her, but after having been covered with filth from head to toe and everything else she'd dealt with, these smells were like a heady perfume to her now.

As always, the place was dimly lit, and to her surprise, a few of the booths actually had what looked like customers in them. Behind the bar, a man toweled a glass dry. He nodded at her as she walked toward the back of the establishment.

Alicia boldly entered the men's bathroom, and smiled at the white-haired man sitting on a stool near the sink. He looked at her over his John Lennon-styled spectacles.

"You're not that same little girl who first showed up here scared of her own shadow, are you?"

She grinned. "Harold, you're adorable."

"Bah!" Harold held out a white towel. "I was hoping you'd stay afraid for a little while. The young ones are always so much fun to mess with."

Alicia took the towel and entered the third of the bathroom's three stalls—the one with an "Out of Order" sign taped to it. She shut the door behind her, then placed the special towel on the flushing lever and flushed the toilet.

Immediately the floor dropped and within five minutes she was walking into the conference room for the AAR meeting.

This would be her first one.

Mason and Brice both stood as she walked into the conference room.

"Good to see you in one piece," Brice said it with a smile. "How was your trip?"

"Don't get me started." Alicia glared at him and shook

her head. "Obluchye to Irkutsk, Irktusk to Bangkok, Bangkok to Delhi, and then finally Delhi to Washington DC. I don't care for your travel agent one bit."

Mason smiled, motioned toward the conference room table and said, "Take a seat. We'll try to make this quick so you can recoup and get some well-earned time off."

Alicia felt a bit weird, their gaze trained on her as she walked around the table and picked a seat. She didn't like being the center of attention. There was nobody else in the room, and she'd hoped that Lucy would be at the meeting. She was probably still be pissed off that Alicia had blatantly ignored her advice and went on the mission.

Mason looked over at Alicia and said, "As you likely already know, we tend to have after action reports at the end of each mission to better understand what we've accomplished, what things remain unresolved, and if there were things that didn't work out as expected, what those things might be." He turned to Brice, "First things first, what was the end result of the mission objective?"

Brice pulled out a glossy satellite image and pointed at a black splotch. "This is a hot off the presses, a satellite image from twelve hours ago. That black spot is the epicenter of what looks like a very significant explosion. From what we can tell, there's a two-hundred-foot-wide crater where a building used to be. It looks like every building in a fifteen-hundred-foot radius was flattened as well. From what we know of the objective, I'd say mission accomplished."

"Any chatter from Beijing or elsewhere as it relates to this incident?" Mason asked.

"You'd have expected something." Brice shook his head. "We've been listening and not even a peep. There were phone calls to the authorities from civilians in the nearest town of Yichun. Evidently the explosion woke hundreds of people up from their sleep, but aside from that, nothing. We're keeping tabs on all avenues of communication, and if that situation changes, I'll be alerted right away."

"Chris said the general's project was hurting for funding. Maybe that's why we haven't heard anything." Alicia frowned. "Does... does anyone know how Chris is doing?"

"I do." Mason's expression was unreadable. "He got out of surgery about twelve hours ago. Evidently that thing that hit him and wedged between his ribs was a chunk of concrete, likely from that massive explosion. The good news is that he'll recover and be back at it in no time."

Even though she knew it wasn't really her fault, Alicia still felt a pang of guilt. "Do you mind if I ask some questions about Chris and some of what happened?"

"Go ahead." Mason nodded.

"So, the whole Chris and his brother thing... how exactly did that work. The entire time I was there, I was confused by how any of this was really happening. How did Chris know about his brother's work, and is his brother really dead?"

"Well, this particular instance is a bit unusual, and it requires a bit of backstory." Mason said as he drummed his fingers on the conference room table. "You were briefed on the whole Manchurian candidate concept, right?"

"I was."

"Well, to make a long story short, Bo and Chris were identical twins born in China and soon after, their parents moved to the U.S. Both parents are academics, and all I can really say is that one of them works for the Outfit, and both kids were part of an experiment. They were tagged with burst transmitters and it helped us advance some of our research on what would end up being what you now think of as the Manchurian candidate process.

"One of the parents decided they wanted to go back to China and literally vanished overnight with one of the kids. That kid, obviously, was Bo. Over the years, we got occasional datagrams of brain patterns from both boys, though neither of them were aware of this."

Alicia's mouth dropped open and before she could ask a question, Mason held up his hand.

"Let me finish answering your question first. For years, we gathered data, and it was purely for research. It helped us understand and decipher how memories work and get stored in the brain. Now, don't think that we actually had deepest or darkest secrets from either of them, we didn't. Think of it more like a scrap book of images or thoughts. Every once in a while, we'd get a new image. A new set of feelings unattached to an image. It was fairly random.

"And then Bo went into the PLA, and specifically into the MSS, which is the Chinese equivalent to the KGB, CIA, and Stasi all rolled into one. We were able to up the frequency of the transmissions, but only to a certain extent. We collected what we could, and even managed to track Bo to Taiwan both the first time and the last time he went.

"The last time he went was when Chris's brother got killed. And just like we were able to transmit memories out of someone's head, we were able to get fragments of Bo's memories into Chris's head."

"But he couldn't remember who he was."

Mason nodded. "That was for his protection. We have over the years figured out how to lock away memories so that others can't extract them, unless of course, they have the right key."

Alicia frowned. "Is that why I can't remember some things? I know you blamed this multiverse thing, but..."

Mason shook his head and smiled. "No, that's not how it works. We don't have the ability to carve out bits of memories and lock them away. It's sort of an all or nothing kind of thing. Maybe someday we will be able to do what you're describing, but that's not something we can do today."

Alicia wasn't sure she believed him.

Brice turned to Mason. "Multiverse?"

Mason waved aside the question.

"Is Lucy okay? I lost touch with her after Taiwan."

Mason grinned. "I heard what happened, and believe it or not, after you ended up blowing her off, the Dragon Lady blamed me for your behavior." He laughed. "I swear, that lady really hates my guts." The director shifted his attention back to Brice. "Anything else on your end?"

"We're still trying to get out of the Taiwanese what exactly it was that they were messing with. Obviously, we know about the prions, but I think they got so scared of whatever it was they were doing they destroyed every record." Brice shrugged. "That feels like a huge fail on my part, but given the circumstances, I don't know what else I would have done differently. This was an unusual set of events."

"Bah," Mason waved dismissively. "They're always unusual." He looked across the table at Alicia and gave her what looked like a warm, almost sincere smile. "You've earned time off to recover. I read the reports and you have lots of bruises and miscellaneous trauma that needs some time to heal. You likely averted a pandemic that might have had consequences far worse than anything we experienced from the Wuhan incident, much less anything else in the past."

"I think we all need a little bit of rest." Brice said.

"What about the general?" Alicia asked. "General Hong? We blew up his facility, but whatever his motivation, he can almost certainly start over. Do we really even know what exactly that place was doing?"

Mason and Brice shared a look, then Mason leaned forward. "You don't need to worry about him."

"Why?"

Mason looked at his watch. "He had an accident ten hours ago. I'm afraid it was fatal."

Alicia shook her head in confusion, then felt her jaw drop as what Mason had *really* just said hit her. "An accident?"

"Do you recall me telling you what our unofficial motto is?" Mason asked.

Alicia shook her head.

"If it's actionable, we act." He drummed his fingers on the table. "There are things that we do for the betterment of our society and the world that inevitably requires things to be done that nobody in the power hierarchy of today's governments would give permission for. From our inception, we knew that was a weakness of organized government—the inability to say 'make it so' for uncomfortable acts that need to be done.

"Had Chris not gotten hit with the debris from the explosion, he'd have disappeared for a day or two, allowing the dust to settle and then he'd return to the base and take Hong out himself. That was his endgame. However, as events come to pass, some plans require in-field revision.

"Alicia, sending someone in to do wet work is much easier than you think. Especially for the Outfit. We have people trained for it. You'll eventually train for it. Sometimes taking one life can save millions."

Wet work was a euphemism for assassination. Something that would get you bloody.

"But—"

He held up a hand. To his side, Brice had been nodding in

agreement with his boss the whole time. "Let me ask you something. Is the world safer without Hong? Simple question. Yes, or no?"

"Yes," Alicia said instantly, and she meant it. But assassination...

"There's your answer. And you already had it. You said yourself he could just start up another variant of the same kind of program again. You're right. We came to that conclusion ourselves weeks ago. So we handled it. Because that's what the Outfit does. When it's actionable, we act. Do you understand?"

"I think I do," Alicia said. But inside, a little of the Outfit's brightness lost its sheen.

Mason looked at Brice and said, "Alright. I need some of this put into a report that I can share with the DC folks. They're asking for an update and I need to give them a sanitized version of something. Obviously nothing about the general for now. Let's you and I at least get the first draft done tonight."

"The job is never done, is it?" Brice moaned.

Mason pushed back from the conference room table. "You know that there's always something around the corner." He looked at Alicia and said, "Young lady, now you have a small idea of what it is we do here. I hope you're prepared."

"It can't all be like this."

Mason and Brice both laughed as if it was the funniest

thing they'd ever heard and walked out of the conference room.

Alicia yelled, "No, I'm serious... you guys, it's not always like this... right? Right?"

Her phone buzzed, Alicia looked at the number and nearly squealed, "Dad!" into the phone.

"Hey baby doll, I just wanted to let you know that I'll be back in the country sooner than expected, likely next week. I hear you're back from Taiwan. How did that go?"

"Um..." Alicia imagined her father's conniption fit if he knew what had actually happened. "It went well. I'm curious, when you're on a mission, they're not always crazy, end of the world type of things that you do, right?"

Her father began laughing and then said, *"Oh, sorry, I have to get going. I'm glad to hear you're safe and sound... don't do anything dangerous."*

"Dad?"

The phone line was dead.

Anything dangerous? Alicia snort-laughed and shook her head.

If he only knew.

AUTHOR'S NOTE

Well, that's the end of *New Arcadia*, and we sincerely hope you enjoyed it.

This was the first, but certainly not the last writing collaboration between Mike and Steve. We wanted to have a section in this book where we can introduce ourselves, give you a little insight into who we are, what our thought processes were with regards to this book, and maybe even where we're going with what will be a series of books with Alicia as its main character.

We are authors with a rather lengthy list of books to our names, but we are by no means similar in how we came to be authors, nor in the type of things we normally write. I guess the easiest way to introduce ourselves is by just diving in, and let's start with the Rothman portion of the Rothman/Diamond duo.

I started this author thing accidentally, and by that, I mean years ago I had two young boys who enjoyed their bedtime stories. And my attempts to create off-the-cuff stories were pretty elaborate and to remain consistent I began to write things down. That was the beginning of a slippery slide into authordom for me.

As to my background, I've worked most of my life in various engineering disciplines, with my formal education being in the hard sciences. And I've spent most of my career in Silicon Valley companies as a designer and inventor of cool things. During that long career, I've traveled the world and seen many things that help bring color to my work. My writing has naturally evolved to focus on stories heavily laden with science, action, and adventure.

I'll hand the virtual microphone over to Steve so he can introduce himself:

I think I've always wanted to tell stories. One day I looked up at my mom's bookshelf, and I saw Tolkien, Lewis, and Brooks up there. Terry Brooks, in particular caught my eye, because the books looked so massive next to the others. I had to know what those were. I read Sword of Shannara when I turned 10-years-old, and never really looked back. Fantasy, Science Fiction, Westerns, and Crime Thrillers. And somehow all of those led me to Horror. The end result of all that reading? I love mysteries and thrillers.

My background is all over the place. I'm an accountant by trade. I lived in Mexico for a year. I've been an editor, book reviewer, art director, and publisher. I love sports almost as much as I love cooking BBQ. When it comes to writing, I tend to focus on character. What they love, hate, hope, and fear. I love writing characters that "solve problems" like Repairman Jack or Harry Dresden. I also like showing heroes placed in situations that push them to the limits. But most of all, I hope the stories I write (or co-author!) entertain.

With the introductions out of the way, let's move on.

Mike has found some success in taking an unusual approach to the writing of his thrillers, many have described his work as resembling Michael Crichton in that both he and Crichton brought real modern science into the matrix of an action-adventure type of story. It could easily be said that Crichton placed the initial stake in the ground for what would end up being the genre known as the technothriller. When talking with Steve, the idea of putting their talents together seemed both unlikely and possibly new and exciting.

Both enjoy the idea of writing thrilleresque stories, and while Mike's approach brings with it heavy amounts of science and international intrigue, Steve has a way with bringing the dark side of human nature to the fore, up to and including elements of the paranormal.

Could we convince a reader of thrillers to enjoy a book that stretched science to its limits? We believe that already to be the case.

However, could we meld the strengths of both authors to produce something that further challenges the audience? As this series develops, you will see elements folded in that test our preconceived notions of what's real and what isn't. Could things that we believe to be figments of our imagination actually be elements of science reality? Could we "sciencify" (a technical term) a novel that had what we've always considered to be paranormal elements in it, and puncture that gauzy veil between make-believe and reality? We believe we can, and it remains to be seen whether that works out as planned or doesn't.

This story was just the beginning of a long, serialized set of stories with a focus on its namesake, Alicia Yoder. Even though each story is set in our world, our time, and with many of the same cast of characters, you'll soon learn that each of the planned stories are independent of each other. Meaning that each book is a self-contained story that starts and ends with each book, but readers of the series will be able to appreciate a growth in the main character as well as those she surrounds herself with.

Fair warning and a sneak peek: starting in book two, we will introduce a new member of Alicia's universe named Bagel. Bagel is not a character to underestimate, and that's all that we'll say about that, for now.

We expect to have a lot of fun writing this, and we hope you all enjoy the ride... it's going to be a tumultuous one.

Thanks for reading *New Arcadia*, and there's lots more where that came from.

--Mike and Steve

We should note that if you're interested in getting updates about our latest work, we have links below so you can join our mailing lists.

M.A. Rothman: https://mailinglist.michaelarothman.com/new-reader

Steve Diamond: https://authorstevediamond.com/newsletter/

P.S. – Did you really think we'd give you such a provocative tease about a mysterious upcoming character named Bagel without giving you a peek at a bit more context? Starting on the next page is a preview of *Operation Thrall*, and maybe just maybe you'll be introduced to Bagel. We hope you enjoy it.

P.P.S. – Even though this is technically the first Alicia Yoder novel, it isn't actually the first novel that she's had a material contribution to. Mike first introduced Alicia in the novel, *Multiverse,* which spawned more than a few emails requesting her to have her own series—which is why we are here! To get a taste of that novel, we've included a small excerpt to that story. We hope you enjoy it.

PREVIEW OF OPERATION THRALL

Alicia Yoder doubled over in pain, clutching at her abdomen for all the good it would do. The cut branches she'd gathered to make shelter for herself and for her dad fell to the rain-soaked ground.

She leaned against the nearest tree and sunk down, scraping her back against the bark. For a moment she forgot to breathe, then took in two, quick, gasping breaths to steady herself. The trip to the Catskills should have been a good test of her survival skills. Instead, barely eight hours in, Alicia wasn't sure she'd make it through the night.

The pain started maybe a month or two ago. The nausea didn't affect her much. Neither did the occasional back pain. But then the hot, angry pain moved into her abdomen, then spread across her pelvic region.

Warning bells rang in her mind as she recalled her trip

back from the Far East a few weeks ago, and the agonizing drive straight to the Georgetown University Hospital in DC. The visit led to an ultrasound, which led to the discovery of tumors on her ovaries. This, in turn, meant a CT scan, a CA-125 blood test, and a biopsy.

When Alicia pushed up to her feet, the nausea sucker punched her, and she lost the two pieces of toast she'd forced down that morning. *Whatever*, she thought, wiping her mouth with the back of her hand. *The bread sucked. Who uses sourdough bread for toast, anyway?*

A few more breaths and the pain and desire to hurl subsided. She didn't want her dad to see her weak. A lesson she'd learned at a young age on the streets of Hong Kong and those same lessons had been reinforced in New York City. Never show weakness. She retrieved the branches, now broken and mostly useless for their makeshift shelter. Lifting her face to the sky, she let the rain patter on her face. It felt good. Maybe it could wash away her worries.

Tumors.

The doctor said ovarian cancer in premenopausal women was uncommon, but the words offered little relief to the anxiety gnawing at her gut. Something inside her wasn't right, and it was getting harder to ignore. All she could do was wait for the test results to come back.

The branches felt so heavy and her arms like lead. She dragged the tree cuttings the rest of the way to camp, no longer caring. Her mind wouldn't turn from the worry those tests could bring.

Levi Yoder—her adoptive dad—had already built the frame of a lean-to, and had a small fire going. He looked up, and frowned when he saw her dragging the branches.

"Alicia, if you won't take something as small as this training seriously, how..."

His words trailed off as those piercing blue eyes took her in. He stood quickly and rushed to her side.

"Sorry, dad. I, uh... I'm not feeling so hot. Must be a cold or something." She hadn't told him anything. Didn't need him worrying about her when he was off saving the world from terrorists or whatever mission the Outfit would send him on next.

"Hey... hey why don't you sit down for a minute. I got this."

Levi gently helped his daughter to the forest floor, then laid the ruined branches onto the frame of the lean-to, forming some semblance of a roof over her head. He jogged out into the trees and returned a few minutes later with pristine cuttings that filled out the shelter and kept nearly all the rain out. Alicia chuckled to herself despite the exhaustion—her frequent companion these days. Even at her best, she knew it would have taken her twenty minutes to find the right components for the shelter. For her father, this sort of thing was second nature.

He sat down next to her, keeping his eyes down on the small fire. Normally he wouldn't have done so. *Don't look right at the fire*, he always said. *You can't afford to have your eyesight impaired if you're in a situation where survival is key.*

She assumed he now broke his rule for her benefit. A way to give her a measure of privacy where none really existed.

Alicia leaned over and rested her head on his shoulder, loving him for the kindness he'd always shown her and her siblings. She wiped away a tear before it could roll down her cheek. "Thanks."

She felt his smile without having to look. "Hey, neither of us wants to be soaked to the bone when we go to sleep."

She shook her head at the answer, but said nothing. They both knew that wasn't what she thanked him for. But his tact—especially when it came to family—was a skill Alicia hadn't managed to learn quite yet.

"How are things at the Outfit?" Levi asked, changing the subject.

The Outfit was an agency that didn't officially exist, but it was part of the government. Sort of. Her father did the occasional assignment for them, and they'd only recently recruited Alicia. She smiled, remembering when she'd first been introduced to the Outfit's US headquarters. To her, it was like the agency from the movie Men in Black, where nobody knew about it unless they needed to know. Sadly, as far as she could tell, the Outfit had nothing to do with aliens, which would have made things much more interesting. "My six-month evaluation period is nearly up. They supposedly fast-tracked processing on my SF-86. It'll be official. I should get my Top-Secret clearance squared away a week from now. It'll actually be official, though I don't see the point. It wasn't like the Outfit actually limited my access to anything, regardless of classification."

"The Outfit does have their benefits, though as you know, they're known for skirting around the rules others follow."

"Can I ask you something?"

"Shoot."

Even after her initial run-in with the Outfit nearly six months ago, the shadowy society still remained an enigma to her. "They've been around since before the Revolutionary War, pulling strings and keeping our government on the straight and narrow—"

"I wouldn't go that far," Levi interrupted.

"Don't believe in miracles?"

He hesitated for a brief second. Had she imagined it? "I can get behind a miracle or two," Levi said. "But keeping the government... how did you put it? On the straight and narrow? Yeah, that's not happening."

Alicia laughed, letting the conversation push her earlier worries into the background. "Fair enough. I guess I just don't get how truly far their reach goes. You know what I mean? Like, how long does a full TS clearance usually take to process?"

"Two years."

"Right. And I'm done in three months? With my background?"

"Yeah... none of the searches will ever learn about your real background. I pulled some strings when adopting you.

You have carefully fabricated and official backstories from birth to my having adopted you."

"Really?" Alicia hadn't realized. After saving her and the other girls from the trafficking ring, she hadn't asked too many questions. Somehow, despite everything, her adoptive father's kindness surprised her. "Well... that's awesome. Same for the others?"

"Of course. But that's not your question. What about the Outfit do you want to know? Not sure how much I can really tell you. I certainly don't know everything about what goes on in that place. I'm just a contractor."

"Why do I even need a clearance? It's obvious that they somewhat run with their own set of rules. What kind of events have they guided through history?" She froze. "Did they kill JFK?"

Her father laughed. Like just about everything with him, the laugh seemed warm and endearing. Even huddled in the cold, by a meager fire, he still looked like he'd just stepped out of a Cabela's advertisement.

"I honestly don't know. The clearance is the easy question. Even though the Outfit skirts by the classification rules on plenty of occasions, you might find yourself on another agency's team that demands proof of clearances. It's easier to have it than not to."

"Makes sense," Alicia said. "And JFK?"

He chuckled again. "No idea. Ask Mason."

Mason was one of the directors at the Outfit.

The rain relented and the clouds above thinned to give

them a peek at the stars. Away from the city, they were so bright. To Alicia, the bright dots of light in the sea of darkness seemed so full of hope and promise.

She felt a growing tightness in her lower abdomen. Fear and dread wormed back into her mind.

"I'm going to go get some more wood for the fire. Build it up a little." Alicia leaned back against the inner wall of the lean-to as her father stood. "We've had a long day testing your survival skills, and you're doing fine, more or less. Let's not push things with any nighttime drills, especially if you're feeling sick. Let's just enjoy the outdoors tonight. We'll get back to the city early. That way you can prepare for your final review with Mason."

"Yeah. Maybe you're right." For all she knew, a message from the Georgetown University Hospital would be waiting for her. *Don't show weakness.* Alicia forced a smile—she was a professional at the art. "I'm not really worried about Mason. It's the shrinks."

"Psych evals?"

"Twice a week."

"Just remember, anytime they ask if you're sleeping well—"

"Like a baby. Couldn't be more rested."

He pointed both fingers at her.

"Don't do that."

"What?"

She exaggerated the gun fingers. "Makes me remember just how old you really are."

He grinned, flashing perfect teeth. "I'm young at heart." He gave her gun fingers again with a wink and walked off into the woods.

Young at heart. He joked, but he didn't look a day over thirty-five. Alicia knew he was closing in on fifty.

The gentle patter of droplets falling from the trees above splashed onto the roof of the lean-to, lulling her into a comfortable haze. With her eyes closed, she took in a few deep breaths. Not the meditation her father frequently practiced, but close enough for her. She'd never been able to figure out how he did it, locking out everything around him.

Alicia's peace lasted a few minutes before the guilt kicked in. Regardless of the pain and exhaustion, she shouldn't be sitting here, doing nothing, while her father collected wood for them. She crawled out of the shelter and slowly got to her feet. How long had her father been gone? Collecting wood shouldn't have taken him this long.

Pulling her jacket tighter around her, she headed off in the same direction her father had gone. The rain had stopped, but the chill of the forest air wormed its way through every gap in her clothes. They didn't fit like they used to. The nurse at the hospital who'd taken her vitals had told her she weighed one hundred and twenty-five pounds. Alicia hadn't commented at the time, but she was down nearly twenty pounds from just a few months ago, and at this weight she was thinner than she should be.

Despite it all, she did love walking among the trees in the Catskills. They didn't judge her. Didn't look at her with pity or commiseration at her upbringing. Neither did the forest remind her of the claustrophobic alleys and filthy beds that had been part of her life on the streets. The trees didn't care about her past, her present, or her future. They simply existed.

She walked for nearly ten minutes, looking for signs of her father's trail. The occasional footprint in mud or newly broken branch, guided her footsteps. Her father wasn't covering his trail, an oddity for him. Alicia wondered if he was more worried about her than himself, and used the walk to clear his mind. She never knew what he was thinking. They weren't related by even the tiniest drop of blood, but in some ways they were more alike than blood relatives.

Low, murmuring voices made her stop short and step behind a large balsam fir. She edged forward, moving tree to tree toward the voices. The quiet talking resolved into two, distinct voices as she drew nearer. One she picked out easily as her father's. The other voice she'd never heard before.

By the sound of her father's tone, it was obvious that he was upset or agitated about something.

"Narmer, just answer the question. What are you doing out here?"

"Can't a man enjoy a bit of nature? Levi, you know how I am about the forest." It was a man's voice. Old. And... somehow the voice sounded gauzy, almost as if it wasn't completely there. Yet this Narmer person came off as oddly playful. Alicia had a knack for voices. Being able to judge a person by their voice... hearing intent in their tone of voice... it had saved her on more than a few occasions as a kid.

"No," Levi said. "Not you. Not after all these years. Someone like you doesn't just show up."

She walked closer, careful not to let even the smallest twig snap or creak underfoot. In a tiny clearing, her father stood talking with an old man. Levi still held an armful of wood for their fire, but he stood ready, right foot back and his weight balanced between it and his leading foot. Alicia saw the tension in his body, ready to explode at any moment.

The old man, on the other hand, wore a lazy smile. He waved a dismissive hand and lowered himself to sit on the trunk of a downed tree. The man's clothes were threadbare, but he didn't seem to feel the cold like she did. He had an eyepatch over one eye, and one leg was gone below the knee with a wooden peg in its place. Alicia blinked. An actual peg-leg. The man couldn't have stood out more in this place... or, she supposed, this time. Everything about him felt out of place, as if he didn't belong in this world.

He set a polished, wooden cane against the tree next to him and sighed. He looked up at the forest's canopy, and when he spoke, it was with wistfulness. "You know, Mister Yoder, where I grew up, we didn't have forests like this. Just... sand and desert scrub. Even sand and deserts have their stark, flowing beauty... but I think I prefer the green, here. In my travels I've seen nearly every forest. I never grow tired of them."

There was something about his voice that caught Alicia's

attention. Her mind flashed back to one of the characters from Men in Black and a shiver raced up her spine. She half-expected this old man's skin to slough off and a giant cockroach to emerge from the skin suit he was wearing.

"Why are you here?" Levi asked again.

The cripple sighed. "My time is coming to an end. I came to see if you'd reconsidered your place in history."

"My place in... are you joking? I'm out here training with my daughter. I don't believe in any of your nonsense, and I told you that years ago."

"I had children once. Wives." Again, the wistfulness. "A curse, wouldn't you say, to outlive your wives and children? Though I suppose it doesn't have to be. Burdens and gifts are often the flip-side of the same coin, I think."

Her father stiffened with anger at Narmer's words. No... Alicia recognized it for what it truly was. Rage.

"You don't get to lecture me about loss... or *gifts*." Her father spat the last word. "I don't have time for riddles, old man. My daughter doesn't feel well, and I'd rather spend my evening in her company than yours. Tell me what you want."

"Time. Yes. For most people it is finite. But not quite so for you. And yet you refuse to believe. Do you not look in the mirror? Has not every benefit I mentioned to you been verified?"

"I'm done listening to you." Levi turned to walk away.

"Wait." The iron in Narmer's voice stopped her father in his tracks. "Here. Take this." He held up a piece of paper. Thick parchment, and even from where she stood, Alicia could see the texture on the paper. It reminded her of old papyrus she'd seen on display at the Met in New York City. "I'll be here for a few more weeks. Come see me if you change your mind."

"I won't," Her father walked to the old man and snatched the paper from the cripple's outstretched hand. Her father calmed all at once, his rage vanishing, replaced by sadness. He bowed to the old man. "Goodbye, Amar Van." Then he said something in a language Alicia didn't recognize before walking out of the clearing.

Alicia kept behind the trees, unmoving. Her father obviously knew the old man. Obviously respected him by the way he'd bowed at the end. But her father's wariness couldn't have been more obvious. Just who was this... Narmer?

"Do you intend to stand behind that tree all night, young woman? Or perhaps you could humor an old man and come introduce yourself?"

Alicia cursed silently, wondering what had given her away. A scrape of her coat against bark, maybe? Maybe she'd snapped a twig and not noticed? Walking back to that warm fire appealed to her tired mind and body, but curiosity about the old man won out. She stepped out from behind the tree and walked into the clearing.

Up close, that man looked even more ragged than from afar. The threadbare clothes looked moth-eaten, and hung off his body like tattered remnants of a burial shroud. He patted the spot on the log next to him. She should have walked away. Should have run away. But the man's voice had an odd sort of magnetic effect that pulled her close until she sat beside him.

"Who are you?" Alicia asked. "How do you know my dad?"

"I met your father years ago. When he was trying to find himself. In those days he still carried grief with him."

"Grief? About what?"

"That's a question for your father, I believe." His laugh carried a dry brittleness in it. "My name, young woman, is Narmer. I've gone by hundreds of names over the years, but that one is the truest I have. The one I think I would like to carry with me to the afterlife. And you, my dear?"

"Alicia. Alicia Yoder."

He patted her on the leg. "It is good to meet you, Alicia."

"How did you know I was there?"

"I heard you breathing."

Alicia scoffed, and before she could think to keep her mouth shut, she said, "Impossible."

"Oh, my dear, you truly have no concept of what is possible and what is impossible." The words were a rebuke, but they weren't said unkindly. Then the old man sniffed the air, and his eyes fell to look at Alicia's abdomen. "Ah. You have my sympathy."

"I don't know what you mean," Alicia said. But she did know. He couldn't possibly know she was sick... especially down there.

"If you say so." He smiled at her, then, and his expression

turned into one of curiosity. “Tell me, my dear, do you believe in miracles?”

“I… I don’t know. I’d like to believe they’re possible.” She hesitated. Alicia didn’t know this man in the slightest, but something about him made her want to continue talking with him. “I think… I think sometimes people go looking for miracles… and that doesn’t seem like a smart play.”

“Oh?”

She nodded. “I think people should work hard. They should always try and do their best. Maybe when people are always working toward a goal, they might have opportunities open for them, they just need to recognize them as the chances they truly are. If they grab onto the unexpected opportunities, for a lot of people, I think they see those events as miracles. Sorry. I don’t know if that makes any sense.”

“It does to me.” Narmer stared off in the direction her father had walked. “Then there are those that experience the miracle, and refuse to acknowledge it for what it is.”

After a moment of quiet, Alicia frowned. “Narmer, how do you know my father?”

“Your father is a special man. He was given a gift. I’m sure you’ve noticed he’s a little different than most men? Tell me, Alicia, do you want to be special?”

“No.” The answer came out instantly, without hesitation. “I think of special as being the center of attention, and that’s something I hate. If special means being able to help more people than I otherwise could, then that’s okay, I suppose. I mean, what does being special even mean, anyway?"

"Indeed, that's a question that demands contemplation." He patted her on the leg again. "Well, I've taken enough of your time. Go to your father. Spend time with him." He pointed at her abdomen. "And don't worry too much. I'm sure you'll be fine."

Narmer pushed away from the log and limped off into the forest without another word or backwards glance. *What a strange man*, she thought, watching him go. He walked into the shadows, and was gone.

"What am I doing," Alicia jumped off the fallen tree and stared in the direction the man had vanished. A pang of concern washed over her as she wondered whether the crippled man could find his way safely to the nearest road. With a deep sigh she followed after the old man.

She'd barely walked a few feet when out of the same shadows Narmer had disappeared into, a small cat appeared.

Black as night, with bright golden eyes that seem to drink in the starlight, the cat walked straight up to her, curled around ankle and began to purr.

Alicia reached down and picked up the cat, cuddling it high against her chest. The kitten felt so small and thin, like it hadn't eaten. It was starving.

In the distance, she heard her father calling for her.

There was no sign of Narmer in those shadows. Not even a single track from his peg-leg. Alicia shook her head in confusion, and made her way back to camp and to her father, not sure what she would tell him about her encounter with the old man.

"So how was your trip?"

Alicia shrugged. "Not bad. I wasn't feeling too well, so we cut it short."

"I'll say. You look pale." Rebecca Baker popped the trunk of her car and put Alicia's pack inside it. "You're probably anemic and need more iron in your diet. Have you tried colloidal silver? Stuff works on everything. Seriously. I take it to keep the flu away. I haven't had strep once since I started taking it six years ago."

The woman prattled on, but Alicia didn't mind. She got in the passenger side of the woman's old Jeep Wrangler and leaned back against the headrest. Becca was her neighbor across the hall in their apartment complex, and had taken to Alicia like a mother hen. She'd lost her husband of forty years the previous November to a stroke. A sweet woman. She was one of Alicia's only friends.

They pulled out of the Acela train station parking structure in DC and headed to their apartment building on Wheeler. The train from New York to DC only took a few hours, and her friend had been waiting for her.

Becca talked the whole time, filling every opportunity for silence with recommendations for herbal treatments for sickness, her latest recipe discoveries, and how she'd found a TV station that ran The Ray Bradbury Theater. Alicia smiled and nodded, but didn't really engage in the conversation.

The kitten curled up in her lap, sucking on its tail. The little, black bundle of fur always seemed to be curled into a circle like this.

"That is an adorable kitty," Becca said. "I didn't know you were a pet person."

"I'm not," Alicia said. "I found him out in the forest. Couldn't leave him out there. I mean... look at him?" She rubbed the kitten behind its ears.

"Hey, you won't get any argument from me. You know I love little furbabies. Did I tell you I've been training my little sheepadoodle to talk to me?"

Alicia raised a disbelieving eyebrow. "And how do you do that?"

"I'll show you when we get upstairs."

Somehow the trip from the train station to their apartment building on Wheeler Road passed in a blink. Alicia hadn't paid any attention to the drive. She'd seen it all before, and it didn't have any sites she cared to notice in those passing miles.

When she'd turned the phone back on after landing, there'd been a missed call and message from the hospital. She hadn't had the courage to listen to it yet.

"How old is your dog now?" Alicia asked the question, not really caring, but not wanting to be rude to her friend.

"Just two years old. Well... in human years. In dog years?

I have no idea. I don't know that I believe the whole seven-to-one dog years thing. No. I don't know about that."

Alicia smiled as the older woman spun off into a story about how she'd found an article about dog years. Becca was in her mid-sixties. Had she always been this chatty? Alicia cringed as she imagined the lady's poor husband having to listen to that for forty years.

They pulled into Becca's covered parking spot and pulled her bag out of the truck. Her friend insisted on carrying it to the elevator, where she punched the button to the third floor. After the short wait, the door slid open, and Becca marched off down the hall to her apartment, 310. Alicia's was across the hall, number 311. Her neighbor opened the door and waved for Alicia to enter.

Alicia felt torn. It was either go into her friend's place and have her ear talked off, or go into her own apartment and listen to the message waiting for her on the phone. She veered to the left, went into Becca's place and took a seat at the kitchen table.

Becca already had the gas stove on and a teapot going. Her dog stood up on hind legs next to Alicia trying to get a view of the kitten. Seeing the dog, her new kitten reached out a paw and swatted at its nose. Alicia chuckled and reached down to scratch the dog under its chin. Becca had named the little black dog, Brees, after the old quarterback of the New Orleans Saints. The woman was a diehard football fan, but hated the Washington Commanders.

A few minutes later, Becca brought two mugs over, the steam from the hot apple cider wafted up from both mugs.

Becca sat down and stared at Alicia for a long moment and frowned. “You don’t look good. Are you okay?”

The question caught Alicia off guard. Her friend rarely took the direct approach. “I’m just not feeling good, Becca. I… I went and got checked out at Georgetown before I went on the trip with my dad. I have a message from them, but don’t really want to listen to it.”

“Need me to do it for you?” From anyone else, the question would have been nosey. From her neighbor, it was an offer of kindness.

Alicia shook her head. “No, I appreciate it though.” She took a sip of the cider and changed the subject. “So you’re training Brees to talk?”

“I certainly am! Look over there. You see that mat with the buttons sticking out of it?” Becca pointed to the floor by the sliding glass door leading to her balcony.

Alicia saw a small, foam hexagon. It had seven buttons sticking up out of it, each with a simple picture on them.

“I got my little Breesy these buttons from BabbelPet. I just record an easy word into each, and my sweetheart can press one to tell me what she wants.” She looked down at her dog and pointed to the buttons. “Go tell mama what you want, Breesy. Tell mama what you want.”

To her astonishment, the black dog walked over to the foam pad, looked down at the buttons as if considering, then pressed one with her paw. Becca's voice broadcast from the button's speaker saying, *"Ball."* Brees looked up expectantly.

"Huh. How 'bout that. What do the other buttons say?"

"My little pupper is amazing, isn't she? She knows 'ball', 'outside', 'treat', 'now', 'play', 'stick', and 'mama'. She uses that last one to get my attention, then usually presses one of the other ones to tell me what she wants. I saw it on the internet. Some bigger version of my Breesy had a setup with, like, thirty buttons. She was having a full-on conversation with her owner." As Becca spoke, her southern drawl became more pronounced the more excited she got.

"That's... that's actually pretty awesome." The cat in her lap squirmed, then jumped down. It walked over to the buttons and stared down at them. The kitty batting at one and it did nothing. Realizing that he must not have hit it with enough pressure, the kitty reared up and slammed its front paws onto the button. *"Outside."* Brees backed away from the cat, whining. The kitten repeated the call for 'outside' and looked up at Alicia.

Becca whistled. "Well that is something, alright. I tell you what, I have a bunch of extra buttons. I'll give them to you. Brees has trouble with more than seven. But maybe the little kitty can learn some words too!" She vanished down the hall, then returned with a box containing two hexagonal foam pads and buttons enough to fill out the foam holder.

"Thanks, Becca." Alicia took the box. The cats she'd known back on the farm were pretty fickle creatures, so she doubted this cat would use the buttons, but she didn't want to be rude. "Look, thanks for the ride and for the cider. I'm going to head home and listen to that message."

"Alright, dear. You let me know if you need anything. Anything at all. I'm here for you."

"Thanks, Becca. I know you are. You're the best."

Alicia stood and gave the older woman a tight hug. She grabbed her bag, and then reached down and scooped up the kitten that had ran across the room and wrapped himself around her ankle. It was time to walk across the hall to listen to the message she'd been dreading for days.

Alicia stared at her cell phone, too afraid to touch it. Next to her, the kitten curled up again into a little circle, sucking on its tail. For some reason it reminded her of a bagel.

"I guess that's what I'll call you." The cat looked up at her, cocked its head, then walked over to sit in her lap. Within a minute it was again curled up into a little ball, the tip of his tail stuck in his mouth, purring as he closed his eyes. "Bagel." The cat opened one eye and then closed it. "I guess the name fits you, doesn't it." The purring got louder. Alicia shifted her gaze to her phone and took a deep breath.

She grabbed the phone and pulled up the voicemail before she could change her mind.

"Hello, this message is for Alicia Yoder. This is Doctor Kim Reynolds. I need you to give our office a call. We got the results for

your biopsy, blood tests, and CT scan back. Please give us a call as soon as you get this."

When the message ended, Alicia pulled the phone away from her ear and stared down at it. "That's it?" She played the message two more times, wondering if she was missing something. "They couldn't be bothered to just tell me what's going on? I gotta call them back now? Idiots."

Her anger wasn't fair, and she knew it. But she didn't care. She dialed up Doctor Reynolds. After five rings, someone picked up.

"This is Doctor Reynolds' office. Lance Andrews speaking."

It was the doctor's assistant. Great. The guy was a moron who had a constant tone of condescension. "Hey, Lance, this is Alicia Yoder. I'm returning the doctor's call. She left a message saying my results were in?"

"Yes, she had to leave a message since you apparently didn't pick up."

Alicia felt her grip on the phone tighten. "I was out of town."

"Ah. Well give me one moment. I'll see if Doctor Reynolds is available. Let me put you on hold."

Rather than going silent, the line stayed live. Alicia heard muffled scratching noises, and realized the idiot must have forgotten to hit the "hold" button on the office phone, and was carrying it pressed against his shirt.

"Hey, Kim. Alicia... der's... hone. You want me to... her?"

Alicia only caught a few words at a time over the scratching. Heart thudding in her chest, she turned the volume up on her phone as loud as it would go. She couldn't make out the reply from the doctor.

"OK, I'll tell... Yoder to come... morrow. Do you wan... her... positive for ovarian cancer? OK... leave to... "

She didn't need to hear the whole conversation. Four of those words crashed down on her like an anvil. Positive for ovarian cancer.

"Miss Yoder are you still there?"

Ovarian cancer.

"Miss Yoder?"

Alicia blinked at the cell phone. All the moisture in her mouth vanished, leaving her struggling to form any coherent word.

"Y-yes."

"Doctor Reynolds is in the middle of a consultation that she can't put off. She apologizes. She needs you to come in tomorrow to go over the results. Is the afternoon fine? Say, 2:00 p.m?"

"What's... what's going on?"

"I'm afraid that's best discussed with the doctor. Are you available at 2:00 p.m?"

"Yes."

"We'll see you tomorrow at two. Goodbye for now."

The line went dead, but she hardly noticed.

Ovarian cancer.

Bagel stirred in Alicia's lap as tears fell from her face onto the kitten. It looked up at her, gold eyes filled with concern, then nuzzled her stomach.

Alicia brought up her dad's number, about to call it, but

stopped. What would she tell him? How would he react to the news? Instead, she put the phone down and opened her laptop. A few searches told her the news.

Stage Two had a five-year survival rate of seventy percent.

Stage Three's rate dropped to thirty-nine percent.

Stage Four only seventeen.

She shut the laptop and leaned back. Everything was gone.

Even if she survived, there was no way the Outfit would let her remain as an operations agent and go out in the field again. Chemo would likely cause her to have permanent medical side-effects. The Outfit couldn't send someone medically compromised into the field, and she understood why. Would they even let her be a desk jockey?

Probably not, she thought. *I wouldn't let me help.* Forget even being an employee. There's no chance they'd let her even be a contractor like her father.

She walked to her room, Bagel in-hand, and fell into bed.

Her tears flowed hot down her cheeks until she fell asleep.

Dreams were a funny thing for Alicia. When she was younger, she'd never had dreams, only nightmares. Nightmares of shadowy men and women towering over her, the only light coming off them was from their evil, red, glowing eyes. After being rescued from that life, the nightmares largely faded away to be replaced by the typical fears of a student. Anxiety-raising dreams about failing a test or somehow being in class with no clothes. But usually, her dreams were nice, innocuous dreams of nonsense.

She'd forgotten the taste of fear from nightmares. But they'd returned like a bad penny.

At first, they came only as feelings. Foreboding and dread doing their best to suffocate her. Then the bad dreams took shape. Massive, fleshy tumors swallowing her, bit by bit. Then the tumors turned dark, and they grew the same glowing eyes as her abusers. Alicia tried running from them, but her feet sank into a ground made soft from the cancer's poison, holding her fast.

She recognized the nightmares for exactly what they were, but her sleeping mind wouldn't let her escape by waking up.

The nightmare tumors faded away, replaced by dreams of the old man from the woods watching her, telling her she would never be special and she would never help anyone ever again. Those words, though dreamed, hurt worse than the cancer.

She even dreamed of Bagel. The kitten crawled onto her stomach, sniffing and then pawing at her abdomen. Alicia knew he was trying to get to the tumors under the skin and flesh. In the dream, Bagel was a dark silhouette like the ghosts of nightmares past, but her mind's eye focused on his bright, brilliant gold eyes shining hopefully. The cat continued pawing at her skin, but not enough to scratch it. It made a gagging sound, then threw up on her exposed belly. The vomit looked like liquid gold, and it spread all across her stomach, shifting and moving in the dark like a living thing.

Sunlight stabbed into Alicia's eyes, waking her. As bad as she felt in the Catskills with her dad, she felt so much worse now. Every joint hurt, from her fingers to her toes. Her muscles ached, and her head throbbed worse than any hangover she'd ever felt. It was worse than waking up after the sex trafficker drugged her when she was a child.

Bagel licked her cheek. The poor thing was probably hungry.

When Alicia rolled out of bed, her legs gave out from under her. She crashed down onto the wood-patterned laminate flooring she'd installed the previous summer. The only positive of her current position was the bare floor felt wonderfully cool against her skin.

She wiped a fever sweat from her face and crawled into her apartment's living room. Bagel followed cheerfully beside her, rubbing against her side. Alicia couldn't even find the strength to shoo the kitten away. She got to the couch and the coffee table where she'd left her phone the night before, grabbed it and called Becca.

"Hey there, Alicia! How are you this morning?"

"Please… " Alicia's voice came out in a rasp. "Please come… over… please… "

Less than a minute later, her neighbor knocked at the door. Once. Twice. Then the woman let herself in with the spare key and rushed to Alicia's side. Becca's hand felt cold against Alicia's forehead.

"Oh, my dear. You are burning up. I don't need a thermometer to know you're way too warm. Let me help you up to the couch."

Alicia let herself be pulled and rolled onto her couch. Her neighbor was a lot stronger than she looked. A moment later Alicia felt a cool washcloth pressed to her forehead. "Thank you, Becca." Her voice came out as a barely intelligible grunt.

"I put a tumbler on the table next to you, straw and all. You need to sip on that. I don't know, sweetie. You might need to go to the hospital, you're burning up."

"It's just a fever," Alicia whispered. "Probably from the cancer."

Becca stayed oddly quiet for what felt like an eternity to Alicia. She managed to get her eyes open. Had her eyelids ever felt so heavy? When her eyes focused, she found Becca sitting on the floor next to her, one hand stroking her hair, and the other wiping her own tears away.

"I'm so sorry, Alicia. What… I mean… where?"

"Ovaries."

"I'm so sorry," Becca said again.

"Do me… a favor?"

"Anything, honey."

Alicia waved a tired hand at her kitten. "Get Bagel some food? Pay you later."

"Bagel, huh? Don't worry. I'll go get some right now. You try and get some rest."

Alicia didn't hear her neighbor leave. She faded in and out of fever dreams for the rest of the day. Somewhere, alternating between sweating through her clothes and shivering under three blankets, Becca helped her into the shower where she sat on the tiled floor letting the water fall on her for the better part of an hour. She didn't feel any sense of embarrassed modesty when the older woman undressed her. Those feelings had long since been driven away by her time on the streets.

"Looks like your fever gave you a rash, dear. Strange spot for it, though."

Alicia looked down through bleary eyes. Sure enough, a huge, angry rash covered her entire abdomen. Something about the placement of the redness tried to make it through her exhausted mind, but she pushed it away.

The next day, Alicia's mind felt clearer, though she admitted to herself that was a particularly low bar. She could walk, more or less. Shower herself, thankfully. Becca brought by more cat food for Bagel, who was doing his best to eat twice his weight in tuna. The kitten already seemed larger than when she'd first spotted him, though that was probably a trick of her remaining fever.

She managed to have some pho delivered from the local Vietnamese place, Pho-nominal. She'd tried both chicken noodle and matzah ball soup, neither of which worked when she felt like crap, nor did they taste good. Pho, though, always worked. Especially with a little of her homemade chili paste.

As she drank the leftover broth from the soup, Alicia downed a few ibuprofens and some Tylenol. Her body still felt like she had the world's worst flu. She could barely move without feeling aches and pains. The worst part of all of it was a ringing in her ear that just wouldn't quit. She'd fired pistols and rifles without ear protection, so she was familiar with tinnitus. This was like that, but on steroids. Like the ringing was mixed with a weird sort of static.

At one point, the ringing in her ears was so loud she almost missed the buzzing of her phone. She grabbed it and recognized the number on caller ID as Doctor Reynolds' office.

"Crap. I forgot about the appointment." She tapped the phone to answer. "This is Alicia."

"Hey there, Alicia. This is Doctor Reynolds. We missed you at the office yesterday. I'm just calling to see if everything is alright."

"Right. I'm so sorry, Doctor Reynolds. I came down with something. I've barely been able to stand since the night before last. I spent all day yesterday out for the count."

"Can you tell me your symptoms?"

The doctor was all business. Alicia even detected a little worry.

She took a sip of water and cleared her throat. "Excuse me. Sorry about that. Uh... bad fever. Aches and pains everywhere like you wouldn't believe. Could barely think straight or open my eyes. Constant headaches. And I've got this ringing in my ears that won't go away."

"Alicia, you should have had someone take you to the hospital. Especially in your weakened state."

Through all the pain, fever, and general feeling of garbage, anger burned to the surface, white hot. "My weakened state? And why do you think I'm in that state, doc? Maybe if you or your condescending prick of an assistant would tell me what the hell was going on with my test results, I could make some actual decisions. So how 'bout it? Feel like doing your damn job today?"

Alicia regretted the outburst almost instantly. She'd always had a temper. Always expected people to give their best, and hated when people cut corners. She knew yelling at the doctor wouldn't do any good. The mental image of her father's disapproving frown came to mind.

Screw it. Doc had it coming.

The lie wasn't quite enough to convince herself.

Reynolds sighed on the other end. *"You're right. I apologize. Look, Alicia, the tests show—"*

"Ovarian cancer? Yeah. Tell your assistant to actually hit the mute button next time he puts a person on hold." Hold back, hold back... nah. Screw that guy. "You know, I'm pretty sure my neighbor's dog can communicate better than he can. She uses little buttons. Can press them easily with a damn paw. Need me to set up a training session for your pet monkey?"

"I'll... I'll have a talk with him. But regardless of the poor manner in which you were given the news—"

"Overheard."

"—the fact remains the same. The biopsy and blood work confirm that the growths we found are malignant. Cancer."

"What stage? Don't sugar coat this, please."

"The CT scan showed the tumors weren't just on your ovaries. They've spread, and were large enough to spot through the imaging. This puts you in Stage Three."

"Less than a forty percent chance of making it five years. What... what are my options."

"There's always new treatments that are improving the survival rates. That's why we wanted you to come in yesterday. To go over some of this." Alicia noted how Reynolds didn't deny the life expectancy. *"We need to get you started on chemotherapy treatments as soon as possible. We can have our oncologist, Doctor Sandoval, get this all set up and squared away. I suggest a consultation as soon as you are feeling up to it."*

Her anger evaporated as quickly as it had flared up. All her plans. All the goals and good intentions. All of it gone. "Alright. Give me a couple days, and I'll see where I'm at. Is this the cancer kicking my teeth in right now?"

"Fever, nausea, aches and pains... all of that is pretty

common. But not really at the level you are describing. And not the ringing in the ears. But, look, everybody is different. Even though medicine is constantly evolving, we don't have all the answers for every ailment."

"Right." Alicia closed her eyes and let out a long breath. "Sorry, Doctor Reynolds. It's been a day."

"No apology needed. Just come in as soon as you can."

Alicia agreed and hung up. Bagel crawled into her lap. The kitten was a needy little beast. "And what do you want?" The cat gazed at her with its golden eyes. There was something mysterious in those glowing orbs. Like liquid gold, their color seemed to flow.

Liquid gold.

The dream came back, hazy at first, then a bit clearer. Alicia pulled up her shirt, vaguely remembering Becca mentioning something about a rash. The skin still looked irritated, and just on her abdomen. When she put her hand of the patch of redness, the skin was hot to the touch. She looked down at Bagel.

"Was that a dream? Or... " She couldn't even finish the thought out loud. It was absurd.

Stage Three Ovarian Cancer.

Thinking about it deflated her. Alicia sunk deeper into the couch. The world suddenly seemed so large and uncaring. She was just a grain of sand in a desert.

In the privacy of her home, where no one but her kitten could see her weakness, she relented to the sadness and cried herself to sleep.

Three days after the fever hit her like a dump truck full of bricks, it vanished like it never existed. In its absence Alicia felt... wonderful. No aches. No pain. Zero nausea. All the fogginess clouding her brain before was swept away, as if by a strong ocean wind. The world seemed brighter after having been effectively bedridden for days.

She sat up on the couch, planting her bare feet on the wood laminate flooring. Curling her toes, she felt the grain, and for some reason it brought a smile to her face.

"Food."

The sound of Becca's voice came from one of the BabbelPet buttons.

"Food. Food. Food. Food."

Bagel slammed his front paws repeatedly over the button on the hexagonal foam pads and stared at her. Sure enough, the kitten's bowl was empty. In just three days the cat had filled out substantially. It seemed twice the size Alicia remembered him being back in the forest. But there was no way. It must have been severely malnourished. Maybe it hadn't even been a kitten at all, but a cat in desperate need of twenty cans of tuna. Unbidden, memories of some of her sisters shoved their way to the surface. Memories of their nearly skeletal bodies after her father had rescued them all.

She slowly stood, then straightened with a sense of astonishment. Muttering a small prayer of thanks to whatever higher power had taken away her aches, Alicia was halfway to the bathroom to take a shower when Bagel hit the buttons again.

First, *"Food."* Then *"Now."*

Alicia raised her eyebrows. "Jeez, you're serious, aren't you? Well, I better not keep His Royal Bagel-ness waiting." She walked to the kitchen, feeling a bounce in her step that had been gone for months. After popping the top from a can, she dumped the tuna into Bagel's bowl. The cat pounced on it, eating it all within seconds, then it looked up at her while licking its lips.

"Alright... I guess I'll give you another." She popped another can into the bowl which Bagel attacked, but at a slightly less ravenous pace.

With her cat occupied, Alicia hit the shower. When she got out, she took a minute to look at herself in the mirror. The rash was gone, and the recent pale color of her skin had returned to a normal healthy color. Her reflection still showed a too-thin doppelgänger. She pulled at her skin, checking for tenderness. Nothing. Aside from the weight loss, she looked more like herself than ever.

Along the edge of the left side of her ribcage were rows of scars like hash marks from her days living a horrific existence on the streets. On the right ribcage were two small tattoos. One of the Deftones pony logo, and the other of Jamiroquai's buffalo man. She'd gotten the tattoos while at Princeton to remind her of the music that had driven away suicidal thoughts she'd had before her father had rescued her from the streets.

Alicia felt good as new.

Too good.

Instead of happiness, dread grabbed her by the neck. She was feeling great in contrast to having felt like death warmed over for the last couple days. Alicia still had a veritable death sentence hanging over her. This was the calm before the storm. Alicia rushed to her phone, and called Reynolds to make an appointment before things got worse.

— end of preview —

PREVIEW OF MULTIVERSE

Michael Salomon lurched into a sitting position and felt a wave of dizziness as he blinked the sleep out of his eyes. His heart raced, and he was having difficulty catching his breath as the gauzy memories of a dream fled from his now-conscious mind.

Something had just happened, and he wasn't exactly sure what it could be.

Definitely not a dream. Not with the growing anxiety he felt. Some kind of nightmare...

He glanced at the clock on his nightstand. It was just past seven. He'd gotten to bed only four hours earlier, but waking up at this time was habit. During the school year he'd be frantically climbing out of bed to go teach physics at Princeton. But it was the summer, and he dedicated all his attention to his research.

That was what had kept him up late last night. A discovery that ended with him leaving the lab after two a.m. in a state of shock.

He had wanted to tell someone. Anyone. But it was late, and he couldn't trust himself to talk to his colleagues until he could verify everything with a clear mind. Triple-check the data. Then, and only then, would he risk his reputation.

He stood up from the bed, only to immediately sit back down with a sudden bout of vertigo. Maybe it was his body telling him he needed more rest.

And then he caught the scent of bacon.

He didn't remember making any bacon when he got home from the lab. He had been too exhausted to do anything but go directly to bed. But when he opened the bedroom door, the scent was unmistakable, wafting up the stairs from the kitchen.

And something more.

Someone was humming.

Standing at the top of the stairs, he was about to yell out an empty threat that he had a gun, but his words were choked away when he saw a woman approaching the base of the stairs, carrying a coffee mug. She had straight dark hair hanging to her mid-back, and naturally tanned skin. And she was very pregnant.

Maria.

Their German shepherd puppy, Percy, followed her every step, his nails clicking on the wooden floor.

Before Michael could say a word, Maria's face lit up.

"You're awake!" She held up the steaming mug of coffee. "I was going to bring this up to you and tell you I made breakfast."

He merely stared, not believing that this could be real.

Maria waved for him to come down. "The baby is really moving," she said, putting a hand on her stomach. "Come down and feel her."

The puppy looked up at him and barked joyfully.

Michael's skin felt cold and clammy, like he was on the verge of passing out. But he managed to walk slowly down the stairs, unable to take his eyes off the woman he'd loved for nearly a quarter of his forty-two years on this Earth.

Maria grabbed his hand and put it on her stomach. "Do you feel that?"

He nodded. "What—" He cleared his throat. "What day is it?"

Percy whined for attention.

"You poor thing, you're barely even awake." Maria smiled, handed him his coffee, and scratched the top of Percy's head. "It's Thursday, and you practically passed out the moment your head hit the pillow. You didn't even get undressed."

That part was true. He was still wearing the same clothes from last night at the lab.

Still unbelieving, he pressed his hand to Maria's belly once more, feeling the movement as life stirred within her.

Their baby.

His throat tightened with emotion, and he felt like he was about to explode.

"Ay, *mi amor*. What's wrong?" Maria wiped away an unbidden tear that had rolled down his cheek. She wrapped her arms around him. "Whatever it is, it'll be fine. Did something bad happen at work?"

He kissed the top of her head, a storm of emotions raging through him. "I guess I just had a nightmare."

"What about?"

"I don't want to say it out loud."

"Come." Maria grabbed his free hand and gently pulled him toward the kitchen. "Have a seat, and I'll serve up breakfast. I'm sure everything will look better after you've gotten something in your belly."

Michael sat at the kitchen table and watched as his wife of eight years, pregnant with their child, busied herself in the kitchen.

He watched, knowing it was impossible. Because his memories told him of a cascading set of events that had led to Maria disappearing.

First was the late-term complication with the pregnancy. Their daughter was delivered early, and though she should have lived—the odds were with her—she didn't make it. That was the beginning of the end for their marriage. There were arguments. Bitter and nonsensical fights. And then, one day, Maria left and never came back.

He vividly remembered the pain of waking up and

finding her gone. Her clothes still in the closet. Her car in the garage.

He filed a missing persons report with the police. They told him she was an adult and maybe she'd just needed time away.

But Maria had literally *vanished*. Gone from his life.

For years.

Until now.

And then there was Percy. The puppy was now watching his mom prepare scrambled eggs, his tail wagging furiously as she scooped some into his bowl on the counter.

Percy was alive... and still a puppy. He had whined for weeks after Maria disappeared. And then one day he escaped from the back yard and got killed by a car.

But apparently that never happened.

It was all a lie. A nightmare.

Percy hopped from side to side with anticipation as Maria mixed his puppy kibble with the eggs. When she set it on the floor, he dove in and devoured it.

Michael smiled at the sight. His wife was really here with him, and as his gaze trailed down to her bulging belly, it took all of his self-control to not break down and begin sobbing right then and there. Their daughter wasn't dead. She was having a little party inside Maria's belly.

Everything was good. Everything was as it should be.

Maria set down two steaming plates of scrambled eggs and bacon, poured herself a glass of orange juice, and sat down beside him.

He sipped the coffee. It was hot, strong, and black. Just like she'd always made it.

She looked longingly at his mug and sighed. "That's the one thing I do miss. My morning *tinto*."

Tinto was what Colombians called a black coffee.

He smiled, reached under the table, and patted her belly. "It won't be long. Would you prefer that I don't drink coffee while you're pregnant?"

Maria gave him a hard look. "Why, are *you* pregnant? Don't be silly. Besides, the orange juice is good for the baby." She took a sip, then pointed at his plate with her fork. "Don't let your food get cold."

"Yes, ma'am." Michael smiled and shoveled a forkful of eggs into his mouth.

Yet even as he chewed, he felt a nagging sense of wrongness.

But then Maria smiled. He returned the smile as he took a bite of bacon.

Everything was perfect.

It was just past ten, and Michael was driving south on US-1 heading in to work when he saw a cluster of brake lights up ahead. Traffic slowed, and then stopped altogether. He sighed, not seeing any cause for the traffic jam. It was a simple two-lane highway, and never got backed up.

"Someone must have gotten into an accident," he muttered.

As he sat in the car, making no forward progress, his mind drifted back to last night's experiments. His area of research had to do with superluminal particles, otherwise known as tachyons—a niche field that occupied one of the darkest recesses of special relativity. And there was good reason for that: no one had ever detected a tachyon. They were the stuff of science fiction.

Tachyons were particles that could go faster than the speed of light. And if there was one thing that everyone understood—or misunderstood—about Einstein's groundbreaking theory, it was that *nothing* could go faster than the speed of light.

This wasn't exactly true.

To be more accurate, Einstein said that nothing that *initially* moved below the speed of light could be accelerated to move beyond the speed of light. And thus the question arose: could tachyons exist?

Up until last night, that question had gone unanswered.

Michael was roused from his thoughts at the sound of tires screeching behind him. He looked in the rearview mirror and saw a vintage Cadillac swerving, seemingly out of control. No cars had stopped behind Michael, and the barreling Cadillac was no more than fifty feet away from crashing right into him.

Everything seemed to slow. Michael saw the panicked look on the driver's face as he wrestled with his steering wheel. The driver had clearly lost control of the giant boat of a car. It fishtailed, smoke billowing from the tires.

The professor braced himself for impact.

And... the Cadillac skidded to a stop beside him, facing backwards. The driver was literally within arm's reach.

Under normal circumstances, Michael would have thrown his entire inventory of curse words at the man who'd nearly hit him, and would likely have invented new ones for good measure. But he was shaking with the sudden dump of adrenaline into his bloodstream, and he found he couldn't form a coherent sentence. The world was spinning, and he thought he might throw up.

He needed to gather his wits.

So he turned off into the breakdown lane, moved ahead several car lengths, and pulled into the entrance to a parking lot. It was for some kind of medical complex—a sign read "Rothman Orthopedics." But he barely noticed it. He just needed air.

He parked, got out, and took in a slow, deep breath. He felt as though the ground beneath him was tilting. He'd never passed out before, but he was sure he was about to.

Clinging to his car door to keep from collapsing, he closed his eyes and focused on his breathing.

In his mind's eye he saw a verdant field of grass.

It was more than an image; it was a crystal-clear vision, unfolding as though he were experiencing a dream through a camera lens.

He saw a man in the distance, kneeling. Michael involuntarily moved toward him, despite the fact that the closer he got to the figure, the more anxious he felt.

The man was in a graveyard, kneeling before a tombstone.

Michael's breath caught in his throat. He recognized the man before him.

It was *him*.

But not exactly him. An older version of him. He was thinner. Too thin. A noticeable amount of gray in his hair. A scraggly beard.

Then Michael looked at the tombstone, and his blood ran cold.

Felicia Batsheva Salomon.
We had you only one day, but know this: If love
could have saved you, you would have lived forever.

Below the inscription were two dates: birth and death. They were the same date.

And the date... was tomorrow.

Michael's tires screeched in the driveway as he parked, jumped out of the car, and rushed into the house.

"Maria!" he yelled.

He heard the dog's bark in response, coming from the back yard.

His heart pounding, Michael raced to the sliding glass door leading to the back yard and yanked it open. "Maria!"

"Honey? I thought you were going into work?"

Maria was sitting on a lounge chair in partial shade from their patio umbrella. She looked uncomfortable.

He rushed over and gingerly scooped up her hand. "Baby, are you feeling okay?"

She shrugged. "I'm feeling very pregnant right now. So, the usual. But also my lower back is really hurting today. I thought this chair would help but... no. What are you doing home?"

Michael couldn't explain. "I—I want to get you checked out by the doctor. You look... overly tired."

"Why today? I already have my appointment set for tomorrow."

He pasted on a smile. "Just do me this one favor. It's your job to be pregnant, and my job to be worried, right? I just want to make sure everything is okay with you and Felicia."

Reluctantly, Maria allowed him to help as she slowly levered herself up from the lounge chair. "I haven't even showered yet."

"No one cares about that. Please, just humor me."

"Fine." She rolled her eyes. "But at least let me change my clothes."

He gave her a quick kiss on the forehead. "Deal."

The ultrasound technician placed warm jelly onto the business end of the wide transducer and then placed it on Maria's belly. "Okay, let's take a look at the little cutie and get some measurements."

Maria gripped Michael's hand as the sound of a rapid heartbeat played through the ultrasound machine's speaker. She looked over at the technician. "Is that Felicia's heartbeat?"

"It sure is. Felicia is a beautiful name. It means 'smile' in Spanish, doesn't it?"

"Close, but not exactly. It's more related to *feliz*, which means happy."

The technician continued moving the probe across Maria's belly with one hand while working the machine's keyboard and mouse with the other. "Do you have a middle name picked out?"

Maria smiled at Michael. "We're not sure yet, but I was thinking about Batsheva. It's his grandmother's name; she passed not too long ago. What do you think, honey?"

Michael nodded, but a chill raced up his spine. That was the name on the tombstone.

Felicia Batsheva Salomon.

The technician stopped suddenly and lifted up the probe, making the screen go black. "Wait here a moment," she said. "I'll be right back with Dr. Sakata."

Though her voice was calm, Michael spotted the look of concern on the woman's face as she got up from the stool and left the room.

Maria squeezed his hand. "I should ask Sakata if there's anything I can take for my lower back. I'm not sure I can handle another eight weeks of this."

Michael gave her a warm smile, but inside, he was freaking out. What had the technician seen? There shouldn't be any big surprises in the beginning of the eighth month; it should be smooth sailing at this point. At least, that's what all those damned pregnancy books said that Maria had made him read.

The door opened, and Dr. Sakata walked in. "Hello, Mr. and Mrs. Salomon. I understand we're doing a wellness check. Did you have any spotting or other symptoms that made you come in today?"

"Spotting, as in bleeding? No." Maria hitched her thumb at her husband. "He's just worried, and wanted me to get checked. The only new symptom I have is back pain. But I guess that comes with the territory."

The doctor sat on the stool. "Well, let's have a look."

As the physician slid the probe across Maria's belly, the ultrasound screen showed various structures that meant nothing to Michael. Still he watched closely, his eyes moving from the screen to the doctor's expression and back, looking for some kind of reaction.

Sakata stopped on one fuzzy image that looked like all

the rest, clicked something on the keyboard, and zoomed in. He shifted the angle of the transducer slightly.

The sound of the baby's heartbeat thudded loudly in the room.

"Is there something in particular you're looking for?" Maria asked.

The doctor glanced at her. "You said you're having back pain?"

She nodded. "It's much worse today. I normally don't sleep on my back, but I fell asleep that way waiting for my husband to get back from work." Maria gave Michael an accusatory glare, then squeezed his hand and blew him a kiss.

Sakata zoomed in on different parts of the image and clicked more buttons, causing small printouts to roll out of a slot in the machine. After about a minute of that, he lifted the transducer, wiped it off, and then wiped down Maria's belly with a fluffy white towel.

"Well," he said, "let's start with the baby. She seems to be under no distress and is about where we'd hope she'd be for a gestational age of thirty-two weeks. That's all good. But it's also good that you came in today." Sakata held up one of the images and pointed at something that was hard to make out. "Maria, you have a minor placental abruption. That means that the placenta has partially torn from the wall of the uterus."

Maria gasped. "What does that mean for the baby?" Her

eyes welled up with tears and she squeezed hard on Michael's hand.

"Like I said, it's minor. But I would like to keep you overnight for some tests. We need to check the blood chemistry of the baby and make sure she's still getting everything she needs. It's likely the tests will come back okay, but you two should prepare yourself for the possibility that we may have to deliver early."

All Michael could see at that moment was the birthdate on the tombstone. His voice sounded far away as he said, "But she's only thirty-two weeks..."

Sakata patted the air and tried to smile reassuringly, with minimal success. "A fetus that reaches thirty-two weeks' gestation has a ninety-five percent chance of survival. The important thing is that you're here and we know about this issue. I'm going to prescribe antenatal betamethasone, which is a corticosteroid to help with the baby's lungs. It'll help them mature in anticipation of a possible early delivery."

Maria asked with a quavering voice, "You think we'll deliver early?"

Sakata smiled, and this time it seemed genuine. "We'll do everything we can to keep your little one inside you for as long as possible. We're just preparing for other eventualities." He leaned forward and patted Maria's foot, then shifted his gaze to Michael. "I'll have the nurse give you a list of things to get from the house. I'm going to call admitting and get your wife checked in for tonight."

"How long do I have to stay?" Maria asked.

"At least through tomorrow morning. By then we'll know more. If this is a developing issue that needs immediate treatment, we'll address it then. But it may well be that we can treat this with careful monitoring and bed rest."

"Bed rest, as in *at home* bed rest?" Michael asked.

Sakata nodded. "*If* things are stable, then yes." He gave them both a sympathetic look. "I know this isn't what you wanted to hear. But at least we know about it now, and you're where you need to be. In the meantime, let's try our best not to worry about things that may well not happen."

As the doctor left, Michael could think only of the tombstone.

He leaned down and gave Maria a kiss. "It'll be okay."

"Th-thank you," Maria stammered as she let out a shuddering breath.

"For what?"

Maria began practicing the breathing techniques she'd learned in one of their many pregnancy classes. "For feeling paranoid today. You probably saved the baby."

Michael leaned down and held his wife close so she couldn't see the worry on his face. He wanted to believe her, believe the doctor, and assume everything would be all right.

But he couldn't. His mind's eye couldn't look away from the haunting image of tomorrow's date carved in stone.

Birth... and death.

His fear wouldn't lift until tomorrow had passed safely.

It's only a vision, not a prophecy.

He held his wife tightly and tried to believe it.

Michael stood over Felicia's incubator, staring down at the newborn delivered only eight hours earlier. The last thirty-six hours had been the most harrowing experience of his life. Maria had spent the night in the hospital, but after some observation this morning everything seemed to be perfectly fine. There was even talk of being able to go home on bed rest. And then suddenly Maria was being wheeled into the operating room for an emergency C-section. Throughout it all, the memory of that tombstone weighed heavily on his soul.

"Mr. Salomon?"

One of the neonatal intensive care unit's nurses approached with a growing frown. He knew that he'd breached the hospital's protocol by entering the NICU without having checked in with one of the nurses, but once Maria was out of recovery and had fallen asleep in the hospital room, he'd needed to see his little girl.

"I'm sorry," he said quickly. "There was nobody at the desk, and I just wanted to make sure she's okay."

The nurse paused at the foot of the incubator, shook her head, then checked the digital readout on the monitor. "Heart rate is one thirty-five, respiration is at fifty, and her blood oxygen is ninety-eight. All within a very healthy range."

"She's so small," he said.

The woman picked up the clipboard attached to the lower frame of the incubator. "Three pounds, fifteen ounces, sixteen inches long, with a head circumference of eleven and a half inches. All good sizes for someone her gestational age." The nurse's voice took on a more upbeat tone. "Felicia's had quite a birthday, maybe you should—"

"Honey, how is she?"

Michael turned and his eyes widened. His wife was walking toward him, dragging along an IV pole on wheels. He rushed over to her.

"Maria, what are you doing on your feet? You just had surgery, are you crazy?"

She smiled and patted his cheek. "I'm okay. The doctor said I'm supposed to get on my feet and walk around." She looked to the nurse. "Is she okay?"

The nurse smiled. "She's doing fine. I'll leave you two alone to visit for a little bit." She glanced up at the clock on the wall. "We change shifts in just a few minutes, at midnight. I'll let the new shift nurse know you're here, but you should check in with her as well."

Michael gave Maria his arm to hold on to, then led her over to the incubator, where she gazed down at the sleeping baby.

"She's beautiful," Maria said.

Michael agreed. "Are you sure you're okay to stand? I can bring a chair."

"I'm fine." She squeezed his arm and put her hand on the clear plastic of the incubator, unable to take her eyes from Felicia. "She's a miracle."

They both stared down at the baby, and Maria began softly reciting a prayer.

"God bless Felicia behind the plastic wall.

"She has been taken from my womb without warning and I long to hold her in my arms.

"Lord, I ask in your name that Felicia be healed.

"God give her the strength to make it through another second, minute, hour, and day, as each moment is a blessing and a triumph from heaven.

"Lord, we are at your mercy for the life of our child. Please leave her here on Earth and know that we will provide all the love and understanding that Felicia needs. We accept the challenge and will be your humble servants, dear Lord."

They both said, "Amen," and Michael kissed the top of Maria's head.

"It all happened so fast." Maria looked up at him with a serious expression. "It's a miracle we were even in the hospital already when everything went wrong." Her voice quavered with emotion. "How did you know?"

"Know what?"

"You know, about getting me to see the doctor."

He looked up at the wall clock and watched it tick over to midnight. Somehow, seeing that big hand point to twelve lessened the fear that had been gnawing at his guts ever since he'd had that vision. That tombstone would never be real. It was now the next day.

He met Maria's gaze and smiled. "You'd think I was nuts if I told you."

Maria arched an eyebrow.

"Okay, fine," he said. "I saw it in a nightmare."

"Saw what?"

"Felicia's tombstone."

Maria's eyes widened.

Michael pointed at the clock. "It's past midnight, thank God. But that damned tombstone had yesterday's date on it."

"That's awful." She pressed her lips together and held a troubled expression. "Why didn't you tell me about your nightmare before heading off to work?"

Michael winced as he recalled the screeching of tires that had led to his vision. "Because... I hadn't had it yet?"

Maria looked confused.

"I guess it wasn't exactly a nightmare," he explained. "Is there such a thing as a daymare? On the way to work, someone almost rear-ended me on US-1, and I was so freaked out I pulled off the highway and parked. That's when the nightmare hit me. It was the strangest thing, but it was so vivid. Just like—" He cut himself off. That morning's memories—of not having Maria by his side and all the rest—

it was still a raw emotion that he couldn't stand to even verbalize. "It was just like watching a movie."

"It was just a dream," she said, taking his hand. "I'd say I'm sorry you had to see it, but I can't. Because it gave you the warning that saved Felicia's life." She looked down at their daughter once more. "It truly is a miracle."

As Michael rinsed his mouth and put the toothbrush away, he heard the dog whine. He turned from the bathroom sink and saw Percy gently reaching up with one paw to touch the top of Maria's leg. It was almost as if the dog was finally noticing that something was missing—namely the baby.

Maria was struggling with a wide elastic band wrapped partially around her midsection. "Come here and help me with this abdominal binder," she said. "I need you to pull it tight across my belly while I pull the other side."

"Isn't that going to hurt your incision?"

"They told me I have to use this thing every day," Maria huffed. "Just help me get it on."

As she gripped one end of the band, Michael pulled on the other.

"Harder!" she groused, more impatient than usual this morning.

Reluctantly, he pulled the elastic band taut around her

midsection and pressed it flat on the Velcro portion so it would stay.

"Ah, that's better," she said with a sigh of relief.

He was doubtful as she walked out of the bedroom. It had been only a week since the surgery, and she was supposed to be taking it easy. Maria didn't seem to understand what "taking it easy" meant.

Michael followed her down the stairs. "Are you sure you don't need any help today?"

She shook her head. "Stop asking me that. I'm fine. I just need to get everything ready for the baby." From the moment the doctors had said Felicia would likely be able to come home tomorrow, Maria had thought about nothing else. "I love you, but you drive me crazy asking me if I'm okay every five seconds of the day. Go to work. Show the world how smart I know you are."

"What about food and—"

"Are you kidding me? Our neighbors and your colleagues have filled our refrigerator with more food than we can possibly eat in the next month." Maria pulled him down for a kiss, aimed him at the front door, and gave him a light push. "Go, before I have to kick you out." She pointed with authority in the direction of the door.

Michael got the message. It was time to get back to work.

Michael slowed as he approached the bridge spanning across Washington Road and turned right onto the private road. Despite Princeton's prestigious name and reputation, it always amused him that there were utterly no signs here indicating that he was now on the campus. After a quick left, and then another, he approached Jadwin Hall, where most of the physics labs were located. As it was the beginning of summer session, there wasn't much competition for parking spots, at least compared to other times of the year, and he actually managed to park close to the building.

As he climbed the six steps to the side entrance of the hall, a voice shouted, "Michael!"

The chair of the department was standing by the entrance, with a tall, slim, blonde woman standing next to him.

"How goes it, Herman?" Michael said, walking up to the entrance. "Why are you standing outside in the humidity?"

The man held up his ID and shrugged. "My badge isn't working." Something about the professor's deadpan delivery and native Dutch accent always made it sound like he was making a dry joke.

Michael unclipped his own badge and swiped it on the badge reader. The door buzzed and he pulled it open, letting the two into the air-conditioned building.

As they walked in, Herman made introductions. "Michael, this is Doctor Carmel Harrington, a research fellow at the Children's Hospital of Westmead out of Australia. Carmel, this is Professor Michael Salomon. His work on high-energy particle detection in empty space may lead us into places we never imagined possible. More importantly, his wife just had a baby girl." He looked at Michael. "Congratulations, by the way. How is Maria holding up?"

Michael beamed. "She's doing great. We think we'll be able to bring the baby home tomorrow."

"Excellent. You'll have to bring the little one by so we can all coo over her. Only when mother and daughter are up to it, of course."

"Of course. I'll be excited to show her off."

Herman checked his watch. "Actually, Michael, since you're here, would you mind guiding Carmel to the lounge? I'll be escorting her to give a talk at the Lewis-Sigler Institute in a few minutes, but I need to make a quick call first. You can ask her about her research. It's fascinating."

"Not a problem."

As Herman hurried off, Michael led Carmel down the familiar route, past the first-floor laboratories and into the open-air lounge, which was equipped with several well-stocked refrigerators and even an industrial-strength cappuccino maker, which he'd never actually used before.

Michael grabbed a Diet Mountain Dew and Carmel selected a V-8, and then they took seats at a table. "So," Michael began, "what kind of research do you do at the children's hospital?"

Carmel, who looked to be in her mid-to-late fifties, sipped at her drink. "Professor Salomon—"

"Please, Michael is fine."

"Michael," she said. She had a very slight Australian accent. "Are you familiar with SIDS?"

"Sudden Infant Death Syndrome? I know what it is, but not much more." He shuddered at the idea of having a child stop breathing for no apparent reason.

"Well, I've been studying the subject for thirty years. Ever since my son, Damien, died of it."

Michael set down his drink. "I'm so sorry to hear that."

She waved dismissively. "Ever since then, many people have thought I'm mental for being so single-minded in my pursuit of answers. Or really, just one answer. *Why?* Why did my otherwise healthy son die? At the time it happened, I was actually a lawyer, though I had a biochemistry background. I quit my job, went back to school, got my PhD in sleep medicine, and dove into research. And it's been worth it. My studies have identified a biochemical marker that can help detect which babies are more at risk of SIDS."

"That's amazing." Michael leaned forward, elbows on the table. "What's the marker?"

She warmed to her subject. "It's an enzyme called butyrylcholinesterase, also known as BChE. Babies with a low amount of it are more susceptible to SIDS. We believe that the low level of the enzyme represents a dysfunction of the nervous system, and poses an inherent vulnerability to SIDS for those infants. We're currently working on a treatment protocol."

"Wow. You represent quite the inspirational story," Michael said. He couldn't help but think of Felicia. "As

Herman said, I've just had a child. She was born last week, eight weeks premature, and she's coming home tomorrow, the doctors think. I don't suppose this enzyme test is already rolled out to hospitals yet?"

She smiled. "No, that's still a long way off. We haven't even published quite yet. But I'm hopeful that in the next eighteen months we can be rolling out recommendations to government agencies around the world. Your FDA, the UK's NHS, and others."

Just then Herman appeared in the doorway. He nodded at the drinks on the table. "I'm glad to see you don't share Michael's affection for Diet Mountain Dew. I don't know how he can drink that stuff."

Carmel laughed. "Most people say that about me drinking V-8." She smiled at Michael. "To each their own."

"Well, I'm ready when you are," Herman said.

Michael and Carmel stood. "It was very nice meeting you," Michael said. "I look forward to seeing your work put an end to SIDS around the world."

"I was telling her the same thing!" Herman put in. "For physicists, the victories in our research never feel quite so tangible as that."

As Herman and Carmel hurried off, Michael considered what Herman had said. Physics research often didn't provide the same level of tangible results, and yet...

He thought back to the work he'd been doing the last time he was in the lab, a week ago, on that fateful night before his vision. Would he be able to reproduce those results?

Only one way to find out.

Michael frowned, as he always did, at the name on the sign above the lab's entrance. Although he'd worked in the basement-level lab for nearly a decade now, it had been labeled the "Salomon lab" last year when he attained tenure. That was a thing at Princeton—naming labs after the professors that headed the research within—but to Michael it felt pretentious.

He swiped his badge on the reader and pushed his way inside. He found Ken, one of his post-doc researchers, already at work, showing a lab notebook to a summer institute grad student whose name Michael couldn't recall.

"Hey Ken, were you able to get any of those higher-speed CCDs from that MIT contact I gave you?"

The post-doc nodded vigorously. Ken Lee was a brilliant researcher, and his almost savant-like talent with numbers manifested itself in his ability to solve complex math equations in seconds. Michael loved working with the guy; he was practically a human calculator. But Ken also had severe speech apraxia, making it very difficult for him to communicate in a verbal manner. Instead, he often relied on a notebook-sized dry-erase board that he always kept handy.

As Ken started to scribble a response, the grad student hopped up from his stool and gave Michael an uneasy look. Michael understood; he had a reputation for being a hardass with the students. "He's hella smart, but will tear you a new one if you ask him a stupid question" was a common comment in his student-based reviews on Rate-MyProfessor. Everyone who made it to Princeton was smart, but Michael felt strongly that smart wasn't good enough. All too often, these kids were lazy and didn't want to put the work in. He wasn't at all forgiving when students asked questions about things that were clearly explained in the textbook.

Michael finally remembered the kid's name. "Josh. This isn't going to be like one of my regular classes. You take your cues from Ken. He knows what he's doing, and you'll learn a lot. If you have any questions, ask. I'd rather you ask a question than stare dumbly at us and not learn anything from this summer's experience. Got it?"

Josh nodded. "I totally get it. Thank you for letting me join for the summer, Professor."

"Don't thank me yet." Michael grinned. "You'll probably work harder than you've ever worked. You'll need to keep up."

Ken turned the whiteboard toward Michael, with his response to Michael's question about the CCDs.

"Yesterday we received a dozen high-speed CCDs direct from Professor Johnson's photonics lab. I've incorporated them into the rig, and combined with the new synchronizer, I think we can get

frame grabs in the vacuum chamber with a timing resolution as low as 250 picoseconds."

"That's fantastic. At 250 picoseconds, how far will a photon travel?"

Ken wiped the board with his sleeve and wrote, *"Approximately 7.5cm."*

Josh raised his hand.

Michael grinned. "We're not in the classroom; there's no need to raise your hand. Just ask your question."

"Um." The grad student hesitated for a second. "Professor, if I understand correctly, you're trying to capture proof of certain high-speed particles in the lab's vacuum chamber, right? So, I was curious about why you need a faster cycle time for the cameras. The vacuum chamber has a diameter of one hundred twenty-two centimeters—a full four feet—and the CCDs we had before had a timing resolution of around one nanosecond, so that would mean we could get an image of, let's say a photon traveling about thirty centimeters across the chamber. Meaning we'd get anywhere from three to four images. So... why is that not enough?"

"Very good question," Michael said. "You're just thinking of the wrong kind of particles. You're thinking of luxons—massless particles that always travel at the speed of light, such as a photon. But what if I told you that we're trying to measure something traveling faster than that."

Josh's eyes widened as he looked back and forth between Ken and the professor. "I didn't think—"

"That there were such things?" Michael said. "That's what we're here to prove."

"Or disprove."

"If you have a proposal on how to prove a negative, I'd like to hear it, but no. Our goal is to positively prove the existence of what I think has been buzzing around us since the dawn of time." Michael turned to Ken. "Are the capacitors charged? We ready to run an experiment with the new setup?"

Ken nodded and made a quick scribble on the whiteboard. *"Ready when you are."*

Michael grinned. "Okay, let's do it."

Michael sat in front of a computer, looking at a live image of the vacuum chamber, as Ken walked over to the wall and flipped a red lever. In the upper right-hand corner of the monitor was another video feed coming from the building's roof.

He looked over at the grad student. "Josh, do you understand what we're doing?"

"Ken's opening up the reflector dish to gather whatever it can. It's the same principle as a satellite dish, right?"

"Yes and no. The dish is certainly receiving whatever signals it's being bombarded with, but we aren't reflecting any of the particles nor are we using an LNB to convert any of the signals received into another form. This dish isn't about to receive HBO or anything." Michael watched as the mirror-like petals of the dish unfolded, resulting in something that looked very much like an oversized—and extremely expensive—funnel. "It's a clear day, so we should get a pretty reasonable stream of signals coming in. When we launch the experiment, the funnel will briefly activate a high-gauss magnetic field that will feed the signals into the routing pipe at the base of the funnel. Do you know why we need the magnetic field?"

The grad student furrowed his brow. "Is it sort of like the same problem a particle accelerator has to deal with—you don't want those particles touching the sides of whatever you're piping them through?"

"Exactly right. It's the same consideration they have at the Large Hadron Collider, at Brookhaven National Labs in New York, at Fermilab, and at the smaller accelerators throughout the world. We may not be as famous as them, but I've got a special flavor of the same concept built in this very building. Right now, you and I are sitting in a heavily shielded compartment for an experiment that will last all of about one millisecond.

"That funnel out there is receiving radio waves, visible light, background cosmic radiation, et cetera. Most of which will, of course, be traveling at roughly the speed of light. That's *not* what we want. So we've set up the magnetic fields with a very unusual configuration. The incoming stream of particles will curve, as they do in any accelerator, but we're also forcing the beam to pass through an aperture, such that those particles going at or below the speed of light will bend too far and not make it through the aperture. It's like a race where you have cars going around a track. The slower cars will make the turns as they're supposed to, but a car going too fast will fly right off the track. Those are the particles we're looking for."

Josh grinned. "This is *so* cool. And I was thinking more about the faster cycle time on the cameras. With your setup, even if a particle came screaming into the building at three times the speed of light, meaning it would travel about 22.5 centimeters in 250 picoseconds, we could still catch multiple images of it as it passes through the chamber."

Just then Ken motioned for Josh, who hopped off his stool and joined the researcher at an L-shaped table with a single monitor and keyboard. Michael took the opportunity to look over the equipment. At the heart of it all was a high-density compute cluster, connected by a thick black cable to the synchronizer with the banks of CCDs—in effect tiny cameras capturing whatever light was visible in a 64-by-64 square of pixels. The CCDs were arranged in a grid pattern, and the captured data was fed to the synchronizer, which mapped all the data into an image in the compute cluster's memory.

Michael turned to Ken. "Hey, now that we're pumping CCD frames across to the compute cluster at four times the previous speed, can the computer's memory handle a full millisecond of that data? These are better resolution CCDs than we used before, right?"

Ken began scribbling, and Josh looked over his shoulder and read the words aloud.

"Sorry, Professor, I forgot to mention that. Yes, the CCDs are higher resolution. We have plenty of total memory on the cluster to spool to, but the expected four million frames we'd receive in the span of a millisecond would overwhelm our bandwidth, and the caches can only hold so much. Across all the data channels we have interconnects for, and given that each DIMM has a peak transfer rate of about 35 gigabytes per second, *and* we have no more than 128 data channels we can feed, that gives us a peak spool of roughly 4.5 terabytes per second, or 4.5 gigabytes per millisecond. With these CCDs all pumping a portion of what ends up being a 768K image, the L1 caches will get filled faster than we can flush it across—"

"Okay, I get it. We need a bigger rig. How much wall clock time can we get spooled to memory?"

Using the heavily stained sleeve of his lab coat, Ken wiped the board and wrote a number down, which Josh again read aloud. "Roughly 1.4 microseconds."

Michael let out a groan. He hadn't taken into consideration how close the upgrades would take them toward their current data transfer rate limit.

"Okay, how long does the captured data take to spool to storage and start again?"

More scribbling, and Josh said, "Flushing the caches to memory and then to non-volatile storage will take almost a minute. We also have a limit on how many 1.4 microsecond bursts of data we can store on the storage array currently installed."

"That's fine. I figure if we don't find anything in a particular 1.4-microsecond image run, we can go ahead and delete it. Are we ready on your end?"

Ken gave a thumbs-up.

Michael went back to his console, pulled up the control application, and hovered the mouse arrow over the "go" button.

"Here goes nothing."

He clicked.

A loud thunk reverberated through the lab as several activities all happened seemingly at once.

"Ken," Michael said, "start saving the data and get us ready for another." He kept his focus on his screen, waiting for the first image as he replayed in his mind the steps that had just occurred.

The stream of particles, mostly photons, were captured from the rooftop and routed into the funnel. The conduit through which the particles entered had a very strong magnetic field applied to it, keeping the stream from contacting the walls of the pipe. As the particles entered the building, they raced around the circumference of the basement lab at unimaginable speeds, and on the last loop of their path, those particles traveling at or less than the speed of light were winnowed out. If anything remained in the pipe, it would have flown straight into the vacuum chamber.

The monitor flickered as the first of roughly 5,800 frames of visual data was received. Michael advanced it manually, adding 250 picoseconds with each click—a time period about two billion times shorter than the time it takes for someone to blink. The images all showed nothing—just the darkness of the vacuum chamber.

With his mouse, he highlighted the main portion of the vacuum chamber image, avoiding the time code. Michael clicked the "auto-scan" button, allowing the computer to start flying through the images, looking for any differences in the area he highlighted. In only a second it stopped at the end of the series with a popup message.

"No changes."

Michael nodded. Not unexpected. He glanced at the wall clock. It was ten a.m.

Josh called out, "We're ready."

The professor moved the mouse over the "go" button and repeated the process.

It was going to be a long day.

Michael grimaced. It was seven in the evening, an hour past when he'd told Maria he'd be home. She was used to his shenanigans, especially during the summer, but with the baby coming home tomorrow, he couldn't keep doing this.

"We're ready, Professor." Josh sounded tired.

Michael's obsession wasn't fair to these two any more than it was fair to Maria. "Okay, guys," he said. "This will be the last one for the day."

He clicked "go" again, and the familiar thunk blasted through the room while Michael stared bleary-eyed at the monitor.

The first image came up looking like it always did, with the edges of the dark vacuum chamber only barely visible as varying shades of black and dark gray. Michael had long ago quit searching the images manually; he clicked right away on the auto-scan and waited for the computer to pop up the same message it always—

Wait.

Michael's eyes widened in disbelief.

There was a change.

In the 4,438th image of the series, on the left-hand side, was a tiny bluish smear.

As he zoomed in, he heard footsteps behind him. "Professor?" said Josh. "Is that what I think it is?"

There was a squeak of a dry-erase marker on the whiteboard, then Josh added, "Ken says it's the same color as what he saw in the core of the Advanced Test Reactor at Idaho National Labs."

Michael couldn't wipe the grin off his face. "One second, guys." He zoomed back out, then advanced to the next frame.

A chill raced up his spine.

The blue smear had elongated slightly and had advanced halfway across the screen. He pointed at the tail end of what now looked almost like a minuscule blue comet. "Look at how short that tail is. Evidently the Cherenkov radiation dissipates very quickly. No wonder nobody has ever seen such a thing."

He went back to the previous frame, grabbed a ruler from the table, and placed it against the monitor where the faint blue light had first appeared. He then moved forward one frame and shook his head in amazement.

"The particle has traveled roughly one third of the way across the chamber in 250 picoseconds." He looked over at Ken, who'd already started scribbling while smiling ear to ear. He turned his whiteboard around.

"5.333c!"

Michael advanced the frame once more, and the blue smear was still just visible near the right-hand edge.

They had done it.

"Save this data!" Michael almost yelled. Ken raced back to the compute cluster and tapped quickly on his keyboard.

Michael's heart thudded in his chest as he kept advancing and rewinding through the three frames of evidence.

"Professor, it's saved," Josh announced as Ken got up from his chair with an excited expression.

Michael rose to his feet and fist-bumped them both. "Gentlemen, we just captured a particle going over five times the speed of light."

— end of preview —

ADDENDUM

Even though *New Arcadia* is very much a mainstream thriller, we couldn't help but include nods toward science in one form or another. Given that, we feel somewhat compelled to either explain some of the science or maybe give a bit more detail than the story otherwise demanded.

Obviously, our goal in this addendum isn't to give you a crash course on college-level science, but instead give you enough information or keywords so that you have the data necessary to do more research, if you're interested.

Alicia's Contact Lens:

The idea of a contact lens that can deliver real-time information to the human eye has been around in movies for years, and a staple of many a thriller. But until recently, it's been a thing of science fiction, in that the technology hadn't been developed to properly merge the matrix of the contact lens itself with something that could deliver visual cues to its wearer.

But during CES 2022 (Consumer Electronics Show) just such a technology was presented by InWith Corporation. Its claim was to be the first company to develop the world's first soft electronic contact lens. The lenses work in conjunction with a smartphone or another device, presumably paired via BlueTooth, and it allows the lens to present real-time information.

The details are scant, but the real triumph in technology is the marrying of an smart-device with the contact lens, such that visual elements can be displayed onto what amounts to be the world's smallest TV screen—the contact lens itself.

And borrowing from concepts that already exist such as AR (Active Reality) – which is a form of Virtual Reality that takes your current sounding and overlays things that aren't really there.

An example of such a thing in today's world would be the game Pokémon Go. It's played by millions of people on their smartphones around the world and it allows users to look through their phones at their surroundings and the application overlays certain game elements to what the user sees. They might be looked at the beach in front of them, and a monster appears on the sand, as an example.

Well, with what has recently been developed, the contact

lens that Levi is using can easily be envisioned to do something a bit more practical. In the software world, we have many algorithms to enable facial recognition and ultimately it works through a means of capturing an image of what someone is looking at (a person's face) digitizing it, and then using that algorithm to turn it into a stream of numbers.

These numbers would be communicated from the contact lens to the phone it's wirelessly connected to, and with an internet connection, the phone could use that hash of numbers, which represent the face, and search for a match.

Once a match is found, information about that person can be pulled from various online sources, and the information discovered can be broadcast back to the contact lens.

In other words, the contact lens acts both as a camera of sorts and as a miniaturized TV.

So, even though what I described in the book might have seemed fanciful, it is by no means science fiction. I'd even hazard to guess that in some classified sections of the Intelligence Community, we might have exactly this type of device deployed with our agents in the field.

Multiverse – it's a thing?

In *New Arcadia*, we make references to gaps in Alicia's memory. Director Mason hand waves a bit and talks about something having to do with the multiverse. There's two things about that reference: one is a real science thing, and the other is a veiled reference to another book called Multiverse which is actually Alicia Yoder's first real POV role. Reading that book might give some insight on what caused the memory gaps. However, let's focus a bit on the science aspect of the topic known as the multiverse.

The existence of a multiverse is something that has been debated in the physics community for years. A hypothesis that there are many (possibly infinite) copies of our universe that all exist in parallel to each other. Take the sum total of all the matter, energy, time, and space in all of these universes, and you have the "multiverse."

Although the idea has long been popular in science fiction and fantasy novels, many well-regarded figures in the scientific community (e.g. Stephen Hawking and Michio Kaku) are supporters of the concept. A related theory, known as counterpart theory, hypothesizes that in multiple copies of a given world, each item or event is not necessarily identical, but a copy in which variability may exist. Taking it one step further, there is something known as "many-worlds interpretation." This is a mechanism by which one can conceive that the actual world we live in is but one of many possible worlds. And more to the point, for each different way the world could have evolved, there is a distinct and separate world that represents that outcome.

If that seems confusing, welcome to the multiverse.

Prions:

We encounter, although only at arm's length, a veritable boogieman that's known to the science world as a prion.

What is a prion, you might ask.

The technical definition would be an abnormal, pathogenic agent that is transmissible and is able to induce abnormal folding of specific normal cellular proteins found mostly in the brain.

More simply put: a prion is a type of protein that can trigger normal proteins in the brain to fold abnormally. This abnormal folding causes various types of brain damage.

The affected proteins in the brain are still not completely understood, but this abnormal folding leads to brain damage and the characteristic signs and symptoms of various prion diseases.

Prion diseases are usually rapid onset and always fatal.

Those who ingest these pathogenic agents can see various types of symptoms, including memory impairment, personality changes, and difficulties with movement.

As noted in the book, these dangerous agents are very difficult to eliminate. Even when chemically treated and desiccated, they retain their ability to infect other proteins for years.

Prions cannot be destroyed by the proper cooking of meats. And as stated in the book, extreme heat is one of the only sure ways of destroying the prions.

By exposing prion-contaminated material to temperatures of roughly 1100°F, it doesn't completely destroy the infectivity of the material, to actually eliminate the risk from such material, temperatures of 1,800°F are needed. Just to compare, aluminum melts at 1,200°F.

That's some seriously resilient boogieman.

And folks should realize that this isn't some obscure weird science thing that we dug up out of the archives, these things do affect people and animals. Many may have heard of "Mad Cow disease" which is formally known as Bovine Spongiform Encephalopathy, but it's not the only prion-induced disease. Below are a list of various diseases attributable to prion infection, and let's just hope nobody gets the crazy idea to use it in the way it was implied in *New Arcadia*.

Human Prion diseases:

- Creutzfeldt-Jakob Disease
- Gerstmann-Straussler-Scheinker Syndrome
- Fatal Familial Insomnia
- Kuru

Animal Prion diseases:

- Bovine Spongiform Encephalopathy (BSE)
- Chronic Wasting Disease (CWD)
- Scrapie
- Transmissible mink encephalopathy
- Feline spongiform encephalopathy
- Ungulate spongiform encephalopathy

Gun Stuff:

There's a moment where Chris tells Alicia to make sure she carries with a round in the chamber. This is real deal advice. Gun enthusiasts rarely agree on anything, but they do agree that carrying with the chamber empty is a pretty bad idea.

Most lethal encounters happen within 15 feet. Imagine having to draw a gun to protect yourself (or your family, or the public) and taking 1-2 extra seconds to rack the slide and chamber a round. Or imagine the person trying to protect you has to do the same thing. In a lethal encounter, that 1-2 seconds means you're dead. It's harsh to say it so bluntly, but this isn't about feelings. It's about logistics and facts. The best professional instructors around the country don't mince words about this. Steve's literally been to those classes. If you want to learn more about self-defense, and contextual awareness, these folks are a great bunch:

https://citizensdefenseresearch.com

Brainwashing:

In this story, we do refer to people's memories being either augmented, blanked, etc. References to the Manchurian candidate, which was a movie regarding the topic of what's now euphemistically called brainwashing.

What's the fact versus fiction on this?

Well, in the story, I have the scientists talk about some things that seem oddly specific about how memories work and are absorbed into our consciousness.

Below is a quote from the book.

"We've found that repetition helps the memories stick. And it's not just pure repetition. On the third run we induce a slow-wave sleep to consolidate the memory—"

"I thought something like that required REM sleep," Mason interjected.

"No. The slow-wave sleep that comes right after you fall asleep is when memory consolidation occurs. So I induce that state with a slow-wave frequency generator and then trigger delta waves with about ten milliamps of current through the electrodes attached to the agent's forehead and the base of his skull.

The above quoted material is accurate.

Memories are stored as electrochemical deposits up in our gray matter, and the way the brain handles memory is an entire area of study that many people are working on.

Instead of getting hyper-nerdy on the details like this:

Delta waves can be triggered with just a slow wave frequency generator - about 10 milliamps current with electrodes on forehead and base of the skull.

Induce sleep with steady delta waves - 1-4 Hz. Add in some brief burst of 25Hz, very brief, only 1/10th second at a time

Let's up-level it a bit and talk about how people learn.

Humans encode memories in two ways: visually and through memorization.

If I asked you what the phone number is to the house you grew up in, you might remember that, even if you haven't lived there in decades, yet you likely can't remember the local Chinese restaurant's phone number. Why? Because your use of the home phone number was repeated so often, it metaphorically wore a groove into your brain and it would be pretty hard to dislodge that information. Whereas with the Chinese restaurant, you probably look it up on your phone or have a calendar with its number, and don't have to memorize it.

That's an obvious example of rote memorization.

Now, an example of visual memories is one where you're paying attention while focusing on visual cues. Before the advent of navigation and handheld computers, if you needed to get somewhere and you had basic walking directions, you'd be paying pretty careful attention to where you're going, and after once or twice, you wouldn't need directions anymore. You'd simply know how to get there. We're visual... but only when our minds are engaged. Contrast that to a scenario where you've been somewhere many times, but only as a passenger in a car, you never drove or walked there yourself. If you're suddenly asked to go there, you might have trouble recalling exactly how to get there, because your mind wasn't visually engaged.

So, during the "programming" session for Agent Xiang that Mason witnessed near the beginning of the book, you're witnessing what in essence is a version of visual programming, with some liberties taken.

If you want to read more about memory consolidation, here's an interesting article that might lead you down a few paths of knowledge.

https://www.ncbi.nlm.nih.gov/pmc/articles/PMC3270580/

The Chinese and several other governments have experimented with what's described in the movie Manchurian Candidate. Has anyone actually broken the code to duplicate such a feat? I don't believe so. It is still within the realm of fiction.

Is it conceivable that such a thing could be done?

Yes.

All we have to do is look at how our brain/memory works and it's about reverse-engineering the technique for actually programming that CPU that we call our brain.

For your entertainment, and because it's appropriate to this topic, I wrote a teaching scenario where I demonstrate how the visual memory works, and I've given a version of this talk to many groups—and without exception—people are surprised at how well the demonstration works.

Example: a discussion between a teacher and someone named Peabo Smith, a student.

"Good morning, Mr. Smith. I'm sure you have a bunch of questions. But instead of asking them, let's dive into a visualization exercise. Okay?"

Peabo wasn't sure what that even meant, but he agreed. "Sure."

"Great. I want you to close your eyes and think of your childhood home. Don't worry if you lived in several places, just pick the one you remember the best. Imagine you're standing outside, in front of it. Do you have that image in your head?"

Peabo closed his eyes and nodded. "I do."

"This next part might sound strange, but eventually you'll see why I'm doing this. Imagine a bunch of naked people on oversized versions of those Big Wheels we used to ride around as kids."

With an uncomfortable smile, Peabo recalled some of the memories he had from the one time he'd ever visited a nude beach. It wasn't a pretty sight.

"Now imagine that these naked people are riding past you. Sweaty. Jiggling. Lots of grunting as they go by. They ride right up to your home, and instead of stopping, they crash into the door, and bodies are flung in every direction. Broken parts of the Big Wheels come rolling back toward you.

"You weave your way past the awkward scene and step into your home. You pause, appreciating the sunlight streaming in, and you notice that it's shining down onto Big Bird. Yes, the same one from *Sesame Street*. I'm sure you're familiar with him.

"The big bright yellow bird from *Sesame Street* waves at you from his perch on an enormous tan horse. Your nose tickles a bit as if you accidentally inhale one of his downy yellow feathers."

Peabo shook his head as he wondered what in the world kind of training this was.

"The inside of your home smells a bit like the horse as you walk into the kitchen, where you find the Swedish chef from the Muppets. He says a string of gobbledygook as he rapidly chops vegetables, which fly in every direction.

"You turn and walk into the living room, and there you find Madonna writhing around on your coffee table singing 'Like A Virgin.' And then you open your eyes.

"Go ahead, open your eyes."

Peabo opened his eyes and saw that the instructor was now pacing back and forth at the front of the classroom.

"Mr. Smith, have you ever seen those people who can stare at a deck of cards, spread out face up, or maybe several decks of cards, and after just a few minutes they can recite, in order, the layout of all of them? Or maybe they can do the same trick with hundreds of phone numbers, or people's names. Ever seen people perform those feats on TV?"

"Sure." There were plenty of times Peabo had wished he could do that kind of stuff when he was studying for tests.

The instructor pulled up a chair, turned it around, and sat facing Peabo. "Would it surprise you to hear that these people weren't savants? Most of the people who can do those things have average intellect as well as average memories. They've simply trained themselves through techniques that I'll teach you. And these aren't new techniques, either; this is stuff that the ancient Greeks used to do all the time. Thousands of years ago, we didn't have near-instant access to the world's knowledge, so it was much more common to exercise the memory in ways that might seem unnecessary now.

"I'll give you an example: do you remember the phone number for the home you grew up in?"

Peabo nodded.

"Okay, but I'd wager that you don't remember most, if any, of the numbers you dial frequently today. Am I right?"

Peabo smiled and nodded. The guy was right. There was a local Chinese restaurant that he called every week, but he'd never needed to memorize their number—it was programmed into his phone.

"Think about it," said the instructor. "Over the years, we've made it very easy for us humans to offload our memories to outside devices. Whether it's papyrus scrolls, books, photos, computers, or smartphones, we created ways of storing our memories so that they'll never be lost—as long as we don't lose the storage device. But before such advances, people had no choice but to remember things... or lose them forever.

"And there's a tradeoff. We now lean so heavily on technology, we've stopped training ourselves to remember things. To have the facts right there"—he snapped his fingers—"whenever you need them."

He drummed his fingers on the back of the chair. "Mr. Smith, what I'm going to teach you to do is something that's already part of our human toolbox. It's just a tool that we rarely use. And when we're done, the way you remember things will have changed. We're going to leverage the parts of your brain associated with spatial and visual recognition, and turn those parts into an assistant of sorts—an assistant that will help you remember things like our ancient ancestors used to.

"I could talk at length about the science behind the technique, going in-depth on the topic of elaborative encoding, but instead, let's talk about something more practical: something called the baker/Baker paradox. It goes like this.

"Imagine I walk up to a person and tell them, 'Please remember that there is someone named Baker.' And then I go to another person, to whom I say, 'Please remember that there is a person who is a baker.' Now, imagine I come back to these same people some time later and ask them each to recall what I said to them. It is much more likely that the second person—the one who was told about a man who *is* a baker—would remember that fact than it is that the first person—the one who was told about someone with the *name* of Baker—would remember. Do you have any theories as to why that might be?"

Peabo pondered the question for a moment. "Well, when you said the guy was a baker, I suppose I had a visual of some guy with a chef's hat or something, whereas some guy named Baker gave me no such image or connection."

The instructor smiled. "Exactly right. The name 'Baker' is just a bit of data bouncing around in your head, but the *concept* of *a baker* has a bunch of potential cognitive connections it can make. You might remember the smell of freshly baked bread, funny white hats, flour everywhere. All of those things, those details, images, connections... they help you in recalling that random piece of data you were asked to remember."

Peabo nodded. It made sense.

"In general," continued the instructor, "humans are not good at remembering random facts and figures. But we have *exceptional* visual and spatial memories. For example, if I asked you to repeat the first ten words that I spoke to you upon entering the classroom, you'd probably have a hard time of it. But what if I asked you who was riding on the horse?"

Peabo smiled at the image that popped into his mind's eye. "Big Bird. And it was a tan horse."

The instructor grinned. "And now, the lesson begins."

Printed in Great Britain
by Amazon

26645265R00214